LEGACY OF LOVE

THE STRATTON LEGACY ~ BOOK 2

RENAE BRUMBAUGH GREEN

ISBN-13: 978-1-942265-57-3

CHAPTER 1

1896
Lampasas, Texas

Skye Stratton faced her students—all three of them. Forced back tears that burned her eyes, wiped a few that had escaped, and plastered on a false smile. "That will be all for today. You're dismissed."

"Miss Stratton?"

"Yes, Levi?"

"Why are you crying?"

Sweet Levi. "I...my allergies always act up this time of year. The ragweed is terrible."

Levi eyed her a moment, as if he doubted her but didn't want to argue. "I hope your alligators get better."

She wobbled a sincere grin. Would have hugged him, except she knew it would be her undoing. "Thank you. Now run along."

He gathered his things and followed Sarah and Thomas into the hallway of the Lampasas Early School, now filled with whoops and hollers of students from other grade levels. One week into her first-ever teaching job, and she was ready to quit. Not because of teaching. Not because of her students. More because of her *lack* of students. Because she knew why, even though there were seventeen children on her first-grade roll sheet, only three of them had yet to show.

Once the halls cleared, she collapsed into her wooden chair, leaned her elbows on her desk, and placed her face in her palms. *Breathe. They wouldn't have hired you if they didn't think you'd be accepted...eventually. Give it time.*

The logic part of her brain warred with her emotions, but today, right now, she wanted to cry. Needed to cry freely. She wanted nothing more than to curl into a ball and sob until her throat was raw. But she couldn't. *Just suck it in until you get home.*

Footsteps approached her door. She stood, grabbed the eraser, and started cleaning the chalkboard. If she looked busy, maybe whoever it was would pass on by.

"Miss Stratton?" She didn't recognize the creamy bass voice.

"Yes?" She turned, willing her eyes to drink back the moisture that still threatened to spill, and caught the man ducking to enter her doorway. Brown curls waved away from a strong, sculpted jawline, except for a single rebellious chocolate-brown lock that flopped over one eyebrow. Winter blue eyes seemed to look right through her, as if he could read her thoughts. That probably wasn't hard, considering Levi had done it just moments earlier. The man held his hat and an envelope in one hand.

"I'm sorry to interrupt. I can see you're busy. My name is Alan McNaughten, and I'm the Indian Agent for this region. May I have a moment of your time?"

Indian Agent? Her heart paused its rhythm, then slammed into her ribs to make up for the lost beat. Surely it hadn't come to this. She was white. Well, half white. The adopted daughter of upstanding members of the community. Both *white*. "Perhaps you should tell me what your business is before I offer my time."

One side of his mouth quirked up, as if he wanted to laugh but thought better of it. "There's a school on a reservation in East Texas, just a few hours southeast of here. They've been without a teacher for several years now. I was given your name, told you might be interested in the position."

She sucked in a silent breath. So, they were already trying to get rid of her. "Who told you that?"

He shifted his weight from one boot to the other. Swallowed. Licked his lips. Any humor that was present a moment ago was gone. "That's not important."

"I'm sorry, Mr. McNaughten, but you were misinformed. As you can see, I already have a job. Good day to you." She swirled around in what she hoped was a dismissive gesture and picked up the chalk to write next week's spelling words on the board. She didn't hear any retreating footsteps, so she kept writing.

Still no sound.

She turned, slowly, and allowed her eyes to trail his length. "I'm sorry. Do you need me to show you the door?"

There was that half-smile again. What a horrible man. Why wouldn't he leave? "I know I've caught you off guard, and for that I do apologize. I can see you love what you do. I'm offering you a chance to do it in a place where you'll truly be wanted. Needed. Accepted."

She gulped a threatening sob, pushed it back down to her stomach. How did he know she wasn't accepted?

"Here are the terms of employment." He stepped forward and laid the envelope on her desk. "I hope you'll consider it. I'll give you the weekend and stop back by on Monday. Good day, Miss Stratton." He placed his hat on his head, only to have it knocked off when he ducked back through the doorframe.

Served him right.

~

*A*lan rubbed Fiona behind the ears, gave her a sugar cube, and swung into the saddle. He thought about hanging around the schoolhouse for a while in hopes of getting another glimpse of the tiny, pretty, spitfire schoolteacher, of her gold-brown eyes with green flecks, of her dark wavy hair boasting random sun-kissed streaks of amber. Bad idea. She already didn't like him. No need to give her more reason to deny his request.

Instead, he flicked the reins and guided Fiona down Main Street toward the clean, modest hotel that would be his home for the next week. The sounds and smells of small-town Texas filled his senses. The rumble of wagon wheels competed with children's shouts, their small feet pounding on the wooden boardwalk, mothers calling after them to mind their manners. To his left, a blacksmith pounded his anvil. Up ahead, a group of pipe-smoking old men sat on benches discussing politics or the weather. Lampasas may not be *his* hometown, but it could've been. And it felt good to be home.

A man waved from a carriage parked in front of Smith's Mercantile. Colt Stratton.

Alan fought back a wave of nausea and reined Fiona to a halt. "Good day, Mr. Stratton."

"Did you speak to her?"

"Yes, I met your niece."

His eyes took on an acid glare. "Don't call her that."

Alan held his gaze but said nothing.

"Did she agree?"

Alan surveyed the townscape, drinking it in. No need to waste his visual energy on the likes of this man, even if he did have to be polite. Even if he did have to play the game. "She'll consider it over the weekend and give me an answer on Monday."

"I'm sure I don't need to remind you of all the strings I pulled to get you this post. I can cut them loose just as easily."

"Understood."

Without another word, Colt clicked to his team and left Alan in the dust. The dust tasted better.

Ten minutes later, he lay on his borrowed bed at Wilson's Boarding House, empty boots flung on the round braided rug at his feet. He pulled the letter from his chest pocket, where he'd kept it since he first opened it three months earlier. He unfolded it and read its words again, even though he had them memorized.

June 21, 1896

My dear son,

I hope this letter finds you well. I know you are turning Washington, D.C. on its ear, as you've done to everything you've attempted since the day we laid eyes on you. Do you ever get tired of hearing how proud we are of you? Never in our dreams did we think we'd have a son in Washington, of all places. God has placed you there to be a light, to influence our government with important change. We only wish it were closer to Texas.

Your mother still battles consumption. As always, she puts on a brave face, but she seems to grow weaker and smaller each day. I know you're busy, but I thought you'd want to know. If you can make time for a trip home, I think it would do her good. If you can't, that's all right.

We love you so much. You fill up our hearts. God truly smiled at us the day he brought you into our lives. Thank you for writing so faithfully. Your letters are the highlight of our days.

Ever faithfully,

Dad

The day Alan received that letter, he decided to come home. Back to Texas, no matter what it took. Washington D.C. had plenty of politicians, but his parents only had one son. They'd loved him, cared for him, given him everything since they took him in at age four.

His memories before that day were fuzzy, blurred. Lots of laughing, dancing women. His mother, beautiful in bright red dresses to match her bright red lips. Men, coming and going, when he had to play in the closet and not make a sound. Then, Mama was gone.

He remembered the feelings. Scared. Alone. He missed his mama.

He remembered that day…leaving everything he'd known behind. One of the other ladies took him to a house, set his bag of clothes on the steps beside him, and rapped on the wooden door. Grown-up voices spoke over his head…something about Mama being dead.

Alan knew now how lucky he was. If he could remember the lady, Mama's friend, he'd find her and thank her for taking him to the parsonage. That day, he became the preacher's son.

Five years ago, when he set out for D.C., he planned to make his mark…like everyone else who showed up in that town. He'd found a job working for Senator Henry Tyler Morgan.

But Morgan proved to be a hard man. His treatment of the growing negro population in D.C. left a bad taste in Alan's mouth. He wanted out—out of working for Morgan, out of Washington politics—but didn't know how. Senator Morgan was a powerful man, and he liked Alan. Liked the loyalty and work ethic Alan's parents had taught him. The man wasn't willing to cut him loose.

So when Alan met Colt Stratton at a state dinner for Morgan's most prestigious donors, and learned Colt was from Texas, Alan engaged him in conversation. Alan knew how to play the Washington game. Charm someone, compliment them, blow up their ego. Then ask for a favor, which would most certainly come at a high price with exorbitant interest.

After the typical small talk, Alan mentioned to Colt his desire to find an appointment closer to home. Within two weeks, Alan received a letter and got his wish. He was to be the new Indian Agent for a reservation just a few miles from his Livingston, Texas home. The catch? He jumped from being Morgan's lackey to Stratton's.

He didn't want to be anybody's lackey. Not anymore.

A knock pulled his thoughts back to the present, and he shot to a seated position. The sky outside his window was now a hazy gray. "Yeah?"

A woman called through the door. "Mr. McNaughten, you have a visitor."

"Thank you. I'll be down shortly."

Rapid footsteps bustled away, and he pulled on his boots. The only two people who knew he was here, besides the staff at the boarding house, were Colt Stratton and the schoolteacher. Was it her? Had she made up her mind already?

But the guest standing in the small parlor downstairs was a man he'd never seen.

"I'm Alan McNaughten. You wanted to see me?"

The man turned, studied him a moment like he couldn't decide if he'd slug him or greet him. He offered his hand. "Riley Stratton. I believe you met my daughter today."

CHAPTER 2

*A*lan shook Riley's hand and motioned for him to be seated. "It's a pleasure to meet you, sir. What can I do for you?"

The older man studied Alan a moment longer before sitting on the worn, blue flowered sofa. The smell of Mrs. Wilson's butter rolls lingered in the air. A door creaked open and shut from the second floor, where the four guest rooms were located. "You can tell me why my daughter came home in tears. You can tell me why you want to take her away from here. You can tell me who recommended her for this position you offered."

Alan sat across from him in a too-small, too-fancy chair. His knees came up to his chin. He felt ridiculous. "Your daughter may have told you I'm the new Indian Agent for the Alabama-Coushatta Reservation. We need a teacher. I was told she might be interested in the job."

"Why would she be?"

Oh, boy. This was awkward. Alan pulled out his best D.C. diplomacy and plastered on a sympathetic smile. "I was told she comes from a similar heritage."

"A similar heritage?" Mr. Stratton leaned forward, the glare back in his expression. "She was raised right here in Lampasas, eating fried steak and cornbread. She was educated right here. Attends church, right here. Her *heritage*, as you say, is no different than anybody else you'll find in this town. Why single her out?"

"Because she's a teacher. She's young, and she has spunk." He'd witnessed the spunk for himself.

The man's eyebrows lifted, and a hint of a smile appeared and disappeared in a fraction of a moment. "That, she does. How did you learn about her biological history? I know someone must have put you up to this."

"I'm not at liberty to say. But sir, I do believe your daughter can do some good on the reservation. She'll be paid a decent wage, and I'll be close by, watching out for her."

The man eyed Alan as if he would punch him if he didn't be quiet.

"My father is the local preacher there," Alan added. "If you'd like, I can arrange for her to stay in their spare room."

"In the house with you? Are you joking?" The man's voice was tight.

"Oh, no sir. I'll have my own place." In the barn, most likely. He didn't know where all these words came from, but if he didn't stop spewing random thoughts at the man, no telling what he'd end up promising.

Riley leaned back, his shoulders relaxing just a little. "Skye is a remarkable young woman. Gifted in more ways than I can count. She's also sensitive. It's one of her most powerful strengths. One of her greatest downfalls."

Alan had no idea where this conversation was leading, but he figured he'd best just stay quiet and listen.

"She makes her own choices. I have no idea what she'll decide. But if she chooses to go with you, I will hold you personally responsible for her wellbeing. Physical, emotional, all of it. Do you understand me?"

Alan held the man's stare, his heart constricting. Something about Riley Stratton reminded Alan of his own father. Both men had taken in a foundling, loved them as their own. This... this was a good man. He represented a good family. How Riley came from the same stock as Colt Stratton, Alan couldn't fathom. But he knew Riley was serious. And because he was a good man, Alan wouldn't take this moment, this man-to-man commitment, lightly. "Yes, sir. I understand."

Riley nodded, stood, and left.

Alan sat in the empty parlor for another hour, listening to the tick-tick of the grandfather clock. He'd wandered far. So far from the values he was taught. Done many things he was ashamed of. Now he'd dealt with the devil to take an innocent young woman away from her family...how could he live with himself? Though he would soon be on the physical road back to Livingston, he knew he was lost. Mentally lost, morally lost. And he didn't know if he'd ever be able to find his way back home.

~

"No matter how many times you read it, the words won't change." Mama's voice fell on Skye like a soft blanket. The older woman set the hot apple pie on the window sill and wiped her hands on her apron.

"I know." Skye leaned her elbows on the worn kitchen table. "I just... It's a good offer. I'd make more than I'm making here. Still, it feels like a slap in the face."

"Maybe somebody recommended you because they know you're an amazing teacher."

"You and I both know that's not it. It's because I'm Indian. It's because they don't want me here."

"Skye, if they didn't want you, they wouldn't have hired you. You are beloved in this town."

Mama meant well, but she could be so naïve. "Then why aren't they sending their children to school?"

"Maybe they're sick. An outbreak, maybe?" Mama pulled out a chair across the table from Skye and sat.

"Of course." Skye didn't try to hide her sarcasm. "That's why Maggie Colson's siblings are all there, in other grades. And the Bryant family—all those children are in school except Daniel. And I saw Priscilla Hayes walking into the mercantile with her mother just yesterday. She didn't look sick to me."

Mama placed her hand on Skye's arm. "I'm sure there's a logical explanation. First grade is still young. Maybe folks just wanted to keep their little ones home another year."

Or maybe we can accept the truth. I'll never fit in here. I'll never be accepted. I'll be lucky if I can keep this job and be an old-maid schoolteacher, but at this rate, I'll be nothing more than a deadweight spinster aunt.

Skye couldn't bring herself to say the words aloud. They would only hurt Mama. If Mama and Daddy knew how she struggled, how she hated the way people looked at her, how she hated that she didn't belong anywhere, it would break their hearts. Because she knew, in spite of all her mixed up feelings, in spite of the way people in town treated her...she knew her parents loved her.

So she painted a smile on her face and pretended. Her whole life was one big game of make-believe. She brushed the back of her hand across her eyes and studied the words on the page.

"I hope you're not considering this offer."

Skye folded the letter and looked out the front window. "Of course not." She thought of Levi, Thomas, and Sarah. The faithful three. Their parents all worked in The Big Skye, the hotel and resort Mama and Daddy started over fifteen years ago. But what about all the others? Would their educations suffer because of Skye? Was her presence as the first-grade teacher doing more harm than good?

Yes. Yes it was.

"Pray about it. God will show you the way." Mama stood, wiped her hands on her apron, and headed back to the kitchen. She didn't have to work. The Big Skye had grown into an empire. But for as long as Skye could remember, Mama had been a worker. And a pray-er.

The working part had seeped into Skye's character. The praying part?

Well, what Mama didn't know wouldn't hurt her. "Yes, ma'am."

God may answer Mama's prayers. If there was a God, Mama was surely one of His favorites. But Skye learned a long time ago there was no God out there listening to anything she had to say.

~

Sunday dawned bright and sunny, the kind of misleading September day that promises six more months of summer. Skye straightened her plumed hat, pinned on her ivory-and-pearl cameo, and tucked her pink, ruffled parasol under her arm. She did love Sundays. It was the one day of the week she could wear her fanciest clothes without feeling like she was putting on airs. Or at least, no more than anyone else in town.

Daddy waited at the bottom of the stairs, grinning as she descended. "You're as pretty as your mother, and prettier than all others."

She returned his smile. He'd said that to her every Sunday for as long as she could remember. "Thank you, Daddy."

Fourteen-year-old Cordell stepped into the foyer from the dining room, a half-eaten biscuit in one hand. "Awww, I guess she looks all right," he mumbled around a mouthful of bread. "For a girl."

Skye poked him with her parasol and gave her best scowl. "Watch it, little brother. You may be taller, but I can still whip you."

He snickered but held his hands in surrender.

"She's the most beautiful girl in this whole county. Next to Mama." Eleven-year-old Anita scooted around her brother and placed her arms around Skye's waist.

"And next to you." Skye whispered and kissed her sister's blond curls.

"Are we ready?" Mama rushed past, her taffeta bustle rustling behind her, her Sunday school materials in a small carpet bag in one hand. "Get in the carriage. Let's go!"

"I think I'll walk today, if you don't mind." Skye held her mother's eyes. "I think better when I'm alone."

Mama gave a slight nod. "I understand."

"Can I walk with Skye?" Anita begged.

"No. You'll be late for your Bible class."

"So will Skye."

"Anita." Daddy's voice brought the young girl to attention. "Don't argue with your mother."

"I'm sorry, Mama."

Mama swatted Anita's back side. "Get in the carriage."

"Thank you," Skye mouthed to her mother. She watched them load up, watched Daddy flick the reins, watched the cloud of Lampasas dust float behind them. Sunday mornings. If she left here, she'd miss the special chaos that defined their family on that morning. If she moved to East Texas, would she even attend church services?

Probably. They'd expect it of the new teacher.

Friday night, she'd tossed and turned. Yesterday, she'd fretted and fussed. Last night, she resigned herself to the truth. She wasn't wanted here. She was wanted *there*. Could she really pack up her things and leave the only family she'd ever known to make a new start? Did she want to?

And if she did, how would Mama take it?

What if she just left without telling them?

She'd never do that. This job offer...it was a chance to start fresh. It terrified her.

It also thrilled her.

She wanted to take the job. She didn't want to take the job.

Here it was, Sunday, and she was no closer to a decision than she'd been when Alan McNaughton had first dropped the offer on her desk Friday afternoon.

She was so absorbed in her thoughts, she didn't notice the man riding toward her on his horse, from the direction of town. They both turned onto the narrow lane that led to the church at the same time.

"Good day, Miss Stratton."

Alan McNaughton. She offered a pert nod and positioned her parasol so she didn't have to look at him. She didn't like the man. She didn't really have reason not to like him. He hadn't done anything to deserve her ire. But he was the messenger, and sometimes, messengers got shot.

"I was hoping I'd see you this morning."

She heard his boots thud on the ground. Below her parasol, she saw his long legs match stride with her shorter ones, his horse clomping on the other side of him.

She didn't respond other than to keep walking.

"I hope you've considered my offer. I think you'll enjoy the work."

Skye halted, mid stride, and snapped her parasol shut. "Why do you think that, Mr. McNaughton? You don't know me at all."

His mouth quirked up on the left in a lopsided grin that left her heart aflutter, in spite of her dislike. "I know enough."

She clicked her parasol open again, like a weapon, and marched forward. The nerve!

"I know you care about your students. I could see it in your eyes when we spoke on Friday. I also know you're an excellent teacher, or the school board wouldn't have hired you. There were four other qualified applicants."

She'd been aware of other applicants, though she hadn't learned how many. One was a man who'd been fired from three previous positions. Daddy'd heard that much. She pondered this new revelation but didn't pause her steps. Now she had something new to think about during the sermon. Was she really hired because she was the most qualified candidate, or because Mama and Daddy had donated handsomely to the schools over the years? If her qualifications were the reason, why were so few students attending her class?

Still, it didn't change anything. Tomorrow, she'd have to tell Alan McNaughten yes or no. After school. No need to give the smug man any clue of her answer a moment before she had to.

She couldn't if she wanted to, since she still didn't know what her answer would be.

~

*A*lan watched the pert school teacher bustle into the church. He led Fiona to the hitching post and scooted into the back row of the small sanctuary just as the opening hymn began. A burst of pink in the third row from the front alerted him of Skye's location right away. From this vantage point, he could sneak plenty of peeks at her. To the untrained eye, it would seem he was watching the preacher.

His eyes flicked to the elderly man on the platform, holding a hymnal. Nope. No need to watch him for the better part of an hour. His gaze wandered back to Skye, to the dark strands that caressed her long, slender neck. To the delicate lace that lined her collar. To–

He felt someone watching him. He shifted his eyes to meet

Riley Stratton's gaze. The man had turned nearly sideways in his seat and watched Alan with the same intensity—though clearly less pleasure—as Alan watched Skye.

Alan flicked his attention to the preacher and kept it there for the remainder of the hymn and into the next. When he finally dared a quick look in Riley's direction, the man's eyes were trained forward. But he still sat angled in his seat. Better not chance it.

Against his will, Alan's eyes rested once more on Skye, how her jaw moved as she sang, how she held her shoulders in a way that seemed simultaneously confident and humble. He knew better than to ogle a pretty girl, but something about Skye Stratton captivated him, made him curious and excited and hopeful. Hopeful for what, he wasn't sure.

The organist ended the final hymn, and the pastor flipped a few pages in his Bible. The whole scene reminded Alan of home. Dad would be starting his sermon right about now.

The clergyman's voice boomed through the small congregation, bouncing off the walls and shaking the pews, a stark contrast to Dad's soft-spoken drawl. "Today's passage is taken from Luke 12. "For there is nothing covered that shall not be revealed; neither hid, that shall not be known."

Heat crept up Alan's neck and into his face. *Real funny, God. You know I'm trying to get away from all the lies, all the corruption. But I do need a job. As soon as I get home, I'll stop the dirty deals.*

That voice...that clear voice in his head that he knew was God, replied, *That's what you said last time.*

It was true. Each time Alan did business with a snake, he swore it was the last time. Each time he wheeled and dealed and lied to reach a desired end, he felt ashamed. Disgusted. And he promised God he'd never do it again. And he didn't, until the next snake slithered his way.

This time it was Colt Stratton, Skye's uncle. *But this time I mean it, God.*

The service ended after a couple more songs. Alan mumbled through them and slid out of his seat during the last verse. He'd just mounted Fiona when he heard Riley's voice.

"Nice to see you, Mr. McNaughton." Riley's gaze was steel.

Alan leaned over and offered his hand. "You as well, sir."

Riley took his hand, and Alan thought the man might squeeze it off.

Alan didn't flinch, but it took effort.

"Join us for lunch?" Riley asked.

Lunch with the enchanting Miss Stratton? He couldn't imagine a better distraction. "I'd love to."

CHAPTER 3

Skye allowed her father to assist her into the carriage. "Why'd you do that?" Her voice was low so only Daddy could hear.

"You know what they say. 'Keep your friends close and your enemies closer.'"

"Macchiavelli. So you're saying Alan McNaughton is an enemy?"

"I didn't say that, darlin'. But I would like to know a little more about him."

"Macchiavelli also said that the end justifies the means. Do you subscribe to that philosophy as well?"

Daddy chuckled. "You always were too smart for your own good." He climbed into the carriage where Mama, Cordell, and Anita sat waiting. "Follow us," he called to Alan, who nodded and tipped his hat.

Lampasas roads were crowded with pedestrians, horses, wagons and carriages all leaving their respective places of worship. Skye remembered when their church was the only one in town. Now, four churches faced the town square, one at each corner. Each one had a distinct personality. One of them catered mostly to tourists who visited for the healing springs… the springs that provided a comfortable living for her family. At the intersection that led home, they passed Uncle Colt's carriage.

Mama and Daddy nodded and waved, and Aunt Allison waved back. Davis, Skye's seventeen-year-old cousin, lifted one finger. Uncle Colt pretended not to see them, like he always did. Skye had fantasies about seeing him in town one day, throwing her arms around his neck, and kissing him on the cheek. "Hello, Uncle Colt!" she'd say, just to see the man's reaction. He'd probably keel over dead, right then and there. She craned her head to watch the man who'd resented her half-white, half-Indian existence for as long as she could remember. Saw him make eye contact with Alan. He nodded, and Alan nodded back.

Was it her imagination, or was that more than a passing nod to a stranger? They seemed to hold each other's gazes as if they knew each other. Was Uncle Colt behind this job offer?

Was he behind the town's parents not sending their young ones to her class?

Of course he was. It all made perfect sense.

The entire ride home, Skye felt Alan's presence behind her. Her stomach swirled and knotted. She hadn't planned on seeing him today—much less on spending the afternoon with him. She'd have to play nice. Because in Mama's home, gracious hospitality was the rule, no matter if the devil himself showed up. Today, their guest-of-honor might not be the devil. But she wondered if Alan McNaughton, with his villainous good looks and down-to-earth charm, wasn't one of the devil's minions.

~

*A*lan's breath caught when they took a bend in the road to enter a lush garden bursting with zinnias, black-eyed Susans, periwinkles, and a few flowers he didn't recognize.

Their path changed from typical Texas oak trees to lush pines and willows. Everything about this place whispered, *Peace*.

Up ahead, a quaint mansion rested on a hilltop. Could a mansion be quaint? The large white structure boasted two stories, an oversized shade porch, and a balcony that wrapped around the entire house. Feathery ferns and ornamental potato vines hung in baskets on each level, spilling over the second-floor railing in a welcoming wave. Windows and doors off the balcony hinted at the rooms behind. Small tables with chairs were tucked here and there. At the entrance, double doors sported oval glass panes etched with a lacy scrolled pattern. On either side of the doors were porch swings, flanked by more baskets of colorful flowers. On the path leading to the wide porch stairs, a low-to-the-ground sign, tastefully painted in script, read, *The Big Skye Inn*.

Skye *lived* here?

He was fighting a losing battle. Why would she ever want to leave?

Behind the inn to one side, a smaller but just as impressive house nuzzled in a grove of pine trees.

Riley Stratton pulled the carriage in front of the inn, and Alan drew up beside him. Riley handed the reins to a teenage boy before helping his wife, Skye, and a younger girl step down. "Alan, I'd like you to meet my family. This is my wife, Emma Stratton."

The woman gave him a polite nod. "Pleased to meet you."

Alan nodded in return, then slid out his saddle. "Likewise."

"You've met my daughter, Skye, and this is Anita." Riley looked at each of his daughters, who both repeated their mother's polite nod. "And that's Cordell." He gestured to the young man still in the carriage.

"Pleased to meet you, sir." Cordell offered a firm handshake from the driver's seat. "I'll see to your horse as soon as I put away the carriage."

"Much obliged." Alan took Fiona's reins and tied her to a nearby tree. A birdbath rested beneath it, and Fiona helped herself to the water. Alan hoped that was okay.

"Can I pet her?" Anita asked.

Skye followed her mother up the steps, onto the inn's wide porch, and through the fancy doors without a word. Alan pulled his attention back to Anita. "Of course." He pulled a sugar cube from his pocket. "Give her this, and she'll be your friend for life. Keep your hand flat, like this."

Anita offered the cube with one hand and stroked Fiona's forehead with the other. "She's pretty."

"Thank you. I think she likes you, too."

Riley rested a hand on Anita's shoulder. "Why don't you go help your mother and sister?"

The girl sighed—almost a groan, but not quite. "Yes, sir."

"I hope you don't mind. We'll eat in the inn's dining room instead of our private home." Riley led Alan toward the inn. "Leftovers from last night's dinner. The staff has their own worship service mid-morning, after the breakfast crowd. We tried to figure out a way to give them every Sunday off, but we have too many weekend customers. The dining room is closed to the public for lunch, so it'll just be us. Our patrons know to eat lunch in town on Sundays."

Alan had attended plenty of lavish meals in Washington, so the setting didn't intimidate him. But Colt Stratton had led Alan to believe Skye's family was...well, that they were the country cousins. He'd pictured something a little different. "It's a beautiful place. I'm honored to be here."

"We've been blessed, that's for certain. Would you like a quick tour before lunch, or would you rather wait until after?"

"Either way is fine with me." What Alan really wanted was to catch another glimpse of Skye, but he was well aware of the politics of this type of situation. Impress the most powerful person in the room. In this case, he was pretty sure that was Skye's father.

Riley led him down a shaded pathway toward the smaller structure. "This is our home. Far enough away from guests that we have a modicum of privacy, but close enough to keep an eye on things." For the next twenty minutes, Riley showed him various gardens, a recreation area, and finally, the hot springs that bubbled from the ground. "This is what started it all. This is why the people come."

"Do they really heal people?" Alan was fascinated.

"I'm no doctor, so I can't say for sure. Some swear by them. Others say they just feel great and help them relax."

"Nothing wrong with that."

"After we eat, you're welcome to try them out. We keep bathing attire here for our guests."

Alan wanted to, but he had to keep his eye on the prize, which right now was convincing Skye to leave here and teach at the reservation. If he didn't, his job was at stake. If he did, his job was secure for as long as she stayed away from Lampasas. He'd see how things went at lunch. "Thank you for the offer. I'll consider it."

Before long, they were back at the inn, and Riley led them through the wide front door. Inside, the décor rivaled some of the nicest Washington hotels, but it somehow maintained a warm, homey atmosphere. Thick, colorful rugs covered rich wood floors. Sofas and settees with embroidered pillows invited conversation. A room to one side held walls of books and several nooks for reading.

As he took it all in, Alan wondered at Riley's reason for inviting him here. Did he want Skye to consider his offer? What was his game? Yet even as he asked himself that question, he knew Riley wasn't like his brother, Colt. He didn't have a game. He was just a genuinely nice man who loved his daughter and wanted to protect her from lowlifes like Colt. And, by extension, Alan.

"Right this way," Riley said. "I hope you're hungry!"

"Starving, actually." The smell of onions and garlic and some heavenly concoction made Alan's mouth water and his stomach rumble. "Lead the way."

~

"I don't know what Daddy was thinking. Why would he invite him here?" Skye pulled the warming dish of roast beef from the oven and set it on the large wooden kitchen table.

"Maybe he thinks getting to know the man who made the offer will help you make a wise decision."

Skye made an effort to unclench her jaw. Every muscle in her body was tied in knots. "What do you think I should do?"

Mama placed her hand on Skye's. "I want you to stay here. But this isn't about what I want. You're a grown woman with a good head on your shoulders. I want you to consider all angles. I want you to pray about it. And I want you to do what you feel is right. You know your father and I will support you, whatever decision you make."

"Well, I don't see why Skye can't be happy right here." Anita finished placing cookies on a porcelain tray and popped a broken piece in her mouth. "She can marry Mr. Shoemaker."

Skye smiled at her sister and stroked her hair with one hand. Eli Shoemaker, the inn manager, was in his late forties. Older than Daddy. "I don't need a husband to make me happy. You make me smile every single day."

Anita rewarded her with a toothy grin. "There's your answer, then. Stay here so you'll have me every day."

Skye started to respond, but she heard men's voices in the entry hall. She swallowed back a wave of nausea and pasted a fake smile on her face. Let the show begin. She grabbed a bowl of green beans and followed Mama into the dining room.

"And this is where guests eat on most days, and where we usually eat on Sundays." Daddy entered the room, Alan close behind.

"Impressive. And it smells delicious."

"Won't you have a seat, Mr. McNaughten?" Mama smiled her most dazzling smile. "Right here, across from Skye. We just have a few more things to put on the table, and we'll be ready."

Alan's eyes flickered to meet Skye's when her name was mentioned. He smiled, and she averted her gaze. The less she looked into those dangerously captivating blue eyes, the better. Right now, she needed to be clear-headed.

A few minutes later, they all joined hands as Daddy said grace. Then they passed platters of roast, bowls of potatoes and carrots and squash, and a basket of buttery rolls. She took a little of each, but she wasn't sure if she could eat a bite. Time passed with small talk about the weather, today's sermon, how delicious the food was. Skye tried to keep a pleasant expression on her face as she speared a potato a little too forcefully.

"Tell us how you came to be an Indian Agent, Mr. McNaughten. And what exactly does an Indian Agent do?" Mama always knew what to say to guests. She'd taught Skye her number one rule to being a good conversationalist: *Get people to talk about themselves. They'll leave thinking you're the most interesting person they've ever met without you saying a word.* Only right now, Skye didn't want to hear about this man. Except maybe, how did he know Uncle Colt? Now *that* was a question she'd like an answer to.

"An Indian Agent is kind of like an ambassador, I guess. The president appoints a civilian to be the eyes and ears for the government in an area, and to act as a liaison for communication between the Indians and the surrounding people. I stumbled into the position, actually. After finishing my coursework at the University of Texas, I aspired to go into politics. I landed an internship in Washington, D.C. working for a senator."

"Impressive." Daddy leaned forward in his chair as if Alan shared the most intriguing story ever told.

"After working there a while and seeing close-up how things are done, I had a change of heart. I realized politics may not be my calling after all. I'd already decided I'd look for opportunities to return to Texas when I received a letter from my father. My mother's not in the best of health. I needed to come home soon, and I needed a job. An acquaintance of mine knew of an opening that would put me within miles of my parents. I applied and was offered the position."

"So it wasn't a love for the Indian culture or a desire to make their lives better that led you into this line of work?" The words slipped out before Skye had a chance to edit the judgment from her tone.

The room grew quiet. Tension covered the table like a cloud.

Alan held her gaze, quirked that half-smile at her. "No, ma'am. I don't suppose those reasons came to mind when I took the job. But they did occur to me as I took the long train ride from Washington to Texas. I hope I can do some good."

Skye bit back the retort that lay bitter, just inside her lips. She could feel Mama's censuring eyes on her. And truly, she knew she needed censure. Never in her life had she felt such anger as she did at this man. But deep down, she knew he'd done nothing to deserve her disdain. Other than offer her a job. It was his place, after all, to find a qualified teacher. Her anger was misplaced, but right now, it was too much to sort out. She breathed a long, slow breath in through her nose and let it out through her mouth. A trick her other mother—her first mother —had taught her.

Skye offered as much of a smile as she could manage. "I apologize, Mr. McNaughten. That question came out more harshly than I intended. Your new position does put you in a place to help people. I wish you well in your endeavors." She felt, more than heard, the other members of her family exhale in relief.

"No apology needed." His words were as lighthearted and kind as before. "As you know, my business here in Lampasas is exactly that—trying to do something good for the Alabama-Coushatta people of East Texas. I believe you will offer much to those children. You can make a positive difference in their lives for generations to come, should you choose to accept the challenge."

Coushatta? She hadn't known this was a Coushatta reservation. Suddenly, it was as if she and Alan were the only two people in the room. Everyone and everything else hazed away. "How did you know I'm Coushatta? Who told you?" Her voice came out stronger than she felt. More demanding than was appropriate in this setting.

Alan's eyes widened. He looked truly shocked. "I didn't. I had no idea. I was told you had some Indian heritage, but I don't know any specifics."

Skye studied his expression, looking for any hint of deceit. She didn't know what to make of this man.

"Who's ready for dessert?" Mama's voice pulled them from the tense moment.

"I was ready ten minutes ago!" Cordell's comment brought low chuckles from everyone else. That boy could eat an entire bison and still find room for seconds.

"I'm with Cordell." Alan grinned at Mama. "If dessert is half as delicious as the meal, I'd be foolish to pass it up."

Skye followed her mother into the kitchen to help bring the dessert plates. Mostly, she just needed a moment away from the charming, exasperating Indian Agent who was quickly turning her life upside down.

～

*A*lan forced himself not to watch Skye's retreating figure. Too many eyes on him. The vulnerability in her words, her expression when she'd questioned him, was enough to make him want to toss one of the best meals he'd had in a while. He hadn't lied. Colt hadn't mentioned her tribal roots, only that she was Indian. Actually, he'd embellished the word "Indian" with a few unsavory adjectives, but then he'd gone on to describe her as intelligent and capable.

"What will you do if she denies your request?" Riley asked in a low voice.

"I don't have a back-up plan. I guess I'll look for someone else."

Anita tilted her head in compassion. "You'd better get a back-up plan, Mr. McNaughton, because my sister isn't going with you. She already told me so." The girl looked so serious and big-eyed and cute, Alan had to work hard not to laugh.

"I'm sorry to hear that. I'm in town until Tuesday, though, so I hope she'll change her mind."

Anita's wide eyes squinted. "I don't think that will happen."

"You don't know that." Cordell grabbed another roll out of the basket and pinched off a hunk. "Just because you don't want her to go doesn't mean she's not going."

Anita opened her mouth, but before she could speak, Riley intervened. "That's enough. The decision is Skye's, and when she's made it, she'll let us all know."

~

*I*n the kitchen, Skye couldn't stop the silent tears that tracked her cheeks. She kept her back to Mama, hoping they'd go without notice. Hoping she could get herself under control before she was discovered.

"Skye." The softness in Mama's voice just about sent her over the edge of her emotional cliff. Mama pulled Skye into a tight embrace, and the flood came even harder.

Mama rubbed her back. "It's okay. It will all be okay." She led Skye to the long kitchen bench against the back wall and sat next to her. "Do you want to talk about it?"

Skye shook her head. "I wouldn't know what to say. I don't know why I've been so moody and weepy. I don't know what's come over me."

Mama leaned against the wall and held Skye's hand in her own lap. "You've always had a goal in mind. Whether it was winning the spelling bee or learning to sew or becoming a teacher. Now you've finished your schooling and you have a real job, with another offer to consider. It's only natural for you to wonder what's next. It can be unsettling not to know what lies ahead."

Skye kept her eyes on her lap. She didn't think Mama was right about the reason, but she didn't want to contradict her.

Mama squeezed her hand. "You haven't talked much about your first family."

The grandfather clock ticked a loud, steady rhythm. She'd pushed thoughts of her mother's extended family, thoughts of her first mother and father, to the recesses of her mind and slammed the door. No point resurrecting the dead. Dead things brought foul odors.

Mama waited a thick minute before she continued her thought. "But I know you think about them. It's okay to want to know more about your history." She pulled back, placed her hand under Skye's chin, and lifted her face so their eyes met. "You're my daughter. Nothing will ever change that. But it's okay to acknowledge you had another mother before me. She raised a beautiful, strong girl, and I reaped the benefits."

Skye's heart pounded in her chest like iron on an anvil. She'd never voiced her thoughts. Her longings. It sounded strange to hear Mama speak Skye's secrets. "I don't know what to do…"

"Pray about it. God will show you."

Skye wiped her eyes on the back of her hand, mostly for an excuse to break eye contact. Because her relationship with Mama and Daddy's God—the white man's God—was something Skye would never discuss with them. Ever. It would crush them.

~

*A*lan tried to think of something, anything, to change the subject from whether or not Skye would accept his offer. What was taking them so long with that dessert? "This dining room is beautiful. How many does it seat?"

"Sixty. At the height of tourist season, we sometimes feed a few hundred at a meal, coming and going. We're known for our cuisine, so we get quite a few customers from the two other resorts in town as well."

Why would Skye want to leave? Judging from the inn's name, she was at least a shareholder in this place. Why did she even teach school? Surely she didn't need the money. If he didn't need her agreement to secure his own position as Indian Agent, he'd go tell her right now to forget the whole thing. She'd never find this kind of luxury in East Texas.

The women returned from the kitchen. Mrs. Stratton carried a glass tray with a white-frosted cake covered in strawberries. Behind her, Skye carried extra plates and forks, her eyes suspiciously red. That he was the cause, at least in part, made him feel lower than a grub in a potato patch. He could stop this whole charade, but he wasn't going to. And out of all the low-down, dirty deals he'd pulled in Washington, none had made him feel as slimy as he felt right now.

CHAPTER 4

*M*ama's words rang in Skye's mind while she served the cake, dolloping each slice with a spoonful of rich whipped cream. She felt like she was sleep walking, like she'd wake up any moment and this would all wisp away and be forgotten.

Yet, now that Mama'd spoken the words out loud, they couldn't be unsaid. It was true. Skye was curious about her mother's family. Her people. The ones she could barely remember, other than blurry streaks of barely-there moments that slipped away from her grasp the instant she tried to focus on them.

She sat in her chair and moved bite-sized pieces of cake around on her plate, hoping no one would notice she wasn't eating. Around her, their small talk made no more sense than buzzing flies. After a time, at a lull in their conversation, she said the only thing that came to mind. "Mr. McNaughten, would you care to go for a walk with me?"

The surprise on his face showed he thought her bold. Brash, even. She didn't care. She had questions, and there was only one way to get answers.

"I'd be honored, Miss Stratton."

She didn't wait while he made polite conversation, telling Mama and Daddy how much he enjoyed the meal, saying some niceties to Cordell and Anita. She just pushed her chair back and left the room. She'd wait on the porch.

He wasn't far behind. He didn't say anything, just offered his arm. She slid her fingers around the crook in his elbow and they started walking, no place in particular in mind. She knew instinctively he followed her lead.

She didn't say anything for several minutes. He must think her so odd. Finally, when they reached a small table and chairs under her favorite willow tree, the one near the goldfish pond, she gestured for him to sit as she took the opposite chair.

"I can't imagine what you must think of me," she said. "You're probably ready to retract your offer."

"Why would I do that?" He leaned back in his chair and stretched his long legs in front of him, crossed at the ankles.

She hadn't thought through what she'd say...only that she needed more information. "I...I'm usually a very nice person."

That lopsided grin quirked. "I can see that."

She chuckled. "I don't think that's what you've seen of me. But you caught me at a bad time on Friday, and your offer has stirred up a lot of feelings I usually try to push down."

"Why is that?"

She would not be pulled into a conversation about the psychology of her actions. "Mr. McNaughten, how do you know my Uncle Colt?"

There it was. That flash of surprise in his eyes, which he masked with a false look of confusion. "Your Uncle Colt?"

"I saw the two of you make eye contact after church. Please don't deny it. I know what I saw."

He looked as if he'd do exactly that, then shifted in his chair. Leaned forward. Rested his elbows on the table, his face in his palms. He stayed that way for the better part of a minute before dropping his hands and meeting her eyes. "I met him in Washington."

Washington. She knew Uncle Colt took business trips, but she'd never asked where he went. He wasn't an active part of her life. They'd never had more than awkward exchanges at family Christmas parties and birthdays.

"He put you up to this."

Alan shook his head. "I'm not sure I'd put it that way. He knew I wanted the Indian Agent appointment, and he was part of a conversation in which the need for a teacher was discussed. He shared that he knew of someone who might be interested. And he told me about you."

Alan held something back. She could see it. But what? She shifted her focus to the goldfish pond. The bright orange fish always calmed her, the way they floated and darted below the surface, so graceful, as if they didn't have a care in the world.

Uncle Colt probably had some choice things to say about her background. That must be what Alan held back. He was trying to be polite, to be a gentleman. "Thank you for your honesty. I still haven't made up my mind, but I will have my answer for you by tomorrow afternoon, as you requested."

He smiled. "You asked me a question. May I ask one of you?"

"I suppose."

"All this." He gestured at the surrounding landscape. "The inn bears your name. Surely you don't need to teach school. Why do you?"

She couldn't stop the smile that bubbled up for the first time in many days. "I love teaching. I love children. Mama—she was a teacher. I was her first pupil, as a matter of fact. That was before she and Daddy were married, before they adopted me. She made such a difference in my life. I want to do that for others."

"Your students are fortunate to have you."

Her joy dampened a bit. She thought of the students who *weren't* fortunate to have her. The ones who were being kept at home, simply because she was an *Injun.* As long as she stayed in this town, that was how most people would see her.

~

*E*very nerve in Alan's body was on high alert. He'd sunk to a new low by lying—or at least withholding the whole truth, which was pretty much the same thing—about his relationship with her uncle.

The truth was, his job depended on Skye. On his removing her from Lampasas. Why was it so hard to just do the right thing? The more he tried to dig himself out of the mess he'd made, the lower he sank. Like quicksand.

"I…I just remembered I have some paperwork to do." Another untruth. "I should get back to my room. Tell your family how appreciative I am for the meal and the company." He stood, gave her a nod and his best smile, and went in search of Fiona.

Soon, he was on his way back to town. Halfway there, he noticed a rambling path to the left. At the bottom of a slope was a bubbling stream. He led Fiona down the path. Was this one of the springs that had turned Lampasas into a tourist destination? He climbed off the saddle, squatted, and swirled his fingers in the water. It was warm! Not warm-from-the-sun warm. More like a just-right bath with water from the stove.

He looped Fiona's reins around a branch and pulled off his boots and socks. Scrunched his trousers to his knees. Found a large oak tree with a rock at the base, right next to the water, perfect for sitting. His feet dangled in the water, and he wished he could put his whole body in. Maybe he should have stayed at the inn, taken Riley up on his offer to relax in the springs.

But no. This would have to be enough for now. He leaned his head against the oak and closed his eyes. This was a little piece of heaven, a beautiful contrast to the hell he was living.

God, I want to do better. Be better. Why do I keep making the wrong decisions? I'm just trying to find my way back, and I keep getting more lost.

A cardinal flitted past and landed in a tree across the stream.

A scripture he'd memorized when he was nine years old came to mind. He'd memorized it for Miss Sally's Sunday School class. She made the best oatmeal cookies and rewarded them to anyone who memorized their assigned verse. That week's passage included two verses, so he'd hoped for two cookies. Sure enough, she'd made extra for that very purpose. He smiled at the memory, and at the relevance of those words now, all these years later. *Trust in the Lord with all thine heart; and lean not unto thine own understanding. In all thy ways acknowledge Him, and He shall direct thy paths.*

How was Alan supposed to trust God and do the right thing when the right thing would land him in a heap of trouble? If he'd told Skye the truth about his dealings with Colt today, she would turn down his offer for sure. If she turned down the job, the deal was off. Not only would Alan not have a job, but Colt would ruin his name and reputation. He had the money and power to do it. If that happened, Alan might never work again.

Once he got back to Livingston, he'd do better. He'd trust God then. He'd landed himself in this heap. He needed to get himself out of it. Right now, he just had to concentrate on securing his position and getting home.

CHAPTER 5

Skye didn't sleep that night. Again.

How could she leave her parents? Her home? The family who'd taken her in, loved her, and treated her like she was their own? Here, she was safe. Loved. Wanted.

Alan was right. The inn bore her name. Why would she ever leave it?

Then again, how could she stay? For as long as she could remember, the minute she set foot off this property, she'd always felt out of place.

The stares from townspeople.

The whispers.

The pointing, when they didn't think she saw.

Oh, her last name kept anyone from being *too* obvious. Their disdain was subtle, but real.

Would she ever find acceptance? Would she ever feel wanted, anywhere?

She could leave. Take Alan's offer. Maybe things would be better. Or maybe, in a new place where no one knew her parents, where no one cared about her last name... Things might be worse. She might be sheltered, but she wasn't stupid. She knew how *Injuns* were treated.

Or she could stay right here, under her parents' protective wings. But their wings only stretched so far.

Early Monday morning, she dragged herself out of bed, put on her most sensible dress—because weren't schoolteachers supposed to look more sensible than smart?—and pulled her hair into a low bun. Her two nods to fashion, on teaching days, were her parasol and her earscrews. She had four parasols in different colors. Today, she grabbed her blue one to match her navy striped skirt. She'd tuck it away in the supply closet in her classroom when she got there. And she had three sets of earscrews. Today she chose the tiny, dangling pearls. They made her feel pretty, like a picture she'd seen of Queen Victoria. If people were going to point and whisper, she'd at least carry herself like a queen and give them something to whisper about.

The hallway was empty when she entered the school. She was usually early, but today she'd arrived earlier than usual. She needed time to think. Because as of right now, she still didn't know what she'd tell Alan McNaughten when the time came.

Voices floated from the headmaster's office at the end of the hallway. She walked softly, not wanting to alert anyone of her presence or get pulled into a conversation. Just as she placed her hand on the doorknob to her classroom, she heard her name.

"Surely there's something we can do. If we keep Miss Stratton, we're alienating half the county. If we let her go, we're alienating her parents. And we know where we'd be without them."

"Teaching school under the oak tree. I know."

Skye recognized Miss Culbertson's voice. The principal's assistant had given Skye a cool reception since her first day here.

"There's no good answer." Headmaster Steven's voice sounded defeated. He was a kind man who'd welcomed her, which was more than she could say for some of her fellow teachers. "She's a good teacher. Unfortunately, it seems like some parents would prefer a lesser teacher to someone of her…race."

Skye slowly, silently turned the knob and crept into her classroom. The sentiments weren't new to her. She'd heard them all before, in some form or fashion. Still, they stung. But the revelation that she was only hired because of her parents' money? That sealed her decision.

She sat at her desk, pulled a fresh sheet of paper from the drawer, and removed her pen from the inkwell. With broad, clear strokes, she began her letter of resignation. Effective immediately. She'd give it to Headmaster Stevens after she had a chance to say good-bye to her students.

She'd just signed her name when Sarah entered. "Good morning, Miss Stratton."

"Good morning. Place your things on your desk and line up at the door. As soon as the boys arrive, we're taking a field trip."

"A field trip? Why do we want to visit a field?"

Skye smiled. "A field trip is simply a school trip to a location outside the school."

Levi and Thomas entered.

"We're going to a field trip," Sarah told them with a superior attitude. "That's a school trip. Teacher said to line up at the door."

The boys obeyed, though Skye couldn't actually call her wiggly group of students a *line*.

"Students, today is a very special day, and it calls for a special celebration."

The three children jumped up and down. "Are we havin' a party?" Levi asked.

Skye only smiled. "Join hands and come with me." She led her students into the hallway, down the front steps, and across the street to the mercantile.

Glyn Smith, proprietor, looked up when the bell over the door jangled. "Well, well. Hello, Miss Stratton. Who do you have with you?"

The store looked empty, aside from an older woman who browsed through bolts of cloth. The woman gave them a brief glance, pausing her gaze at Skye, frowned, and returned to her search.

Skye returned her attention to Virginia and placed a hand on Sarah's shoulder. "This is Sarah, Levi and Thomas. They've been such good students, I'd like to reward them each with a piece of candy of their choice."

Levi whooped. Sarah and Thomas giggled and clapped their hands.

Glyn smiled. "Why, certainly. Lady and gentlemen, follow me. Let me show you my candy counter." He led the way past shelves and rows of everything from work boots to pencils to iron skillets, all the way to the glass display case at the back of the store.

Glyn's wife, Virginia, approached Skye from the shadows. "Where are the rest of your students?"

"That's all of them. I'd like to purchase each of them their own copy of the McGuffey Reader. Do you have any in stock?"

"I sure do. Let me get them for you."

Skye touched Virginia's arm before she moved away. "I know you don't open the café until lunch. I don't want to be a bother, but would it be possible to—"

"Of course," Virginia said. "It's not locked. Go on in, and I'll be right there. I just finished a batch of cookies. Would you like me to bring a plate?"

"That would be lovely. Thank you, Virginia." Skye herded the children into the café and directed them to take seats at a booth.

"Are we gonna eat breakfast?" Levi licked his lips. "'Cause I already ate, but I can eat again. 'Specially if it's biscuits an' gravy."

"Will we do our schoolwork here today?" Sarah asked. "If we are, I need to go back and get my pencil."

"You won't need your pencil," Skye whispered, fighting back the boulder that seemed caught in her throat. She hadn't thought this decision through. What would she tell these children who'd come to mean so much to her? How would she explain that she was leaving them?

Virginia bustled through the swinging door from the kitchen with the promised platter of cookies. "Here you go! This is a new recipe, and I need you kids to tell me what you think. I can't sell them in the store if they don't taste good."

The children cheered and reached for the cookies.

"I'll be right back with some milk. You can't have cookies without milk." Virginia disappeared into the kitchen again.

"Ain't you gonna have some, Miss Stratton?" Thomas pushed the platter in her direction.

"Not right now. I have something to tell you. Why don't I talk while you eat?" Three heads bobbed their agreement. "I have an opportunity that I want to share with all of you. In another town, just a few hours away, are some children—much like you—who are in need of a teacher. Only there isn't a teacher near them. It's not like Lampasas, where there are plenty of people who can teach school. I've been asked to go and help these children and be their teacher."

Sarah held her cookie in mid-air, and her lip quivered. "You…you're gonna leave us?"

Levi froze, slack-jawed, gooey bits of chewed cookie visible in his mouth.

Skye didn't have the heart to correct him. "I don't want to leave you. After all, you are my favorite students! You'll always be my first class, and no one can ever take your place. But I feel bad that you have so many people who want to be your teacher, but these other children don't have anyone to teach them. If they don't have a teacher, they'll grow up not knowing how to read or write or do sums. They'll have a hard time getting jobs if they can't do those things, which means they might go hungry, and their families might go hungry."

The children stared at her, all glisteny-eyed. This was not going well. An idea came to her. "I was hoping you could help me teach them. You could each be my assistant teachers."

"You wanna take us wit' ya? I don't think my mama would like that." Levi looked so serious, Skye couldn't help but smile.

"I agree. Your parents would miss you very much if you left. That's why I need you to stay here. Once I arrive there, I'll encourage the children to write letters to you, and you can write back. Learning to write will be more fun for them if they have someone to write to, someone who will answer."

"I gotta write letters?" Thomas looked miserable.

"You could send a drawing, instead. Anything you want. Don't you think it will be fun to send and receive letters in the mail?"

"Maybe." Levi didn't look convinced.

"You could draw pictures of things you see here in Lampasas, and they can do the same. It will be like going on a long field trip without leaving home, because you'll learn about a place you've never been." Skye smiled her best sunshine smile, hoping it would catch to the children.

"B-b-but we don't want you to leave." Sarah dropped her head.

"I know. And I will miss you all terribly. But my family still lives here. It's not like I'll be gone forever."

Three pairs of eyes studied her as if gauging what their own reactions should be. She held her face in a smile and lifted her eyebrows more, in hopes they wouldn't see through her false joy.

After a fat moment of no response, Levi popped the rest of his cookie into his mouth and grabbed a second one. "Who's gonna be our new teacher?" he mumbled.

Skye slowly exhaled. "I'm not sure. But I know it will be someone fabulous. Do you know how many people want to be your teacher? So many people. And it's because they've heard what bright students you are, and how pleasant you are to work with. There's a good chance that more students will enroll in your class too. Won't that be fun?"

She didn't wait for them to answer. Instead, she picked up one of the cookies and set it on her plate. "I'll need you all to be my special leaders, though. The new teacher will be nervous. Did you know teachers get nervous? I'll need the three of you to be model citizens, to show the newer students how they should behave in school. It will be your job to make the new teacher and the new students feel welcomed and wanted. Can you do that for me?"

Hesitantly, her three champions nodded.

"Splendid. Now that's out of the way, what would you like to do today? I declare today a celebration day, all day. We can do whatever you want, within reason."

"I saw toads hoppin' all over the place on my way to school today, by the river. Can we go catch some of 'em?" Levi managed to look hopeful and doubtful at the same time.

"That's a wonderful idea! Let's do it. What else?" Skye looked at Sarah and Thomas.

"Can we go to my place?" Thomas asked. "My pa built me a treehouse, and I wanna show it to you."

Thomas's place was actually on The Big Skye property. She'd seen Mr. Brown working on the structure a couple of times. "Of course. I'd love to see your treehouse." She moved her gaze to Sarah, who looked on the verge of tears. "What about you? Did I see you with a kitten the other day?"

Instantly, the girl's eyes brightened. "We have a whole litter!"

"Would you like to show them to us?"

A smile split Sarah's face. "Yes, I would!"

Soon the children laughed and chattered about all the things they'd do, and Skye's heart felt a little lighter. They stayed in the café for another half hour. When Skye tried to pay the bill, Virginia would hear none of it. "Consider it our contribution to the local school system." The woman lowered her voice. "Our town is losing one of the best teachers around, Miss Stratton, as far as I'm concerned. I hope you find what you're looking for."

Skye hugged the woman, not even sorry she'd been eavesdropping. "Thank you. That means more than you know." She herded her three young charges back onto the boardwalk and across the street to the schoolhouse. "Gather all your things and line up. I'll be right back." She left them in the classroom and walked, shoulders back, head high, into Mr. Stevens' office.

Miss Culbertson gave her a cursory nod. "I'll be with you in a moment."

"No need. Please give this to Mr. Stevens." Skye placed the sealed envelope with her resignation letter on the woman's desk. "The children and I will take a field trip, and I'll see each of them home. Good day." She didn't wait for the woman's response. As she walked back toward her classroom, a wave of electricity she hadn't expected pulsed through her core. What was this feeling she had?

Anxiety? No.

Excitement? Possibly, but that wasn't the word she would choose. She inhaled slowly, exhaled. Just before she reached the door to her classroom, it came to her—that word to describe her emotions.

Freedom.

~

*A*lan smoothed the covers over his bed, grabbed his hat, and exited into the hallway. Would he stay here tonight or not? He had no way of knowing. If Skye said yes, he'd stick around a couple more days to secure all the arrangements. If she said no, he'd probably get out of town as quickly as possible. Hopefully without running into Colt Stratton. At this point, he might as well just head home and give up hope of working for the government. He could move back in with his parents until he figured out his next course of action. Colt may have the power to blacklist him in politics, but he couldn't keep him from making a living in his own hometown. Could he?

Maybe Alan could farm. Or preach, like his father.

He snorted. Him, a preacher? God would surely strike him dead before that happened. But surely he'd find some way to make himself useful enough to make a life for himself. Even if it wasn't the life of political service he'd once imagined.

He grabbed a muffin off a tray in the dining room—he'd slept through breakfast—and headed to the stables out back to get Fiona. He had several hours to kill before he met Miss Stratton at the schoolhouse. He might as well make the most of them and do some sightseeing.

When he turned the corner onto Main Street, he spotted Skye, three children following behind her like a mama duck with her chicks. They carried their lunch packs, and she carried a parasol. Where were they going?

He steered Fiona into the shadow cast by the post office and watched. They headed out of town, toward her property. He'd follow them.

No. That might make her uncomfortable.

But he had planned to go out there today. Riley had extended an open invitation, after all. And the grounds were beautiful. Peaceful. Almost holy. Could a resort be a holy place? He didn't know for sure, but that's what he'd felt during his visit there yesterday. Like God's presence lived and thrived there.

He pushed thoughts of the Almighty aside and watched Skye and the children disappear around a bend in the road. He might as well carry on with his original plans. If he happened to pass Skye Stratton on the road, what difference would that make? He clicked to Fiona and headed toward The Big Skye. It didn't take long for him to catch the little group.

She turned and shaded her eyes but said nothing.

He removed his hat. "Good morning to you, Miss Stratton! I see you're in fine company this morning."

Skye nodded like a queen acknowledging a peasant. "Good day, Mr. McNaughten. I'd like you to meet my students. This is Sarah, Levi, and Thomas."

Each child smiled and muttered a "pleased to meet you."

"It's an honor." He hopped from the saddle and led Fiona by her reins. "May I walk with you?"

Skye nodded. "Be my guest."

They'd walked in silence for the better part of a minute when the smallest boy—was that Levi?—said, "There! That's where all the toads was this mornin'!" He pointed off to the left, to a slow-running stream. Sure enough, a toad chorus creaked a low-bass symphony. A couple plopped into the water at their footsteps, causing tiny kerplunk-splashes.

"*Were*, Levi. That's where all the toads *were*." Skye spoke a gentle censure, her smile softening the blow.

"That's what I said!" The boy, oblivious to the grammar lesson, dropped his lunch bucket on the roadside and half-ran, half-skipped to the water's edge. "C'mon. I'll bet we can catch a whole bucketful. Oh, I'll need my bucket."

"Why don't we catch and release them?" Skye said. "There's no need to take them from their home." To Alan's surprise, she lifted her dainty skirt and tromped into the high grass. "First one to catch a toad wins a new pencil."

Alan found a low tree branch and looped Fiona's reins. He'd caught his share of toads in his day. This sounded fun.

Sarah stayed at the edge of the road, clutching her lunch bucket and looking unsure.

"What are you waiting for?" Alan asked her. "You have more than enough pencils?"

The girl turned round eyes on him. "No. But these are new shoes. I don't want them to get muddy."

Alan well remembered the new shoes he got at the beginning of each school year. He'd never thought much about getting them muddy, but then again, he wasn't a girl. He wondered if Skye had ever cared about such things. She didn't seem to now.

"That makes perfect sense, Miss Sarah. Why don't I give you a ride?" He knelt in front of her and instructed her to climb on his back.

She giggled but didn't hesitate.

Soon they stood at the water's edge. Alan found a rock large enough for the girl to stand on and lowered her to it. "Your shoes should be safe here."

The two boys and Miss Stratton both hopped around, trying to catch the leaping creatures without much luck. To his left, he spotted a large, brown toad hiding beneath a fern. Slowly, stealthily, he inched in behind it, grabbing it before the creature had a chance to escape. "Hold out your hands." He placed the fat fellow in Sarah's grasp. She squealed, but she didn't let go. Her smile told him she wasn't afraid.

The others turned at her squeal.

"I believe Sarah's won the pencil!" Alan grinned, satisfied that Skye knew he'd caught one before she did.

"Oh, no, Miss Stratton. Mr. McNaughten won the pencil. He just handed the toad to me."

The two boys stamped through the tall grass to Sarah's rock. "Wow, look at 'im. I've never held one that big before."

Skye eyed the toad before returning her gaze to Alan. "Well done, Mr. McNaughten. I shall reward you and your assistant each with new pencils when we arrive at our destination. Now, let's have a look at this creature. My, he must be ancient. I've never seen one this large."

"Can I hold the frog?" Thomas held out his hands to Sarah.

"You may each have a turn, but first, I'd like us all to note that this is a toad, not a frog. May I?" Skye gently took the toad and held it where the boys could also see.

"What's the difference?" Sarah crinkled her nose.

Skye motioned for Sarah to scoot over on the rock, brushed off a section, and took a seat. "Many people don't know the difference between a frog and a toad, but after today, I hope you'll never confuse the two again. Do you see this toad's skin? Touch it. It's dry and rough, like leather. A frog has shiny, smooth, wet skin."

Alan watched the children stroke the animal, who looked bored. Too old to care, probably.

Skye handed the toad to Thomas. "Frogs are semi-aquatic. That means they live in the water and on land. Toads like the water, too, but they can live away from the water for a long time. They mostly stay near the water when they're breeding."

"How do they breed?" Levi asked.

Skye's face flushed from neck to cheeks. "Perhaps your next teacher will cover that."

Alan's mind reeled in fast forward, and the young teacher's voice faded momentarily. Did she say their *next teacher*? Did that mean she planned to accept his offer? He couldn't help the hope that rose up in him. Hope that had nothing to do with pleasing Colt Stratton and everything to do with the excitement he felt about Skye Stratton becoming a more permanent fixture in his life.

*a*n hour later, the small group was back on the road toward The Big Skye. Alan wondered if his presence miffed Skye, but she didn't seem to mind his company. She hadn't brought up her intentions, and he didn't either.

At the resort entrance, Alan pulled Fiona that way, but Skye and the children kept walking. Should he follow? That would be presumptuous.

"Come with us!" Sarah said, taking him by the hand. "We're going to my place. I have kittens."

Alan lifted his eyes to Skye, and she offered an ever-so-slight nod. He couldn't help the silly half-grin he knew made him look like a love-sick calf. He allowed Sarah to lead him—and Fiona—toward their destination.

Skye kept her pace slower, more dignified, matching her stride with Alan's.

"Thank you for letting me tag along on your field trip."

She smiled but didn't meet his eyes. "You're welcome. I didn't expect to see you this early in the day."

"I'm not trying to rush you. Would you like me to leave? I'd planned to visit your place today and test out the springs—your father said it was all right. You just happened to be walking the same direction."

"I don't object to your presence, Mr. McNaughten. I suppose it's good for us to become more acquainted, since we'll be working together."

Alan wanted to whoop. "So the answer is yes?"

She paused her steps, turned to face him. "The answer is yes." The way she stood, backlit by the sun, made her appear more angel than human.

"I'm very happy to hear that. Have you already informed the school superintendent of your intentions?"

"I have. I resigned. Effective today."

Alan's eyebrows raised. "That was fast."

"I still haven't told my family. I'll need a few days to pack and say my good-byes."

"A week, then? Two weeks?"

She sucked in a long, ragged breath. He hoped she wouldn't change her mind. Should he have suggested a month? "Two weeks should be fine."

They reached the barn entrance. In one corner, the children sat on a pile of hay, playing with four—maybe five—small kittens. Mama cat licked her paws nearby and pretended not to care.

Alan touched Skye's elbow before she entered. "In that case, I think I'll head home now. I'd like to make arrangements for you before your arrival. I'll see that your ticket is purchased for the train." He pulled out his new calling card, which had his Livingston address. "If you need me, you can write or wire me at this address."

She clicked her parasol closed, took the card, and placed it in her pocket. "Thank you, Mr. McNaughten." Did she seem sad? If so, that was an appropriate emotion. After all, she'd just agreed to leave her home. She stared at it now through the open barn door, wistfulness in her gaze.

"Miss Stratton?"

She blinked and met his eyes.

"The students of the Alabama-Coushatta reservation will be fortunate to have you as their teacher."

She nodded her thanks, then walked toward her students and the kittens.

He watched her retreat, and something in his heart swelled in the most uncomfortable yet satisfying way. He cleared his throat. "Ladies and gentlemen, I must bid you good-day. Enjoy your field trip."

The children waved and called out good-byes, but they were absorbed in the kittens and their teacher. Without another word, Alan climbed on Fiona, clicked his tongue, and rode back to the boarding house. He had a lot of ground to cover today.

~

*A*fter a full morning of romping and playing with her three young charges, Skye led the sweaty group to the wide veranda on the back side of the resort. Here, they could giggle and squeal without disturbing the other guests. On the way, she'd asked the cook to prepare them a tray with today's specials and instructed the maître d' to set a table. Might as well toss a lesson in decorum and social graces into the mix.

Sarah's eyes grew round and wide when she saw the table. "This is so fancy, Miss Stratton. Is this for us?"

"Indeed it is. Today is a celebration, remember? I can't think of anyone I'd rather celebrate with."

"A celebration? What are we celebrating?" Mama hovered in the double door leading to the main dining room. Her smile rested on Skye, but her eyes looked unsure. Like she didn't really want to hear the reason.

"Today's Miss Stratton's last day with us," Levi said. "I think it's sad, not happy. But she wants a party, so we're giving her one." The child's words brought a catch to Skye's throat. Had she made the right choice?

Too late now. She'd already resigned her position.

"I see." Mama cast a wobbly smile at Skye before joining them. "May I invite myself to this…celebration?"

Skye had a hard time meeting her mother's eyes. She hadn't meant for her to find out this way. "Certainly, Mama."

"And what else have you done today to celebrate?" Mama turned her attention on the children, who all answered at once with their own renditions of the morning. Mama smiled and nodded as if their words were the most interesting she'd ever heard.

When the chatter died down, Mama stood again. "If this is to be a proper celebration, I think a special cake is in order."

"Mama, no. That's not—"

But the children's cheers drowned out her words. Cookies for breakfast. Cake at lunch. These children would be abuzz with sugar by the time she sent them home. Not long after Mama disappeared, another shadow fell on their little table. She looked up, expecting to see her father. Instead, it was Mr. Stevens. What was the headmaster doing here?

"Miss Stratton, may I speak with you privately for a moment?"

What could she say? She didn't want to cause a scene in front of the children. "Certainly. Students, I'll be right back. Why don't you take turns telling your favorite thing we've learned today?"

Skye followed her boss—*former* boss—to the opposite side of the veranda, close enough to keep an eye on the children's mischief, but far enough away not to be heard.

"What is this?" He held up her letter.

"I'm resigning."

"I know that. Why?"

Skye took a moment to gather her thoughts. She hadn't

expected the man to track her down at home. "It's best this way."

"For whom?"

"For everyone."

"Skye." He didn't often use her given name any more. "I've known you since you were a child. You were my best student, and I know one of these days, you'll be my best teacher. You can't leave."

"I can't be your best teacher, Mr. Stevens, when my very existence causes so many students to miss out on a year of school. And don't tell me you disagree. You know I'm right."

He pressed his lips together. "I'd wager they won't miss a whole year. Right now, your 'existence,' as you say, as a teacher, is new. People need time to get used to the idea. They'll come around. Give it a month, and the controversy will die down. Please, don't do this."

Mr. Stevens had a kind heart. Good intentions. But he didn't understand. No one understood what it was like to be a half-blood Indian in a town where most people hated Indians. "I've accepted another position, at a place where people won't have to *get used* to the idea that an Indian will teach their children. I'll teach for the Alabama-Coushatta Reservation in East Texas. I'm sorry for any inconvenience it's caused you, but I know you had several other applicants for my position. You shouldn't have trouble filling it."

He looked out over the grounds, his gaze settling on the pond. He swallowed, and his Adam's apple bobbed.

How unexpected. She'd thought he'd be glad to be rid of her.

After a time, he faced her, his eyes shiny. "No one can fill your shoes, Skye. But those students in East Texas will be blessed by your presence. If this is what you want, I'm happy for you. I wish you all the best. May God go with you." He nodded, turned, and left.

Soon Mama returned, and they spoke no more of the reason

for this dubious celebration. Instead, the two women instructed the children on how to place the napkin in their laps, which forks to use and when, and how to signal the waiter when they were finished with their meal. After a time, several of the wait-staff entered the veranda, one of them carrying a small, colorful cake topped with sizzling sparklers. The children oohed and ahhed and applauded while the staff held the cake at a safe distance. When the sparks died, the cake was placed in the center of the table and sliced. Strawberry shortcake. Skye's favorite.

"Thank you, Mama." Skye whispered the words.

Mama smiled, her eyes bright and shiny like Mr. Steven's had been. "You're welcome, my beautiful girl. I told you I'd support you, whatever you chose. Just promise me you'll always remember where home is."

"I will." Skye knew this would be hard. Right now, her heart felt like it was in a tug of war. But despite the tight feeling in her chest, she knew she'd made the right decision.

~

Alan scrambled to figure out what all needed to happen in order to get Skye safely to Livingston...and to keep her safe and happy. He'd given his word to her father.

Had he done the right thing?

Aligning himself with Colt Stratton could hardly be the right thing. Had he just pulled an innocent young woman into his dark schemes? Had he ruined her life? It was one thing when she'd been a faceless name on a piece of paper. But now that he'd met her, met her family, seen her with her students... Could she be happy living the simple, ofttimes discouraging life of a reservation schoolteacher?

She'd given up her job. If she decided to return here, to her home, would she be rehired?

Probably not. Not when she'd walked away like this. What had he done?

He pushed the thoughts to the back of his mind and tried to focus on next steps. A train ticket, for two weeks from now, for Skye. He immediately purchased one. Should he purchase two? Her father might choose to accompany her.

He purchased another, then returned to the boarding house and paid his bill. Gathered his things. Before leaving his room, he sat at the small desk and scribbled a note:

Dear Miss Stratton,

I am so pleased you've chosen to accept the position we discussed. Please find enclosed two tickets, one for you and one for a chaperone, for the train leaving Thursday, August 25, at 8 am. You will arrive in Houston at 12:26 pm and change trains. Your second train—to Silsbee—will leave at 1:00 pm. You're scheduled to arrive in Silsbee at 6:42 pm. I've arranged for you and your chaperone to stay overnight at The Hilliard Boarding House. I'll be there as well, and we'll leave by wagon Friday morning for a full day of travel back to Livingston.

Should you need anything in the meantime, don't hesitate to send me a wire at the address I gave you. I've set up an account for you at the telegraph office. I left my forwarding address there, as well, for easy access.

The students of the Alabama Coushatta Reservation are fortunate to be getting such a fine teacher.

Ever your servant,

Alan McNaughten, Indian Agent

He read back over the note and, satisfied, folded it into the envelope. He pulled out a second sheet of paper, pushed down the bile that rose in his throat, and wrote,

S. has accepted the position and will leave within two week's time.

A.

He placed that into another envelope, sealed it, and addressed it to Colt Stratton.

Within the half hour, he'd dropped off Colt's letter at the post office. He decided to deliver Skye's letter in person, in case she had any questions. After that, it was time to go home.

~

Skye had just delivered her three charges to their homes on the edge of the Big Skye property and took the long way back to her house. The winding river gurgled and giggled over rocks and twigs, and lush green moss hanging from weeping willows tickled her skin as she passed beneath. Over the years, this place had soothed her spirit even in the worst of times. Would there be a place like this in her new home?

Sometimes, when she walked here, she wondered what it would be like to talk to her parents' God. At times, she thought she could hear Him talking to her. But she knew better than to talk back or to acknowledge Him in any way. She'd tried that once, and the results were disastrous. Instead, she focused on her breathing, on being aware of her thoughts and emotions, and she tried to be grateful for the good things in her life. Those things usually helped, though the results never seemed to last.

She had just taken the fork that led back to the main house when she heard horse hooves and recognized Fiona's gait. Sure enough, when Skye cleared the trees, there was Alan. He didn't notice her for a moment, and she took advantage of the opportunity to appreciate the fine cut of his jaw, his sculpted shoulders, his straight, confident posture. She wasn't sure she could trust him, but there was no denying...the man was handsome.

If she was going to have to work for him, at least there was that.

He was almost upon her before he noticed her, and he visibly started.

Skye chuckled. "Sorry. Didn't mean to scare you."

"Scared? Pshhhh. I never get scared." Alan grinned, a spark to his eye.

"I'll keep that in mind."

He slid to the ground and dug around in his pack. "I'm headed out. I hope I can make it to Waco before nightfall. But I wanted to give you this first, and answer any questions you might have thought of before I go."

She took the envelope, slid out the letter inside, and skimmed it. "It looks like you've thought of everything." She lifted her eyes to meet his. "I can't think of any questions right now. I'm sure I'll come up with a few the minute you're gone, though."

He made patterns in the dirt with the toe of his boot. "Are you really sure about this?"

She exhaled a long breath. "Are you trying to get me to change my mind?"

He gave her a half smile, and she noticed his canine tooth was a little crooked. Lands sake, he was nice to look at. She looked away.

"Do you make it a habit to answer a question with a question?" His voice was low and rumbly. Intimate.

She fought the wave of heat that seeped into her skin. Why did he do this to her? She was being a silly-headed girl. "Is it a problem if I do?" She grinned a sassy grin. Was she flirting with this man? What was she thinking?

He laughed a loud guffaw. "No, ma'am. I don't reckon it is. But you still haven't answered me."

Oh, yes. Was she sure she wanted to do this? "No, Mr. McNaughton, I'm not sure. But I am sure that if I stay here, nothing will change for me. At least not any time soon. You've offered me a chance to reinvent myself, and I plan to take it."

He studied her for a moment.

She held his gaze, and it felt uncomfortable and safe at the same time. For the life of her, she couldn't figure out why this man had such an effect on her. She'd have to move past that.

"Well then, Miss Stratton, I hope you feel as good about your decision a year from now as you do right now. As for reinventing yourself, I don't think there's need for that. Seems to me you're perfect…for the job, I mean…just the way you are."

She fought with the smile that tugged her cheeks. She didn't want to like this man. Not this much. "Thank you. That's kind of you to say."

He nodded and climbed back into his saddle, tipped his hat. "I'll see you in a couple of weeks, then. Good day, Miss Stratton."

She held up her hand in a half-wave but said nothing as she watched him ride back toward the main road. She had two weeks to get this school-girl infatuation under control. Because one thing was for certain—the last thing she needed was to fall in love with a white man. Or any man, for that matter. Her mixed race had doomed her from the start. She'd never fit into anyone's world, and any children she bore would experience the same heartache. She wouldn't put that on anyone.

No. An old maid schoolteacher was the best life she could hope for, the best future she could imagine. In a remote place, where no one cared that she was a half-breed. Yes, this was her chance, and she was taking it.

~

After delivering the letter, Alan was ready to head home. It would be faster to take the train, and he was more than ready to see his parents again. But several days on the trail, just Alan, Fiona, and God, would give him some time to consider some of the probing questions that weighed on his heart.

Once he was in the saddle, ready to leave Lampasas, he noticed Colt Stratton with his wife and son parking his carriage near the bank. Alan waited for the family to disembark and watched the wife and son head for the store. Alan guided Fiona toward the carriage, not sure what he'd say to the man.

Colt saw him coming, then looked at his family, like he wanted to make sure they weren't within hearing distance before greeting him. He took in Allen's packs and rolls. "Leaving town so soon?"

"Your niece has agreed to take the job. I sent you a letter stating that. I'm headed to Livingston to set up her living arrangements."

"I told you not to call her that." The muscles in Colt's jaw twitched, and his nose flared.

"That's what she is. I'm sorry if that bothers you. I have a question—why are you doing this? She's a beautiful, intelligent young woman with a family who loves her. It's one thing not to like someone. But why not just ignore her? Why do you feel the need to drive her out of town?"

"I don't believe that's any of your concern, Mr. McNaughten."

"This is wrong, and I don't like being a part of it."

"You're free to back out on the deal. Just remember the consequences. We have an agreement, and if you don't follow through with your end, you can forget about this or any other government appointment. I'll make sure you're blacklisted from ever working in politics. Money is power, son, and I've got plenty of it. Last I checked, you don't."

Alan held the man's gaze, and the taste of acid and bile scourged his throat.

A slow, sinister smile spread across Colt's face. "Are we clear?"

"Perfectly." Alan pulled at Fiona's reins, turned around, and galloped away from one of Satan's favorite servants.

The only problem was, Alan couldn't run away from himself.

~

*P*acking proved a harder task than making the decision to go in the first place. What would Skye wear to teach in? She didn't want to appear haughty. How did they dress? In native garb? In white man's clothing? She wished she'd asked Alan before he left.

And what kinds of school supplies did they have? Did she need to take all her books? Should she purchase slates? Not two days had passed, and she already wanted to send Alan a telegram. But it was pointless, since he probably hadn't had time to arrive at his destination yet. She'd wait a couple more days and then send a wire with all her questions.

Before long, her initial hesitation gave way to excitement. What a grand adventure! Would she meet her mother's family? Would they welcome her? The idea that she'd finally be at a place where she belonged, where she might feel accepted by the community, sent butterflies spiraling through her middle. She couldn't help the smile that rested on her face while she prepared for her journey of a lifetime.

"Need some help?" Mama stepped into Skye's room, eying the half-empty trunk.

"I don't know what to take. I should have asked more questions."

"Pack light. Once you arrive and assess your needs, let us know. We'll send whatever you want."

"Better yet—we'll bring it." Daddy leaned against her door

frame. "I know your mother, brother and sister will want to see your new place."

Skye folded a navy skirt and placed it in the trunk. "I'd love that."

Papa moved inside and sat in her desk chair. "It's not too late to change your mind. It's never too late, in my opinion."

"I know. But I feel good about this. I'm excited."

Mama sat on the edge of Skye's bed, the strain around her eyes telling a different story than her cheerful voice. "You'll be wonderful. Now, let's look at your wardrobe. Surely you need me to make you a couple of things before you go! You'll need new dresses for a new job."

Mama was an excellent seamstress. Skye needed nothing, but a sewing project would give Mama something to throw her energy into for the next week and a half.

And give Skye something else to focus on besides the grand adventure she was about to begin. This could be the best decision she'd ever made. Or it could be just one more opportunity to find a place where she didn't belong.

CHAPTER 7

*A*lan's trip home was uneventful, other than a couple of thunderstorms. He and Fiona took cover in caves and crevices when needed and arrived in Livingston late Friday evening.

He hadn't warned his parents he was coming. He wanted to surprise them. Three years, he'd been gone. Now, as he stood on the porch and removed his hat, he wondered whether he should knock. Normally, he wouldn't. But he didn't want Ma and Pa to think it was a break-in. Preacher or not, Pa wasn't past putting a bullet in a man's chest to protect his wife. Well, more likely in his leg. Alan knocked three times.

He saw the kerosene lamp flicker through the window. Slowly, the door scraped open a crack. The light blinded Alan to who was behind it. He smiled, waved. "It's me."

"Alan?" The door flung open, and Alan was pulled into James McNaughten's embrace. "Is it really you? Get in here, boy! Why didn't you send ahead? Let us know? Your mother will be fit to be tied. She would have made a special meal and put fresh sheets on your bed."

"That's why I didn't let you know." He backed out of his dad's hug. "How is she?"

Pa's gaze dropped to the floor momentarily. "That cough of hers is getting worse." He lifted his eyes to Alan's and smiled. "But she'll be better now. I guarantee it. Come. She's asleep, but she'll want to be awake to see you."

"Maybe you should let her sleep. I don't want to—"

"Nonsense. You're the best medicine she could have, and I know she'll want a big dose as soon as possible." He led Alan into their small bedroom and perched on the bedside. "Susie? Sue, honey. Wake up. Look who's come to visit!"

Alan watched the tender way his father roused his mother. In all his twenty-eight years, he'd never seen another love like theirs.

"James? What is it? What's wrong?" The lamplight flickered over Sue McNaughten's gaunt cheeks. She must have lost twenty pounds since Alan last saw her, and she was a small woman to begin with.

Alan moved beside his father. "Howdy, Ma. It's me."

Her eyes blinked, confusion clouding them. "Alan?"

"Yes, ma'am."

A broad smile split her face, her eyes widened, and she tried to push herself up on her elbows.

"Don't get up." Alan leaned over and embraced her. "I wanted to surprise you. I'm here to stay, so we'll have plenty of time to catch up."

She tilted her head to the side. "To stay? That's wonderful. But why? What happened to Washington? To your political career?"

"It's taken a new direction. You're looking at the new Indian Agent for the Alabama-Coushatta Reservation."

The silence that followed his statement was louder than a creek full of August bullfrogs. Ma and Pa looked at him like he spoke Mandarin, not English. Alan didn't say more. Just smiled as if being an Indian Agent was his lifelong dream come true.

Pa broke the silence. "That's wonderful, son. I couldn't be prouder of you."

Ma's eyes glistened in the low light. "You'll be wonderful. I don't know why we didn't think of it before. You're perfect! You have such a kind, decent heart. I can't think of anyone better for the job."

"I'm not sure about that, Ma. But I'll do my best." It felt wrong to be the recipient of his parents' pride when he knew the only reason he got the appointment was because he was willing to deal dirty with the devil.

"James, there are fresh sheets in the trunk there." Ma nodded toward the chest. "Make sure his bed is made."

"I can make my own bed." Alan kissed his mother on the forehead, grabbed the sheets, and exited. "I'll see you in the morning," he called over his shoulder before Pa followed him into the hallway and shut the door behind them.

"She may not sleep a wink, now." Pa's grin warmed Alan to his core. "But that's all right. It's so good to have you home, son."

"It's good to be here."

Pa stood in the hallway, holding the lantern, blocking Alan's way to his room. "Do you want to tell me about it now or later?"

No use asking what Pa meant. That man could always see straight through to Alan's soul and love him anyway. "I'm tired. Can it wait 'til morning?"

"Sure thing. Sleep well." He moved aside and handed Alan the lantern as he passed. "I love you, son."

"I love you too, Pa."

He made his bed quickly, climbed out of his boots and outerwear, and slid into the most comfortable place on earth. Each time he closed his eyes, Skye Stratton's face appeared in his mind, same as it had the past two nights on the trail. There was something vulnerable beneath that beautiful, confident exterior.

Almost like one of those raspberry-filled hard candies from Green's General Store. The outside was nice, but once you broke through the hard shell, the sweetness exploded. He wondered what it would take to break through her shell, and if he even wanted to.

Would they remove him from his post if he married someone of mixed Indian heritage? Did he care? And why on earth did the word marriage even enter his mind? He was perfectly happy as a bachelor. He sighed and tried to push thoughts of the pretty schoolteacher out of his mind.

He was bone weary. And there was something about home that felt sacred and holy. He may be dirty right now. But if he wanted his sins washed clean, he knew this was a good place to start.

He only hoped he hadn't done too much, gone too far, to ever really come home.

~

*S*kye waited as the postmaster sent the wire. How long until Alan received it? She wondered when she could expect a reply. She thanked the man, exited the small building, and nearly ran headlong into her Uncle Colt.

"Oh, I'm sorry."

"Oh. Skye. How are you?"

That was more acknowledgment than he had ever given her. And right there on a public street?

"I'm doing well, *Uncle Colt.*" She spoke a little louder than normal and bit back the grin that threatened. She knew he hated when she called him that in public. She kept her eyes wide, her expression innocent. There! She saw the slightest cringe. Served him right.

"How do you like teaching?" His words may have been neutral, but there was cruelty in his eyes.

"I'm sure you've heard I've accepted a new position. I'll leave in about a week."

"I see. Well, I wish you every success in your new job." He lifted his hat before heading down the boardwalk.

Something inside her wanted to call, "You're welcome to come visit any time!" But she knew better than to bait a bobcat. She turned to head the other direction only to find a trio of mean church ladies eyeing her, their fans covering their mouths to keep their noxious gossip from reaching her ears.

A week ago, she would have lowered her eyes and kept walking. Today, she looked each of them in the eye and smiled. "Good afternoon, ladies. It's a lovely day, isn't it?" She held her head up and brushed past them as if she had no idea they hated her. Soon, if everything worked out the way she hoped it would, she'd never have to look at them again.

~

Sunday morning dawned clear and bright. Alan could have stayed in bed longer—he hadn't slept that well since…he couldn't remember when. But there was no way he'd miss hearing Pa preach his first Sunday back.

He'd bathe in the creek out back; no need to fill the tub. He still had some old Sunday meeting clothes in his wardrobe. He hoped they still fit. The clothes from his pack were all wrinkled and smelled like horse sweat.

Ma was in the kitchen, fixing breakfast. She looked so small.

"I hope you're not doing that for me. I've been fending for myself for a while now."

Ma grinned. "I hate to think what you've been eating, if you had to cook for yourself. Sit down and grab a plate."

He obeyed, and she piled three flapjacks and two hefty sausage links on his plate, her hands shaking as she worked. With slow, strained movements, she poured a cup of coffee and, after spilling a couple of drops on the floor, set it on the table before taking the chair across from him. "I may be ailing, but I'm not dead. I love cooking for you, sweet boy."

Alan chuckled. Ma hadn't changed a bit.

"Your father's already at the churchhouse. I'll walk over with you as soon as you're ready."

He eyed the flapjacks and savored the scent of warm, maple syrup. He wished she hadn't done all this, but he did love her cooking. "Ma, Pa wrote to me and said you were…not well." Alan could see that was true.

"Pshaw. I'm fine. This consumption gets me down from time to time, but I'm too ornery to die."

"You're the opposite of ornery, Ma. But you do have a stubborn streak, so you may be right." He watched her bring her own coffee to her lips with unsteady hands.

She sipped, then set her cup down. "I said I'm fine. Pray, then eat."

Alan hadn't said a prayer aloud since he'd last sat at this table before leaving for D.C. "Dear Father, thank you for this food. And thank you for home. Amen."

Ma coughed. "Amen. Now tell me more about how you ended up as the Indian Agent. You've been here since last night, and I feel like you're holding back."

Alan cut into his flapjacks. "Can it wait until this afternoon?" He still had to figure out exactly what to say to his parents. Would he tell them the whole story, or the version he wanted them to believe?

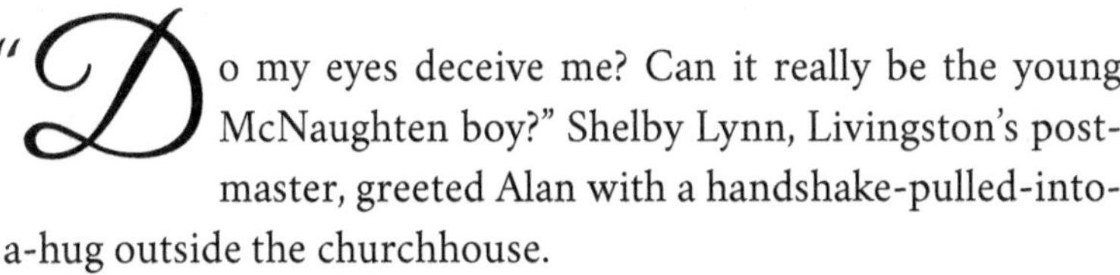

"Do my eyes deceive me? Can it really be the young McNaughten boy?" Shelby Lynn, Livingston's postmaster, greeted Alan with a handshake-pulled-into-a-hug outside the churchhouse.

"Not so young any more, I'm afraid." Alan smiled at the man.

His wife, Debbie, hugged him next. "Young is a matter of perspective. Trust me. You're still a whippersnapper."

The service was over, and people practically tripped over themselves to reach Alan. Though Ma and Pa raised him, the entire congregation claimed him as their own. A picture of Skye as a little girl flitted through his mind, and he wondered what it had felt like for her, being adopted. Apparently, her experience was different from his.

"I should have suspected you were headed this way," Mr. Lynn said. "I received a wire earlier this week addressed to you. I placed it in your parents' post box, but your father only checks his box on Monday. It didn't seem urgent, so I didn't deliver it. I'll be glad to get it for you, if you want. Somebody named Stratton, I believe."

That could be one of three people. Skye changed her mind? Riley checking in? A veiled threat from Colt? "Yes, I'd appreciate that. I'll meet you at the post office at two o'clock, if that works for you."

"That'll be fine. Just ring the bell." The Lynns lived above the post office, so at least they wouldn't have to go out of their way.

"Alan McNaughten. I do believe you've grown taller since you've been away."

An overpowering scent of drug-store manufactured lavender and roses assaulted Alan's senses and itched his throat. Margaret Tusselhoff. Alan turned toward the voice and tried not to cough. "Miss Tusselhoff."

"What is this 'miss' business? We've known each other since we were children. Call me Maggie." She fluttered a pink-and-white feathered fan in front of her face.

Was she flirting? Please, no. "It's a pleasure to see you again. I believe my mother has lunch waiting for me. I'd best not be late."

"Oh, dear. I was going to invite you to eat with my family. How about next Sunday?"

"My schedule is already occupied for next Sunday, but thank you for the invitation." He turned to leave, pretending not to hear her protests or her suggestion for any day of the week, any day at all.

Good gravy. The last thing he needed was Maggie Tusselhoff. Poor girl. She wasn't bad to look at. She just tried too hard to impress. The result was not impressive.

They had leftovers for lunch. Alan was more than happy to take charge of the reheating while Ma rested in the cushioned chair in the parlor area of the large room, and Pa sat at the table.

Pa cleared his throat. "When will you spill the tea, as our British friends like to say?"

"I'm not sure there's much to spill. I tried Washington. I didn't like what I saw. I figured out a way to come home." That much was true.

"What didn't you like about it?"

Allan stirred the beans, replaced the lid, and sat across from his father. "Politicians have a tendency to be more self-serving than public servants."

"I could have told you that. It's precisely why we need good men like you up there, making the decisions."

"Pa, I...I was becoming like them." Neither Pa nor Ma said anything, so Alan kept going. "I'm not proud of it, but I'm *good* at politics. I'm *good* at the scheming, the manipulation, the *charming* people into agreeing to things that aren't to their benefit. And that's not who I want to be."

"I see." Pa steepled his fingers in that way Alan knew all too well. It signaled a coming life-lesson or mini-sermon. "What's even better is that *you* see. We usually won't change for the better until we recognize our faults. But have you ever thought that those gifts you have are from God? Have you considered how you might use your charisma and charm to help others?

Because that's what you'll be called to do as the Indian Agent. You'll represent a group of people who need a loving, benevolent advocate."

"I hope I can be that. But to be honest, I didn't accept the position to be a 'loving, benevolent advocate.' I accepted it to come home. And I...I wasn't the most qualified for the position. I did something I'm not proud of in order to secure it."

"Would you like to tell me about it?"

He wanted to tell Pa, but he didn't want Pa to know. Which didn't make sense at all. "Not right now."

"All right, son. I'm here when you're ready to talk. But don't be so quick to rule out God's providence in your life. I think, despite your choices, He may have you exactly where He wants you."

"I hope so." Alan finished reheating the simple meal and spooned rice and beans into bowls. He and Pa ate at the table, while Ma stayed in her chair. When they finished, he put the dishes in the bucket to soak, told his parents he was going for a walk, and left them to their afternoon naps.

He had just reached for the bell at the post office when the door swung open and Shelby handed him an envelope. "Here you go, Alan. I'm so proud of you for your new position. Indian Agent! One of our own, a real federal officer. Let me know if I can ever be of assistance, ya hear?"

"Thank you, sir. I'll keep that in mind."

Alan waited until he was down the boardwalk a ways before he opened the message. He sat on a wooden bench and read the contents.

Packing—What kinds of supplies needed—Is gen. store available for more purchases—S. Stratton

He couldn't help the grin that warmed its way from his belly to his lips. She hadn't changed her mind. But in the next breath, the grin gave way to a frown. Was he ruining her life by bringing her here?

Nothing he could do about it now. The wheels were already turning.

As for the answer to her question about school supplies, the truth was, he didn't know. Now was as good a time as any to ride out and visit his new charges.

CHAPTER 8

The reservation was an hour's ride from town, too far for Miss Stratton to travel alone. Just outside the reservation boundaries, he stopped and let Fiona drink her fill from a clear creek. Should he just ride in, unannounced? He hadn't received any training for this post other than, "Take care of things, and make sure they don't bother the white folk."

All right, then. He was in charge. He'd ride in. He didn't bring any kind of ID with him. He wished he'd thought to tuck his card-sized Indian Agent certificate into his pocket before he left. He'd do that next time.

When Fiona was satiated and he'd worked up a little more fortitude, he entered the reservation gates and followed the narrow trail. The fresh, homey scent of pine needles calmed his nerves. He compared this setting with the scrubby oaks back in Lampasas. He may be biased, but Central Texas was a far second to the Piney Woods in terms of scenic beauty. Soon, he came to an opening in the thick, tall trees, and it was like a veil was pulled aside to reveal simple log structures and tepees. Brown-skinned people, dressed mostly in white-man's clothing, with the occasional headband or beaded necklace, went about their business. Many of them cast curious glances his way, but for the most part, they ignored him.

An older man rose from a bench and walked into the road, blocking Alan's path. His expression was neutral, wary but not threatening.

Alan slid from his saddle and extended his hand. "How do you do? My name is Alan McNaughten, and I'm the new Indian Agent for this reservation."

The man took his grip. "John Scott. I am the tribal chief."

Alan felt a brief moment of panic, but he forced his expression to remain calm. A chief? Alan knew how to deal with senators. He'd even met President Cleveland once. But a chief? Were the rules different? How was he supposed to act?

He decided to treat him with honor and respect, same as he'd do with a senator. "It's an honor, sir. I'm here as your representative. I'd like to be of assistance, any way I can."

The man—should he call him John? Mr. Scott? Chief?—didn't look excited or impressed. He didn't respond at all, just stood there, waiting for Alan to continue.

"Er...would you mind showing me around?"

Scott called out something in a language Alan didn't recognize, and a man appeared at his side. "This is Alan McNaughten. Indian Agent. Show him the reservation." To Alan he said, "This is the second chief."

The man looked to be in his late twenties or early thirties. He wore a white shirt and black pants, and his hair was cut short. He extended his hand for a firm handshake. "John Walker." Were they all called John?

Walker motioned for Alan to walk beside him. "This is our main part of town, what you would call Main Street, I suppose." His English was impeccable, and he pointed out the structures as they passed. "There is our general store, our church, the saloon. Down there is the school."

"I've secured you an excellent teacher. She will arrive in a week and will hopefully start classes soon after. I understand you've been without a teacher for some time now."

Walker's eyebrows rose, but he didn't comment. They kept walking through town, to a bend in the path that led to more small structures, many with thatched roofs. Several women stood around a fire, and the smell of roasted venison made his stomach growl. Small children played tag or helped their mothers add sticks to the fire. Some older boys, probably around age twelve, stared at him and whispered. Walker spoke to them in their native tongue, then turned back to Alan. "This is where we live. We try to keep our structures close together, both for safety and to leave our remaining land free for hunting, fishing, and farming."

Alan took it all in. It looked like these people got along pretty well without an agent. Still, he saw room for improvement here and there. Some of the houses could use repair, and most of the children were barefoot. That was fine for now, but he needed to make sure they had shoes for winter. "Can we head back to the schoolhouse? I'd like to get an idea of what's there and what we need to purchase."

Walker led him back to Main Street. He didn't seem to be much for small talk.

Alan wondered if he was naturally quiet, or if he just didn't care for white people. Or Indian Agents. "May I ask you a question?"

Walker's answer was to pause and look at Alan.

"Where were you educated? It's clear from your speech you've had schooling."

The man continued walking toward the schoolhouse as he spoke. "My people are extremely *educated,* as you say. We are educated by nature, by life. As for the education you refer to, Reverend Jacob Whitley and his wife, Sarah, lived here with us for many years. They taught us to read and write the white man's language. They taught us to do sums. About three years past, they both met the Creator. Jacob in January, Sarah in March of the same year. My people still mourn their passing."

Three years with no teacher. And apparently, no pastor. That was a long time in the life of a child, the life of a village.

Walker led him into the one-room schoolhouse. It was bigger than he'd expected, and well-kept for a room that had been in disuse for several years. He knew there were around five hundred people on the reservation. How many of them were school age? Would this schoolhouse be enough? He counted the desks—forty-eight. "How many students do you anticipate will attend school?"

"They only receive formal schooling from age five to age twelve. We currently have about forty children in that age range."

"Forty children and no teacher..." Alan muttered under his breath.

"They have been taught by one of my cousins. I believe you would call her a distant cousin. I'm sure she will be relieved to have someone with more experience."

More experience? Not necessarily. But Skye did have more than a sixth-grade education. "Do the students have what they need?"

Walker led him to a shelf behind the teacher's desk, where stacks of crumbling primers and cracked slates rested. Their supplies needed updating, but he wouldn't have the foggiest idea what to order. He'd message Skye to wait until she arrived. They could order supplies from Livingston.

He examined the room more closely. The chalkboard was scratched and worn. Some sandpaper and a fresh coat of paint should fix that. What else?

Probably best to wait for Skye. She could better assess the students' needs.

Forty students. That was a lot. "I hope your cousin will

continue on after Miss Stratton arrives. I'm sure she'll appreciate the help, especially at first."

"I will let her know."

There was so much more to learn, so many questions to ask. "Do you have a few minutes to sit and talk?" Alan motioned to one of the larger desks, and Walker sat. Alan took a seat across from him. "It looks like your people are self-sufficient. I'll be honest. I'm not just new to your reservation. I'm new to this job. I really do want to help in any way I can. Is there anything you need? What can I do?"

Walker held himself straight and stiff, and Alan had a hard time reading his expression. After a pause, the man answered. "Agents have visited before, but they rarely return. As long as we stay on our land and do not bother your people, we are left in peace."

"Is that what you want? To be left in peace?"

Walker held his gaze. "We do not want trouble. When we venture into the white man's territory, there is trouble."

Alan soaked in his words and the unspoken message behind them. "How often do you need to leave the reservation?" Even as he spoke the words, he realized their implication. These people were prisoners here. Peaceful, hardworking people, forced to stay within their government-imposed boundaries. No wonder Walker looked at him with such distrust.

"We trade in Livingston and Silsbee when we need supplies. I usually go alone. People feel less threatened if they see just one of us. If two or more go, we are often confronted for a fight. Alone, I'm merely insulted, and if I don't respond, nothing comes of it."

Nothing Walker said surprised Alan, but it distressed him nevertheless. "How should I address you and Mr. Scott? Forgive me for not knowing the proper etiquette. Should I call you chief? Mister? Sir?"

A look of surprise shuttered across Walker's eyes before his expression returned to neutral. "Our people address both Scott and me as *chief*. The white man uses mister or just plain "Walker," or "Scott.""

"Which do you prefer? Mister? Would you be offended if I called you Chief?"

One of the muscles in Walker's cheek twitched. "No offense will be taken. Do as you please."

Alan considered the man's words, and the lack of honor shown to these people. "In that case, Chief Walker, I hope you won't mind introducing me to some of your people. I don't plan to be an absentee agent."

Chief Walker stood and gestured for Alan to follow him. After meeting several people—men and women—who looked at him with wary politeness, they returned to Chief Scott. The man nodded what Alan assumed was a dismissal, but the older man said nothing more. Soon, Alan left the reservation with more questions than he'd had before he arrived.

The days passed quickly, and Alan returned each day to the reservation, learning the people's needs and their ways. There was still much to be done to prepare for Skye's arrival, but it would have to wait. He was due to meet her in Silsbee tomorrow. He hitched Fiona to Pa's buckboard—nothing fancy, but well-hinged for a smooth ride. The journey would give Alan a chance to do some figuring in his head.

"You sure are taking extra care for your appearance," Pa said as Alan buttoned his freshly-starched, second-best shirt. "This school teacher…she caught your eye?"

"Of course not," Alan lied. "Nothing wrong with wanting to look my best for the journey. Besides, I won't even see her until tomorrow evening. Are you sure it's okay if Skye—er, Miss Stratton—stays here while we make more permanent arrangements?"

"You know it is. Your ma will enjoy having another woman around. The bigger question is, will you be okay in the barn?"

"I s'pose I'll have to be."

"Very gallant of you, son. We'll do all we can to make her feel right at home."

Ma leaned against the doorway. "I'll have your room all ready for her by the time you get back here tomorrow. Fresh flowers and everything."

He loved seeing Ma with some of the old spark in her eyes. "I'm sure it'll be great, Ma. I know she'll love being here with the two of you. She may not want to leave."

After a few finishing touches on his hair and clothes, Alan grabbed the carpet bag containing his best shirt for tomorrow, hugged his parents, and set out for the short drive to town, where he'd grab a few supplies. He was just doing his job. But he felt pretty sure most parts of his job wouldn't put the same spring in his step as the thought of spending time with Skye.

He'd just stopped outside the general store for a few items when a familiar, grating voice called his name. "Alan! Yoo-hoo, Alan."

Margaret waved a handkerchief from across the street. Why did he look? Why didn't he pretend he didn't hear her?

Because that would be rude, that's why. "Good morning, Miss Tusselhoff."

She left a cloud of dust in her wake as she hurried across the street to greet him. "My, you look spiffy today. Where are you off to?"

Her too-strong cologne assaulted his senses. "Silsbee. I don't have long."

"Silsbee. The train station? Surely you're not leaving us. You just got here."

"No, nothing like that. I'm just taking care of some business."

"Business? I see. I heard you're the new Indian Agent."

"That's correct."

"I can certainly understand why they chose you. You're such

a strong, forceful figure. Goodness knows those savages need someone powerful to keep them under control."

A bitter taste settled in Alan's mouth. "You've had trouble with the local Indians?"

"Not trouble, exactly. But just knowing they're out there, only a few miles away... Let's just say I'll sleep better at night knowing you're handling things."

Alan tipped his hat. "Miss Tusselhoff, I do apologize, but I have a long journey ahead."

"I understand." She moved in. Brushed something off his shoulder.

He was pretty sure whatever it was existed only in her imagination. He stepped back.

"Will I see you at church on Sunday?" Her voice was low, intimate.

"Uh...perhaps. I'm not sure if I'll be back in time." He planned to give Skye the option to rest for a day before traveling back here.

"Well, soon then."

"Good day, Miss Tusselhoff." Alan tipped his hat, stepped around the woman, and stretched his stride as long as he could to get away from her. He much preferred Skye Stratton's cool reception to Margaret Tusselhoff's warm one.

He looked at his watch. He wasn't really in that big of a hurry to get to Silsbee. He was, however, in a hurry to get away from that husband-hunting headache in high heels. Tomorrow evening, he'd see Skye. That made his heart beat faster, his blood pump warmer than it should.

CHAPTER 9

*A*s planned, Alan stopped by the reservation on his way to Silbee. He was greeted with stares, but the people seemed less alarmed with each of his visits. More curious. Chief Scott sat outside his home in a rocking chair, taking advantage of the shade of a thick copse of pines. Alan reined in Fiona and brought the buckboard to a stop.

"I did not expect to see so much of our new agent." The man's voice was welcoming.

"I pick up your new school teacher tomorrow at the train station in Silsbee and thought I'd swing by. I have something I'd like to discuss with you."

Chief Scott motioned to a young man, probably fifteen or sixteen, who was working in a garden alongside the log home. "Bring Agent McNaughten a chair."

The boy nodded. Soon he returned with a sturdy wooden chair and placed it next to the chief.

"Thank you," Alan said. The boy nodded and left them in the shade.

"What can I do for you, Agent McNaughten?"

"The teacher I told you about. For now, she will stay with my parents. But it's more than an hour's drive, so we'll need to find her a place closer to the reservation. Possibly on the reservation, if you feel that's safe."

Chief Scott's expression didn't change, other than one ever-so-slightly raised eyebrow. "A white woman, staying on the reservation? I can't imagine that will be acceptable to her."

Alan shifted in his seat. Cleared his throat. "She is half white. Half Indian. I'm not sure what her preference will be, but right now I'm exploring options."

The older man stopped rocking but said nothing.

Alan knew from his time in Washington to let silence exist, especially when exchanging ideas. Often, the best ideas came after some good thinking time. After several minutes, he was about to say they didn't have to decide anything today when Chief Scott spoke.

"This young woman has had a difficult life."

Alan wasn't sure how to answer that. In some ways, yes. In other ways…? She'd certainly lived a life of luxury few in these parts could relate to. "I suppose in some ways, she has."

"Does this woman want to be one of us?"

"I'm not sure. I think she wants to learn about her heritage. And she wants to be accepted."

The man nodded, looking into the distance. "Few of her background find acceptance from people, no matter their race. If she wants acceptance, she'll have to look to God. If she chooses to live on the reservation, I will see that she is not bothered. You must understand, however, that if she lives here, she will say good-bye to her former way of life. Once she makes her residence on this reservation, the white part of her world will never see her in the same way."

Alan thought about that. With Skye, things were more complicated than he'd considered. He leaned his head against the high back of the chair. He'd certainly had his own struggles in life. But he'd never had to consider what it felt like to not be accepted simply because of the color of his skin.

He'd had people make comments about his lineage plenty of times. Still, he couldn't help but think that Skye's situation was going to be a whole lot harder than he'd first anticipated. "Thank you for your insight. I suppose, if it's preferable, we could build her a dwelling place just outside the reservation. But I worry about her safety."

"Why don't we wait until she gets here. Let her make the journey from your parents' home for a few weeks. Then we'll ask her what she'd like to do."

Alan nodded. "That sounds wise." He sat for another minute, neither man speaking. The towering pines whooshed and whispered around them, and somewhere behind him, a mockingbird sang his heart out, probably calling for his mate. The young man worked the garden, the swoosh of his feet among the plants adding to the melody. "We'll stop by in two days' time. I'd like to give her a tour and introduce her to some people. Is it possible for her to meet the lady who has been teaching?"

The chief dipped his head in one slow nod. "It will be arranged."

"Thank you." Something about this place was peaceful. Chief Scott was someone he'd like to be friends with, and he could've stayed longer. But he and Fiona still had a long way to travel, and he wanted to arrive in Silsbee before nightfall. He stood, tipped his hat, and held out his hand.

Chief Scott did not stand, but he returned the handshake with a solid grip. "Good day to you, and safe travels."

Alan climbed into the wagon and signaled for Fiona to move forward. This short visit had given him even more to think about. He'd come in search of answers and solutions. But the more time he spent with these people, the more questions he had.

~

The days swooped by, and before she knew it, Skye was ready for the journey. She decided to wear one of her nicer suits for travel. The pale blue silk skirt would keep her cool on the journey, and the gauzy linen bodice with matching blue silk embellishments offered a breezy top layer over her chemise. The two-piece outfit was more comfortable for sitting than a dress. She took her time and combed out her long, chestnut-brown hair, then braided it in one braid down her back before curling it into a bun at the nape of her neck. After securing it in place, she tucked a few pearl-head pins here and there. Instead of a parasol, she'd take an embellished accordion fan with delicate blue butterflies and pink roses painted on the paper. It might come in handy on the train.

She studied her reflection by the flickering kerosene lamp. How long until she sat in this room again, in front of her dresser? Her honey-brown eyes looked back at her. With her dress, posture, and composure, no one on the train would guess her true race. Plus, Daddy would be with her. They'd probably assume her mother was French.

She tucked her brush and hand mirror into her carpet bag. She ticked back through her packing list, wondering if she'd forgotten anything. She'd included one additional for-nice dress and several plain cotton ones for teaching. She had one formal dress, wrapped in tissue paper at the bottom, just in case. That should get her through the fall, anyway. Mama and Daddy would bring her warmer things when they visited.

All too soon, she and her family stood on the platform with her single trunk, waiting for it to be loaded, waiting for the call to board. Mama, Cordell, and Anita huddled around her, their mouths smiling, their eyes solemn.

"Can I come with you and go to school with the Indians?" Anita's face turned serious. "I could help."

Skye hugged her sister. "I wish you could. You would be a great help. But this is something I must do alone."

Mama turned away, dabbed her eyes. When she faced Skye again, her smile was in place. "You'll be wonderful. And we'll visit soon."

Cordell pumped a fist in the air. "Yeah! Daddy said we might miss school to visit you."

"Remember, I'm a teacher, little brother. You can always attend my school while you're away from your own."

Cordell snorted but said nothing.

Daddy placed a hand on Skye's back and looked at Mama. "I know you're not ready, but it's almost time for us to leave." Skye was glad her father would accompany her, even though she'd told him it wasn't necessary. She'd be in Silsbee tonight, and Alan would meet her there.

Mama and Anita clung to Skye like she was going to China, not Livingston. Even Cordell wrapped his arms around the little group.

The conductor had just called "All aboard!" when a commotion broke out at the ticket window.

"Please, sir! I must get on that train. This telegram just came, and my mother is in a bad way."

The ticket master shook his head. "I'm sorry, ma'am. I told you. I only have one available seat."

"But I can't leave Charlie behind! He's five years old. Please… I'll hold him in my lap." The woman neared hysteria.

"If we weren't so crowded, I'd be inclined to let you both ride for one ticket. But we're at capacity. You and your son will make the ride uncomfortable for everyone. I'm sorry."

The woman gathered her son, collapsed onto a nearby bench, and sobbed.

Skye looked at Daddy. Was he thinking what she was thinking?

He held her gaze, disappointment filling his eyes, but he gave a slight nod. In two long strides, he was at the bench. "Pardon me, ma'am. I couldn't help but overhear your conversation. I'd like to offer you my ticket."

The woman looked at him with red-rimmed eyes. "Really? Oh, sir! Thank you so much. I don't know how I'll ever repay you. My mother…"

Daddy knelt to her level. "What is your mother's name?"

"Nellie."

"I will keep Nellie in my prayers."

The woman thanked Daddy, took his ticket, and purchased the remaining ticket.

Soon, after Skye gave a last, wistful hug to each member of her family, Daddy pressed a few extra coins into Skye's hand and spoke low in her ear. "I just now placed my six-shooter and some extra ammo in the bottom of your carpetbag, just in case you need it. Be careful. We'll visit soon."

Skye caught her breath, then grinned. Thanks to Daddy, she could handle a gun better than most men she knew. She also knew enough to hope she didn't need to.

Mama moved in for one more embrace and whispered, "Remember who you are and whose you are."

"I know, Mama."

Her heart pounding, Skye gripped her coins, her carpetbag, and her courage and boarded the crowded train. The moment she was secure in her seat, she heard the whistle blow, and she turned to wave at her family until the train rounded the corner. She was really doing this. Her heart pounded in time with the rumbling wheels.

Breathe in. Breathe out. Breathe in. Breathe out.

This time next week, you'll be living a whole new life.

Skye sat wedged between a paunchy gentleman to her left and a buxom woman to her right. The woman was absorbed in some type of penny novel and paid little mind to the others on the train. Across the aisle facing her was the little boy, Charlie, next to his mother, who was so distraught she did very little mothering. On Charlie's other side was a feather-topped middle-aged woman who looked like she enjoyed children from a distance. She heard the woman introduce herself as Mrs. Marlow to Charlie's mother.

Charlie reached for her feathered hat time and again, with grubby fingers. The woman flinched and squirmed, trying to keep the costly millinery from getting soiled. After a time, Charlie grew weary of the game and pointed his finger out the window. "Pow! Po-pow!" He leaned over the woman's lap, practically crawling in it, in an effort to be nearer the window.

"What, pray tell, are you doing, child?" Mrs. Marlow looked like she'd entered an outer layer of the underworld.

"I'm shootin' Injuns!" Charlie said.

The man beside Skye chuckled. "Good boy," he said. "The only good Injun's a dead one."

"Pow! Pow-pow-pow!"

Skye grew hot from her nose to her toes. What would the man do if he knew the truth of her heritage? She cleared her throat. "Ma'am, I'm a teacher, and I'm accustomed to children his age. Would you like to trade seats with me?"

Mrs. Marlow gaped at her like a drowning woman who'd just been offered oxygen. "Please!"

After some tight shuffling, Skye settled into her new place next to the small Injun hunter. "Your name is Charlie, right?"

The boy looked at her. "How'd you know?"

"I heard your mother call you that at the station. My name is Miss Stratton. Would you like to play a game with me?"

"What kinda game?"

"First, you must put your guns away. I never play with guns."

"Oh. Okay." He slid his pretend gun into an imaginary holster.

"Thank you. Have you ever played a guessing game?"

The boy shook his head.

"That's all right. I can tell you'll be good at this game because you seem very smart. I will think of something on this train—something you can see. You will ask me questions, but the answer to the question must be "yes" or "no." As I answer the questions, you try to figure out the item I'm thinking of. Do you understand?"

"I think so."

"All right. I've chosen my item. Do you have a question?"

"What is the item?"

"That's not a "yes" or "no" question. Try again."

"Oh…um…is it big?"

"No."

The boy grinned. "Is it small?"

"Yes."

He looked around at all the small items around him. "Is it this button?"

"No."

"Is it my shoe?"

"No."

The game kept Charlie occupied for the better part of ten minutes, when he finally guessed it was his mother's ring.

The woman sniffed, hugged her son, and looked at Skye. "Thank you, ma'am. I'm afraid I'm not myself today. Bertie Calhoun."

"Skye Stratton. And it's my pleasure, Mrs. Calhoun. He's a delightful child."

The feathered woman let out a *hmph* but said nothing more.

~

*A*lan felt as nervous as a lizard in a barn full of cats. Last night, he'd made it to Silsbee in plenty of time to stable Fiona, check into the boarding house, and have a nice, filling supper. This morning, he'd strolled the streets of the small town, looking in shop windows, perusing the general store for new finds or bargain prices. At first, he was bored.

But as the day wore on, he checked his watch more often. Like a watched pot never boils, and a watched train never arrives, he supposed. Around two p.m., he decided to stop by the post office to see if any messages had arrived for him. Not that they would. But just in case.

He gave the man his name, and sure enough, there was a telegram from Skye's father. Due to unforeseen circumstances, she'd be traveling unaccompanied. A wave of uncertainty pulsed through Alan, though he didn't know why. Skye was a perfectly capable woman. And surely nothing would happen to her on a public train. Still, the chief's words played in his mind again, and he thought about how difficult things must be for her.

Of course, no one on the train would know her race. Why, she could pass for French easily. There were plenty of dark-haired, honey-brown-eyed people in the world...though few as attractive as Skye. Still, she knew better than to reveal her background to strangers. Didn't she?

Of course she did.

She would be exhausted. Especially after traveling alone. Was she anxious?

He thought of her set jaw, her determined spirit. Probably not. But he was plenty anxious enough for both of them.

He went back to the general store and looked around for some small gift he could purchase for her. Not from him personally, but from the reservation. Something to welcome her, to thank her for accepting the position. Was that appropriate? He didn't know. And he certainly had no idea what kind of gift he was looking for.

He spotted some brightly beaded items in a far corner of the display case. "Excuse me. Could you tell me about these?"

The proprietor set aside his broom and made his way behind the counter. "Those? Those are a big mistake. I bought those from some Indian traders several years back. Problem is, people around here don't think too highly of Injuns, and they won't buy them. I think they're pretty, but they've turned out to be a waste of money."

Alan looked at the items in the case. A hair clip, a small bag with a long strap, several necklaces, a couple of bracelets, a set of earrings, and a long, narrow pouch. "May I see some of them up close?"

"Sure thing. I'll give you a great deal on whatever you want. I'd love to free up the space." The man pulled out several pieces of jewelry.

But jewelry was too familiar. She might take it the wrong way. "What about the bag? And the small pouch? What is the pouch for?"

"For whatever you want to use it for. Some might use it as a knife case. Maybe to hold a pipe. I dunno."

Alan examined the long, narrow pouch. The beadwork was exquisite, in bright blues and reds, yellows and greens and whites. The pattern formed a tulip at the top, with the stem scrolling and curving the length of the piece. The colors and pattern matched the bag with the strap.

She could probably use the pouch to carry pencils. Chalk, maybe. "I'll take these two items. And I'd like four pencils, please."

The man rang up the items, wrapped them in brown paper, and tied them with string.

Alan took his purchases and looked at his pocket watch. It was only two forty-five. This was turning out to be one of the longest days ever.

～

fter several hours that felt more like years, the train pulled into the station at Houston. This station was much larger and more crowded than the one in Lampasas, and Skye's chest was tight with anxiety. Daddy would know exactly what to do, where to go. She stayed in her seat and watched people around her gather their things and stand in the aisle, waiting their turn to disembark. No point standing in a crowded line when she could stay seated and wait her turn.

It didn't take long. She gathered her bag and allowed Charlie and his mother to go ahead of her.

"Thank you again, ma'am. Was that your father who gave up his ticket? Please thank him again for me.

"I'll do that." Skye held out one hand to Charlie. "It was a pleasure to meet you, sir."

He giggled and returned her handshake. Then he lunged at her waist with a tight hug, nearly knocking her back to her seat. "I wish you were comin' with us."

When he loosened his grip, Skye sat on the bench again so she'd be at his eye level. "Do me a favor, will you?"

"Sure!"

"Be careful about who you aim a weapon at. People—real or imaginary—are just people. You can't tell if a person is good or bad by the way they look. There are good people and bad people from all different races and backgrounds."

"You don't want me to shoot Injuns?" His eyes widened.

"I don't want you to shoot anyone unless you know for sure they plan to hurt you or someone you care about and there's no other way to stop them."

The line dissipated, and Charlie's mother tugged at his arm. "Let's go, son."

Charlie waved one last good-bye and went with his mother, and Skye followed them onto the crowded platform. She looked around, tried not to panic. How long did she have to board her next train? There must be a dozen different lines, all taking people to different places.

A man slammed into her from the left. "Pardon me, ma'am," he said before rushing past.

She spied an empty bench near the station wall and headed that direction. She should have gotten her ticket out before leaving the train. She couldn't very well stop in the middle of the platform and dig through her case. She might be mauled again.

She sat and opened her case, taking no notice of people around her until an old cowboy spit in her direction. The disgusting wad landed on the platform just to her left. That's when she saw him...an Indian man, leaning against the wall in the shadows. He wore moccasins, leather leggings, a white button-up shirt made of broadcloth, and a vest. Half Indian garb, half white. A long silky braid hung over each shoulder. Around his neck he wore some kind of necklace made of stone. Or was it bone?

He stared straight ahead. Didn't blink. Almost as if he tried to be invisible.

Skye searched the crowd for the spitter, but he was gone. An unseen rope cinched her chest, squeezed tight. She couldn't breathe. Couldn't think. What was she doing?

Ticket. Blood pounded her ears like a drumsong... warsong... Panic flooded her veins, poisoned her mind, freezing her will.

"Fear not, for I am with thee." The verse she'd learned in Sunday School whispered through her thoughts, and for once, she wished she could believe the promise.

"Be anxious for nothing, but in all things, through prayer and supplication, let your requests be made known to God." The last time she'd made such a request, she'd been six years old. Her first father died that night. She wouldn't pray again.

Air. She needed to breathe.

In. Out. In. Out.

Her heartbeat slowed. She grabbed hold of her senses.

There. She found the ticket. Searched for a ticket master, a conductor, anyone who might assist her. She couldn't miss her connection.

She spotted the ticket booth, gathered her things, stood. But before moving away, she sucked in one more deep breath and turned to the Indian man. She ducked her head and studied the ticket so others wouldn't notice her talking to him. "I'm sorry for how you're treated. It's not right."

The man said nothing. Briefly, she lifted her gaze to his face, met his eyes. He studied her a moment, and she knew...somehow, she knew that *he* knew they were the same. He gave the slightest nod, then shifted his gaze into the distance again.

CHAPTER 10

Skye boarded the correct train—she hoped—and found a seat next to a staid-looking silver-haired woman with knitting needles and several balls of yarn in her lap. Spread down to her knees was a half-finished pink-and-yellow-and-blue baby blanket. She looked safe enough. Hopefully this leg of the journey would be more relaxing than the first one.

As soon as she seated herself, she noticed a nice-looking man, probably late twenties, in a business suit sitting across from the woman. He smiled at Skye and looked away.

Her stomach rumbled, and she thought of the brown paper package Mama had tucked into the side of Skye's bag. "Lunch," she'd said. Skye didn't know what was in it, but whatever it was, she knew it would be delicious. And probably three times more than Skye could eat in a day.

"Miss Stratton!" Charlie's voice squealed from several seats up, causing several passengers to lift their heads.

Skye waved. Soon, the boy stood in front of her. "Come sit with us! There's an extra seat."

Disappointment mixed with exhaustion in her mind, like watercolors all running together to form a murky gray. How could she say no? She opened her mouth to reply when her elderly seatmate spoke up. "Young man, you should find your seat right now. The train is about to leave, and it's not safe for you to be here. Once we're on our way, perhaps your friend can come and visit you."

"Oh…um…yes, ma'am." Charlie's shoulders drooped, but he didn't argue. Just returned to his seat without another word.

The man across from them chuckled and unfolded a newspaper.

Once Charlie was out of hearing distance, Skye whispered, "Thank you."

The woman smiled. "My son and I were on the earlier train as well. We sat a few rows behind you. I was exhausted just watching you two. You need a break. I know I would."

What a doll.

Skye flicked her gaze to the man—the woman's son?—who grinned. "You have quite a way with children," he said.

"Thank you. I'm a teacher."

He nodded as if that explained everything.

Skye spoke to the woman again. "That's a lovely blanket. Is it for someone special?"

"It's for whoever needs it. I like to keep my hands busy, and it doesn't take long to make a baby blanket. I almost always have one going. Most get donated to orphanages, but I give some away as gifts."

"How thoughtful."

The woman didn't respond. Just kept up the steady click-click of the needles. Soon, a loud hissing sound signaled the train's imminent departure, followed by a lurch forward before the wheels began their familiar clacketyclack. The noise prevented them from speaking for a few minutes.

Skye looked out her window and thought about the Indian man. Would that have been her life, if things had been different?

She knew it would. Yet something about him looked…she

couldn't find the word. Accepting? Dignified? It wasn't that he didn't care. She was *certain* he cared. But something about the way he held himself, so straight and tall and proud, and how he didn't acknowledge the action, led her to believe he'd risen above it.

Of course, she couldn't know what happened inside the man's head. Still, when she thought of him, she felt almost ashamed of herself, masquerading as a white woman when she knew, if all these people knew the truth, they would spit at her too. At least, some of them would.

After about ten minutes, Skye opened her bag and pulled out the brown package. "Have you eaten?" she asked the woman, then nodded to the man. She felt odd eating in front of others without offering them any. "I'm happy to share."

The woman didn't look up from her knitting. "Oh, we had a nibble earlier, at the station. You go ahead. Thank you, though."

"I'm Skye Stratton, by the way."

"Ann Kelly. *Mrs.* And this is my son, David. Pleased to meet you." She set down one of her needles and held out a hand, which Skye briefly took and squeezed. It was awkward shaking hands, seated side by side, but it was sweet.

David offered his hand as well, and Skye shook it.

She settled back in her seat and opened her lunch to find her favorites: two ham-and-cheese sandwiches on thick rye bread, a cluster of grapes, an apple, an orange, a small tub of butter and some extra bread, and three petit fours with tiny pink roses on top. The roses were a little smashed, but they brought a wispy smile to Skye's face all the same. No wonder her case was so heavy.

"Either you eat a lot more than you appear to, or someone really loves you." David smiled, but there was no censure in his expression.

"My mother." At least these seatmates were calmer and quieter than Charlie.

Arranging one of the blue gingham napkins on her lap, Skye removed half a sandwich, a few grapes, and one of the petit fours, rewrapped the rest, and placed the extra back in her bag. She took her time eating, savoring each bite, watching the passing scenery, and missing home more with each turn of the wheel. When she finished, she wiped the corners of her mouth and tucked her napkin back into her bag.

"Where are you off to, Miss Stratton? I hope it's not too forward of me to ask." David seemed pleasant enough. Nothing in his tone felt invasive or threatening.

"I've been offered a job as a teacher, near Livingston."

His eyebrows lifted. "We own some land near there. I've been trying to sell it, but no one wants to buy it. It borders the Alabama-Coushatta Reservation, and you know how people are. I find the people charming, myself."

Should she tell him that that was where she would teach? She opened her mouth, but Charlie appeared at that moment. "Can you come sit with us now, Miss Stratton?"

Mrs. Kelly let out a low harrumph but said nothing. David lifted the newspaper in front of his face, his shoulders shaking suspiciously.

"You're so kind to ask me, Charlie. I'd love to. But first, have you eaten?"

"Yeah. Mama took me to the dining car. They have real tables, and you tell the people what you want and they bring it to you." His eyebrows lifted high on his little forehead, and his eyes sparked.

She almost offered him one of her little cakes, but she figured she'd better check with his mother first. With a wry smile, she caught Mrs. Kelly's eye, who only shrugged. She took Charlie's hand and let him lead her away like a lamb to slaughter. David offered a look of amused sympathy as she passed.

At least she'd had a short reprieve from the boy's boundless energy. It looked like the next leg of the journey would be just as exhausting as the first.

Nearly three hours later, Skye leaned her head back and tried to catch a rest from Charlie's incessant chatter. His mother, poor thing, dabbed at her eyes every few minutes. Skye sure hoped the woman made it in time to see her ailing mother. She was doing all she could to help the woman by keeping Charlie entertained. Occasionally, Mrs. Calhoun patted Skye's leg with her gloved hand as if to say *thank you.*

For a time, Charlie was occupied watching for deer out the wide window, and Skye's thoughts wandered ahead. This evening, Alan would meet her. Would they have dinner together? Surely they would. She tried to tame the thrill of excitement that coursed through her at that thought.

It wasn't as if she was getting attached to the man. But what woman in her right mind wouldn't want to be seen with the likes of Alan McNaughten? She knew nothing would come of it. He was aware of her heritage, and he was white. Still, he seemed kind. That was all this was. A kind man meeting her for professional reasons who happened to be nice to look at. And talk to.

Gracious. She was being silly. She pushed all thought of Alan to the side and focused on Charlie again. Her bag was still in her other seat. She leaned to Mrs. Calhoun and spoke in a low voice. "Do you mind if I give him a sweet? I have some petit fours in my case."

"Yes, that's fine. You are so kind."

Skye took Charlie's hand. "Come with me. I have a surprise for you." They made their way several rows back, and Skye watched the landscape race by outside the window. Was that a horse and rider just outside the treeline? She thought it was, but the train moved so fast, and by the time she focused in on the figure, it was gone. Probably her imagination.

They arrived back at her original seat to find Mrs. Kelly, head to the side, letting out a dainty snore. Her blanket and balls

of yarn still rested in her lap, and one hand clutched her knitting needles.

David greeted them with a smile and moved his long legs to
the side to let them in. Skye had gently taken her seat and
reached down for her bag when a screech pierced her ears.
Something slammed, and Charlie fell into her lap. The
screeching continued, and she held Charlie tight with one arm
and clenched the edge of her seat with the other.

Mrs. Kelly's blanket, yarn and needles flew into the aisle, and
the woman gasped and grabbed the seat with both hands. David
leaned forward and braced one hand on the arm of his mother's
seat, one arm on the opposite side of Skye's seat in a protective
gesture, to hold them in place.

All around Skye, people hollered. A few men uttered inappropriate words. Or at least, in most situations, they were inappropriate. She wasn't sure if this might be one of the situations
in which those words might be considered borderline.

Oh, that screeching! Skye wanted to plug her ears from the
painful noise, but she wouldn't let go of Charlie. He clung to
her, buried his face in her neck. What was happening? Were
they going to die? *Please, God. No.*

Her hypocrisy wasn't lost to her, crying out to God when
she'd refused to speak to Him all these years, but along with her
pounding heart, along with her fierce need to protect the little
boy in her lap, came the words from somewhere deep inside
her. *Please God, please God, please God no.*

After what seemed like the longest hour of her life—which
was probably only about three minutes—the screeching
stopped, the train came to a halt, and Skye braced herself to
keep from sliding forward. People were on their feet, in the
aisles, pushing, shoving, shouting, trying to reach the exit.

Skye held tight to Charlie. "Stay here. Wait until things calm
down."

He said nothing, only clung to her as tightly as before, except now he lifted his head and looked around.

David checked on his mother—she seemed fine—stood, looked at all the commotion, and retook his seat.

A disturbance came from the exit—a different commotion than the pushing and shoving. Ladies screamed. The crowd parted. Two men in broad cowboy hats with bandanas concealing their faces marched down the aisle. Each held two guns, one in each hand.

"Ladies and gentlemen," the one in front announced, "this is a hold up. Right now, the conductor is being held at gunpoint, and every car in this train is being boarded as we speak. Nice and easy now, hands over your heads. Every one of you."

The other one spoke up. "We have blown up the bridge, and we've plenty more explosives, ready to be ignited. Calmly return to your seats and keep your hands high. Row by row, we'll ask you to retrieve your valuables and give them to us. If we suspect you of holding back, we'll shoot you. If you cooperate, we might let you live."

After some terrified gasps, the car grew silent. It was an eerie contrast to the chaos. Somewhere behind her, a woman hissed, "Injuns."

That's when Charlie spoke up. "He ain't no Injun. His eyes is blue."

"Shh…." Skye whispered, but it was too late.

The man found Charlie and moved to stand in front of them. "You're a smart kid, you know that? You'd better keep your mouth shut or you might get hurt."

Charlie buried his face in Skye's neck again.

Somewhere behind her, a woman sobbed. She was pretty sure it was Charlie's mother.

Her carpet bag, under her seat, had somehow stayed in place. She felt it press against the back of her legs.

The gun.

How could she get it, yet keep it concealed? Should she try?

No. Not yet, anyway. She scooted the bag further under her seat.

They'd want her jewelry, for sure. Her gut tightened at the thought of giving them her brooch. It had once belonged to her paternal grandmother.

She had the pearl pins in her bun. They weren't real pearls, but if she made a show of taking them out of her hair, it might distract them.

Surely they didn't blow up a bridge and hold up an entire train for a few passengers' baubles. Someone on the train must have a real treasure they knew about. That was the only thing that made sense. Which meant their combing this car for valuables was all for show.

At least that was what she hoped. Or maybe they were just trying to squeeze as much out of this robbery as possible.

The blue-eyed man moved down the aisle. When he was a few rows past and the other man had his back turned, Skye whispered to Charlie. "Keep your eyes closed. Stay very still."

Thankfully, the boy obeyed.

She slowly, awkwardly reached down and felt around in her carpet bag. Felt her wallet, grabbed it, and placed it beside her in the seat. Maybe they'd be satisfied if she offered her cash.

She put her hands in the air again. When both men had their backs turned, she used one hand to unfasten her broach and drop it in her open bag. David made a slight gesture with his eyes, and she knew the men were coming. Charlie clung to her. She felt his little hummingbird heart pound with every breath.

Two gunshots went off in the distance. Was that from outside or from another car? Skye's heart pounded in time with Charlie's.

Mrs. Kelly's skin was nearly as white as her hair.

David's lips pressed together in a tight line, the muscles in his face strained.

Both bandits made their way toward the exit, abandoning their treasure hunt. "Ladies and gentlemen, it's been a pleasure. I advise you to stay seated for at least ten minutes."

They were nearly out the door when Charlie shouted, "I recognize his boots and belt! I saw him at the station. He's got red hair and a red beard!"

Skye clamped her hand over Charlie's mouth, but he wiggled too much. She was too late. The man backed into the car again and made his way to their row. "Kid, you're comin' with me." He looked at Skye. "You his mama?"

"Naw. I just met her today! I ain't going with you." Charlie kicked the man's knee.

The man grabbed Charlie around the waist and hauled him over his big shoulder like a kicking, screaming sack of flour.

David stood, tried to block the man. "Sir, I must demand that you let the boy go! We've been cooperative. Surely you know the legal penalty for kidnapping is more severe than armed robbery. You'll never get away with this."

"Put me down! I ain't goin' with you!" Charlie kicked his little legs.

Quick as lightning, the bandit rammed the butt of his gun into David's head and made for the exit.

Time slowed down and sped up and jumbled together in that moment. David collapsed into his seat.

Skye's brain told her to fight, grab her gun, do whatever she could to save Charlie. But her voice, her body wouldn't obey her mental commands.

She just sat there and watched, as if from deep underwater, as the man took Charlie and left the train. The whole scene played out in a minute, maybe less than a minute.

Mrs. Calhoun's screams shook Skye to her senses. The sound pierced through like a knife. Charlie had been in her care, and she'd let him be kidnapped. What kind of person was she?

In an instant, she dug through her bag for the six-shooter.

Gun in hand, she lunged for the aisle, but Mrs. Kelly grabbed her skirt and wouldn't let go.

"Go now, and they'll kill the boy, and all of us as well. Let them get a few minutes ahead. The people on the other side of the train can see which direction they're going. Then some of our men will go after them."

"Let me go!" Skye could only remember a handful of times in her life when she'd shouted. She couldn't recall ever shouting at an elder. But she was desperate.

Men stood, blocked her way, all talking at once. "We'll get the boy back."

"The lady's right, ma'am. We need to be logical."

And, "This is no task for a lady."

She couldn't get past them. A few of them pulled guns from their boots and carrying cases. She tried to block out Mrs. Calhoun's desperate sobs. They'd haunt her for the rest of her days.

David reached for her. A knot on his forehead had already turned a sick shade of purple. "It's all right. We'll go after them. But we need to let them get far enough ahead that they think they're in the clear."

No place else to go, Skye dropped to her seat. Everything in her screamed that she needed to go after them. Now. But maybe these men were right. Maybe that would put Charlie in more danger.

If ever she'd wanted to pray, it was now. Did she dare?

CHAPTER 11

Alan spent nearly an hour talking to Fiona at the livery. Anything to pass the time. He was just reaching for the livery door when it pushed open. John Walker stepped in. He held several braided halters and reins. Had he made those?

"Chief Walker! Good to see you."

The man looked surprised and decidedly uncomfortable.

Outside, a rough-looking group of men stood, laughing and pointing at the Indian man.

Alan held open the door and let Walker pass, then moved outside. "Good day, gentlemen. I'm Alan McNaughten, Indian Agent for this territory. Is there a problem?"

"I'd say there's a problem. You ain't keepin' yer Injuns fenced in."

"This is a free country. He has as much right to do business here as you and I do."

The tallest one spit a wad of dark tobacco juice, which landed on the toe of Alan's boot. Everything in him wanted to punch him, but that wouldn't help matters any. His job—the only job description he'd been given—was to communicate with the Indians and maintain the peace.

Still, in his mind a scene played out, a scene where he landed the perfect upper cut to the man's jaw. Tobacco juice went flying all over his buddies, and the thug landed on the ground, dazed. No, not dazed. Unconscious. Slowly, the other men lifted their hands and backed away, leaving their juice-slinging friend in the dust.

Yeah, that would make a great scene in one of those western penny novels. Probably not the best choice right now. Instead, he tapped his boot on the ground to shake the spittle loose, all while maintaining eye contact with his assailant.

Then he tipped his hat. "Gentlemen." He nearly choked on the word, for they were far from gentlemen. He re-entered the livery and shut the door behind him.

Walker stood with his back to the room, waiting on the owner to finish some paperwork. When Alan approached, Walker spoke in a low voice. "I appreciate your intentions, Agent McNaughten. However, that behavior is nothing new. Please don't feel the need to come to my defense."

Alan shifted his weight from one foot to the other. "The way I see it, it's my job to come to your defense. I'm supposed to help keep the peace."

Walker laughed, a low, humorless chuckle. "If you want to keep the peace, you'll leave well enough alone. Confronting those men will only stir up their hatred."

Alan didn't respond. What could he say? Walker was probably right. But that didn't make what he'd witnessed right.

The livery owner turned his attention to Walker, inspected the leatherwork, and gave him a handful of coins. Very little was said between the two men. When Walker turned to go, Alan touched his arm.

"I have some time to kill. Do you mind if I ask you a few questions?"

"Do as you please."

Alan wondered if there was a hidden meaning in those

words. Was he annoying the man? But there didn't seem to be any irritation in Walker's tone, and he didn't seem to be in a hurry, so Alan continued the conversation "Did Chief Scott speak with you about Miss Stratton's living situation?"

"He did."

"Do you have any suggestions?"

Walker paused. When he spoke, his voice was lower, softer than it had been. "Can we discuss this in private?"

Alan glanced over his shoulder and noticed the livery owner placing the leatherwork on display on the walls. Was he eavesdropping? "Good idea."

Walker followed Alan outside. A single horse was tethered to the railing near a watering trough—a beautiful white Appaloosa with dark gray and black spots like freckles. The horse had no saddle and a single bridle made from a cord of animal hide, similar to those Walker had just traded. He untied the horse and walked beside Alan.

"Let's head to the train depot. I noticed some benches there where we can sit and talk."

Alan hoped Walker could offer some insight for what to do with Skye. Would she become even more alienated from the white community once she started her job? Would the Indian community embrace her, make her one of them? As much as he looked forward to seeing her, worry pierced his heart. At that point, Alan didn't know what would become of the pretty schoolteacher who'd left behind riches for...he wasn't sure what.

~

A few minutes after the outlaws disappeared, Skye watched some of the men exit the train, including David. Before he left, he spoke to Skye. "Don't worry, Miss Stratton. We'll get Charlie back."

The women remained seated. As soon as the aisle cleared, Skye stood.

"They'll find him." Mrs. Kelly held her elbow. "It's not safe for you."

"I appreciate your concern. But that boy was in my care, and I plan to offer whatever aide I can in his rescue."

The woman let her go. Other women, and a few older gentlemen, looked at her as if she'd lost her mind, but she didn't care. She exited through the back door onto the little platform between the trains. With no steps folded out for her to use, she'd have to jump a good four feet to the ground. David showed up before she had to. "I wish you'd stay on board, Miss Stratton."

"Your wish is duly noted. Now help me down."

He complied, albeit hesitantly.

The other men turned to look at her, shook their heads, then went back to their conversations. She marched to the far tree line and tied a length of the pink yarn she'd torn from Mrs. Kelly's skein. All she could see in any direction, besides the train and tracks, was a thick forest of tall pine trees. No houses or barns, not even any dirt trails. It was the perfect place for a little target practice.

David followed along like a puppy with a new toy. "What are you doing?"

Under different circumstances, she'd probably consider him quite a catch. Right now, he was getting on her nerves. She didn't answer. Just tromped back to the group of men and tapped the tallest one on the shoulder. They all gazed at her like a herd of cattle looks at a pesky fly.

"Do you see that ribbon? The pink one?" She waited for the men to nod, then lickety-split drew her six-shooter and shot the ribboned branch clean off the tree.

No one said a word, but their jaws hung open like a bunch of lazy frogs hoping for a fly swarm.

"Gentlemen, I'm going after Charlie. You're free to join me if you wish."

A silver-haired, mustached man stepped forward. "Now, hold on just a minute. No one will argue that you're not a crack shot, Miss..."

"Stratton. Skye Stratton."

"You may know how to fire a pistol, but Miss Stratton, it's not safe. If those men get hold of you, there's no telling what they'll do."

"Then I won't let them get a hold of me." She knew the man was right. But she was used to cutting her own path. Right now, she didn't care what these men, or anyone else on the train, thought about her. And what they didn't know? She wasn't going to volunteer that she'd been tracking and finding her way through forests since she could walk. Her first mother taught her the sounds of nature and what they meant. Her first father taught her to look to the stars to find her way, or in the daytime, to look at the direction the shadows fell. And Daddy? Well, she'd been target shooting with Daddy since before he was her daddy, when he was still her uncle. All she cared about was finding Charlie. She scanned the length of the train until—there. In the back.

An open-air, cage-like car held horses. She headed that way, David close behind her, hoisted herself up to the platform before he could help, and worked the latch loose.

"Miss Stratton, I implore you. Let us handle this."

She turned, ready with a sharp retort. But the look of sincere concern on his face stopped her. "I'll be fine. Are you going to help me or not?"

He looked over his shoulder at the group of men. Whistled to get their attention. Soon, several of them headed their way. They stood around and talked some more, trying to decide who would go and who would stay. Good gravy. At this rate, they'd have Charlie all the way to Mexico by the time this group got started.

She wasn't sure how she'd get a horse off the platform, but she'd figure it out. She appraised each of the animals—there were seven, each in its own little stall—and settled on a light, lean paint horse. He looked fast. Each horse's gear hung on hooks at the back of the stall. She made quick work of it, and soon the horse was in full tack.

A glance at the cluster of men showed they paid her little mind. They seemed to be all hat and no cattle. She leaned her head out the stall window. Up and down the length of the train, more people exited their cars and stood, exclaiming over the bridge, women weeping, men pacing.

Propped in a corner near the exit, secured by a length of rope, were several long boards. Of course! She'd create a ramp. As soon as she lifted the first board, large hands took it from her. She'd almost forgotten David was there. Together they formed the ramp and led the horse down, along with a quarter horse David selected. That would have been her second choice. Maybe he had a few cattle to go with his hat after all.

She'd climbed on the paint's back and was leaning forward, ready to spur him on and hoping he'd obey, when the older gentleman she'd spoken to earlier waved her down.

"Would you like to at least hear the latest?"

"Make it quick, sir. Each minute takes Charlie further from his mother."

"The conductor"—he pointed to a man in uniform—"was able to get off a partial wire to Silsbee before they stopped him. He feels certain they'll send someone right away, and they should be here within the hour. The men were after a bank roll they knew one of the passengers was carrying... It was on the car in front of ours."

The man shifted and lifted his hand to block the sun. "Wait for the authorities to arrive and let them handle it, Miss Stratton. These men won't get away with this. They'll have every Texas Ranger and lawman from both sides of the Brazos looking for them. Some of the younger men will go after them now, try and track them. Why don't you hop down off that horse and trust it to the menfolk? Those bandits won't kill the boy. They'll hang if they do, and they know that. They'll probably just leave him somewhere, where he's likely to be found. They just wanted to scare him…to scare all of us. He'll probably be back with his mother before nightfall. If you go chasing after them, you'll put yourself—and the boy—in more danger."

Ridiculous. Skye clicked and spurred the horse, and he seemed to understand the command. Behind her, she heard David's *hup!* and the following hoofbeats. She was certain others would follow. Well, good. Power in numbers and all that. She knew one thing, though. If she didn't get this party started, they'd stand around all day figuring out which boot was left and which was right.

She scanned the ground, picked up several sets of tracks easily enough, and used her legs to steer the horse into the woods. She'd chosen him for speed, but right now, she needed to take it slowly, figure out exactly where the outlaws went. That wasn't as easy in the shadows of the thick towering pines. She squinted her eyes, searched the pine-needle carpet, and looked for recent disturbances in the landscape. The outlaws couldn't be too far ahead, could they?

David pulled up beside her. "You've done this before." His voice was low, hushed.

"Yes."

"Can you show me what we're looking for? I'm an accountant, as is my father. We ride for pleasure, but we've never had much need for tracking."

That couldn't have been easy for David to ask. She respected his humility. She needed to get a closer look anyway, so she slid off her horse and led him through the dappled light, inspecting the pine needle carpet. "See, here. The pine needles are smooth, covering the ground evenly. Now look here." She pointed to a place where the landscape had been disturbed by a horse's hoof. We're looking for places like this."

David leaned forward. "I don't see a difference."

She showed him several other places, moving forward all the while. She hated that this was so hard. The bandits knew where they were going, and they would have ridden fast. Each minute she spent searching for tracks was another minute Charlie was in danger.

CHAPTER 12

$\mathcal{A}$lan and Walker found a bench. It was early for the train, and the station was sparse. The young chief didn't seem to be in a hurry, so Alan leaned back and stretched his legs in front of him. "Do you have ideas about where Miss Stratton can live?"

"I understand she is half white. I know nothing more of her. However, if she can pass as a white woman, you should let her keep that identity. Just as there are white people who will never accept an Indian as an equal, our people have their own prejudices. Some in our tribe will not accept a half-breed. It could be a problem."

Alan felt the air leave his lungs. He hadn't expected that. He didn't have a response, so he stood, paced the platform, looking in the direction the train would arrive. Some trains were early, right? He walked back to the bench and sat again. "That's not what I wanted to hear."

"Sometimes truth is difficult."

"Was it a bad idea, bringing her here?"

"I cannot answer. Much will depend on her."

Alan nodded. Stood again. This whole conversation made him antsy.

He wandered to the ticket booth. Maybe the man could tell him if the train was on time. "Excuse me, sir? Have you heard anything about the train coming from Houston?"

Wrinkles filled the man's forehead. "As a matter of fact, I received a wire just a few minutes ago. A partial wire, actually. There's some kind of delay, but I'm not sure what happened. You might as well make yourself comfortable, 'cause it'll be a while."

A cold wave passed through Alan's chest. "What does that mean? Can you tell me what the wire said?"

"I'm sorry. That's confidential. All I can say is there's been a delay. I'm working on wiring the authorities now."

"Authorities?"

The man nodded. "Let's just say, from what I could make out, I think the Rangers will need to be called in. Be patient. The authorities will be here soon, and they'll take care of things."

If they were calling the Rangers, then some kind of crime had been committed. His heart slammed against his ribs. He slapped his palm on the ticket window and bit back the words he wanted to spew all over the man. Wait on the authorities, his foot. He called out to Walker to follow him and headed toward the livery, picking up pace to a jog, then a full run. Good thing he'd paid the livery owner in advance.

When he arrived at the stable, he slowed enough to speak to the Indian man. "Something's happened. Her train's been delayed, but the man won't tell me what's going on. I'm going after her. Thank you for your time." At lightning speed, he had Fiona ready, jumped in the saddle, and spurred her full speed out the door. He'd bought the young quarter horse for her speed. Now was her time to shine.

He gave Fiona her head and guided her along the tracks. He heard hoofbeats behind him. A quick glance over his shoulder showed him Walker followed. Alan didn't slow for the man. He just kept riding as fast as Fiona could carry him.

Normally, he would've enjoyed the speedy jaunt, but right now, he felt more nauseated than free. They rode and rode, saying little, following the train tracks for the better part of an hour. He could see the bridge up ahead, and it looked…

What was wrong with the bridge?

He reined the horse in and studied the scene as Walker pulled in beside him. Someone had blown up the bridge.

Walker led out a low whistle. "Dynamite."

Just over the bridge, the train was stopped, and people milled about. Alan and Walker would have to go through the deep, rocky ravine to reach them. Without a word, but of the same mind, they proceeded. Slowly, steadily they guided their animals over the rough terrain. The last thing they needed was for a horse to twist an ankle. When they pulled up the other side, a uniformed man asked, "Are you with the Texas Rangers? The bandits went that way, and they kidnapped a little boy."

Kidnapped? Bile rose in Alan's throat, and he swallowed it back. "No, sir. I was waiting to pick up one of your passengers when I heard about the delay. I had no idea. We decided to come check on things, make sure my friend is okay. Her name is Skye Stratton." He looked around at the faces, but he didn't see Skye. Maybe she was still on the train.

"You're welcome to look for her. I'm sorry I can't help you right now, but I'm trying to get this wire signal working again."

Alan dismounted and led Fiona to a group of women. He felt Walker's presence behind him. "I'm looking for a woman named Skye Stratton. She has dark hair, about so tall."

A couple of the women looked at Walker with suspicion, then shook their heads in answer. Two of them looked down at their hands, and another glanced over her shoulder as if checking on her loved ones' safety.

He asked several more huddled groups until one man said,

"Sounds like that maniac who took off on a horse after the little boy. She's gonna get herself killed."

"What? Are you sure we're talking about the same woman?"

A tall, silver-haired man stepped forward. "Did you say Stratton? That's her, all right. She took one of the horses from the back and sped out after the bandits. She felt responsible for the boy's kidnapping. I told her not to, but I've gotta hand it to her. She demonstrated her shooting ability, and she knows how to aim a gun. One man from the train went with her, and five more followed about ten minutes later. They took all the horses we had on the train."

"Which way did she go? And how many bandits were there?"

The man told him all he knew and pointed to the spot where Skye entered the woods. "Good luck."

And he'd thought her an intelligent woman. Why in the world would she follow them herself? Why not let law enforcement handle it? He looked at Walker. "I can't believe she'd do something so stupid."

"Women often have spirit and intuition men can only strive for. It does not surprise me."

He hadn't expected that and didn't know what to say in response. "Let's go."

Alan thought himself a decent tracker, but soon he let Walker take the lead. The man easily spotted the fresh tracks, but they had no way of knowing if they were from Skye's horse or someone else's.

The longer Alan rode, the madder he got. Angry at Skye for being so foolish. Angry at those lowlifes for kidnapping a little boy. Wasn't it enough to blow up the bridge and rob the train? Angry at himself for taking Colt's bait and bringing her into this situation in the first place. Why couldn't he have just come home without a job? Why did he need a fancy, government appointment?

His pride. He hadn't wanted to return home a failure, a quitter. He'd wanted his parents, his community to see him as a success. So he'd crawled in the mud with Colt Stratton, and here they were.

God, this is all my fault. Please keep Skye safe. The little boy, too.

They'd ridden about fifteen minutes when they came upon a little trail to the left. Several sets of fresh tracks led in that direction.

Walker slowed and held up his hand in a stay-back motion, then pulled a knife out of a sheath in his pocket.

Alan felt for his holster—a necessity in Texas—and made sure his Remington was at the ready.

~

It took a couple hours, but Skye tracked the bandits to a little cabin burrowed deep in the piney woods. She and David circled at a distance, then retreated a little way back. Where were the others? She thought they'd be here by now.

Her heart pounded louder than her thoughts. Fear choked her, and she wondered if she shouldn't go back the way she'd come. That old man had been right. If they caught her, they'd hurt her and Charlie both. She wasn't sure how much help David would be. Could he even shoot that gun of his?

At least he had heart. She couldn't fault him there.

When they were far enough back not to be seen or heard, she drew up beside him. "Somehow, I have to get close enough to the cabin to see in the windows."

"Miss Stratton, I can't let you—"

"I don't need your permission. I'm going to circle around and see if there's a window in the back. You stay here and watch from the front. Can you whistle?"

David grinned. "That, I can do."

"What bird calls do you know?"

"I can do a pretty good whippoorwill…"

"Perfect. This will be our signal." She whistled the low-low-high pattern, and he mimicked the sound. "One pattern means I'm safe. Two in a row means I need help. You answer back with one call when you hear me."

"But Miss Stratton, I…"

She didn't want to hear the rest of his sentence. In her mind, she was already on her way. But good sense kept her from moving forward without hearing him out.

"I think we should wait for the others." His voice was low, unsure.

He might be right. But she didn't know when the others would arrive. They may be off on some other trail, lost.

Maybe she should have waited. Then she'd have the numbers she needed. What had come over her? Panic, that's what. But she couldn't undo her actions now.

"I appreciate the wisdom in your words. But something in my gut tells me we need to move forward."

He paused, then gave a gentle nod.

That was all she needed. She moved toward the structure, not even looking behind her. The closer she got to the cabin, the slower she moved, so slowly that her muscles ached. She was barely to the far side of the structure when the door creaked open and several men spilled out. They mumbled to each other, small talk she couldn't make out. She strained her ears to make out something, anything. Squinting her eyes, she focused on the one who seemed to be in charge.

"Get the campfire goin'…meeting…fifteen min…boy tied inside."

They were leaving Charlie unattended? That's what it sounded like. She just had to wait until they exited, find a way in, get Charlie, and escape without being seen. On silent feet, she inched further to the back of the cabin, her heart pounding with each inch, pounding so loudly she felt sure it would give her away.

A twig snapped behind her, and she froze. Grasped at the gun. Could she shoot a man? Could she? Slowly, soundlessly, she turned her body, craning her neck to see what didn't want to be seen. But before she could turn far, someone placed a hand over her mouth and grabbed her from behind. She struggled but stilled at the low *shhh*.

"Skye, it's Alan," he whispered. "It's Alan."

The words, the voice… She didn't understand how he was there, but he was.

"Don't make a sound," he whispered. "I'm going to let you go now."

What was he doing there? Had he come after her? She was so relieved to hear a familiar voice, but she didn't know whether to hug him or hit him. He'd nearly caused her heart to fail.

He loosened his grip, and she turned to face him. "How…? I don't understand." Her voice was barely a whisper.

He pulled her to him in a tight embrace that both surprised and comforted her. Then he stepped away, holding her at arms' length. "No time to sort all that out now. Walker and I ran into your friend already. They're watching the front of the house."

"Who's Walk—never mind. See that man building a fire? I think he's in charge. They're planning to have a meeting in a few minutes. I want to make it to that back window and see if I can climb in. It sounds like Charlie is tied up inside."

"If anybody's going, it's me."

Skye stiffened. "Charlie doesn't know who you are. If you show up, he'll think you're one of them, and he'll scream."

Alan seemed to consider her words. After a moment, he nodded. "All right. But listen for the whippoorwill signal—David told us about it. Two means danger. And…I don't know how to say this in a gentlemanly way, but those flouncy skirts will not help you get in and out quickly."

She looked down at herself. He was right. "Turn around." Her voice was barely a whisper.

When he did, she unzipped her skirt and stepped out of it. Besides Mama and Anita, no one had ever seen her in just her pantaloons. At least they were new. She held the skirt in front of her, like a shield. "All right. You may turn around." Heat scorched her cheeks. She'd hold her skirt in front of her until it was time to go.

Alan was careful not to look too closely at her, focusing on the cabin. They watched through a narrow break in the brush. Soon, men poured out of the doorway. She didn't understand how so many full-grown men had been contained in the tiny space. One of them had red hair and beard, and she knew that was the one Charlie had seen. Some of the men must have been on the train, while others met them at the bridge. There was no way a man could have ridden from Houston at the same speed as the train.

One man, smaller than average but with a big, booming voice, called the men to order, and they gathered around, sitting on logs and tree stumps. She didn't listen to what he said. Now was her chance.

She dropped her skirt and crept toward the back, making her way to the small, low window. *Please let it be open.* Thankfully, there was no glass in the window. It was just an opening covered with loose hanging oilcloth. She pushed it aside and spotted Charlie, in the center of the room, bound and gagged. The monsters!

He saw her too, and his eyes widened. She held a finger over her lips, and he nodded.

Soundlessly, she crawled in the window, scooped Charlie up, ropes, gag and all, and dropped him as gently as possible out the window before climbing out after him. She held her finger over her lips again and made sure he understood before picking him up and carrying him softly, silently back into the brush, hunched over as far as possible to avoid being spotted. That was almost too easy.

He was getting heavy, and she couldn't carry him much further without standing to support her weight. Once they were out of view, she laid him down so she could untie him.

"I'm going to get you out of these ropes, but you have to promise you won't make a sound. Not a single sound. Do you promise?"

He nodded, his eyes still wide and frightened.

Slowly, so as not to make any unnecessary noise, she was able to free him.

"You're in your underwear," Charlie whispered, eyeing her lace pantaloons.

She pressed her fingers over his mouth. "You promised. No sound at all. Remember?"

He nodded.

"We're going to find my friends. I need you to stay down, and stay right with me. Do you understand?"

He nodded again.

Slowly, painfully, they crawled back through the brush, stopping every few feet to make sure no one heard them. She'd just caught Alan in her view when she heard a commotion.

"The kid's gone! Musta got out through the back window!"

She stood, grabbed Charlie by the arm, and practically dragged him to Alan. She'd left her gun in her skirt pocket. If they were found, they had no protection. The first shot was fired, though from which direction, she couldn't tell. When they reached the hollowed-out brush where Alan waited, gun cocked and ready, she grabbed for her skirt, pulling the gun free. "Charlie, no matter what happens, you must still remain quieter than you've ever been. Quieter than a mouse at midnight." She pointed in the direction she'd left David. "If anything happens to me and Mr. McNaughten, I want you to run that way. Okay?"

Charlie nodded.

Several more shots were fired, but they didn't seem to be coming their direction.

Alan leaned close to her ear. "They're shooting into the woods behind the cabin. I guess they think he went straight back instead of circling around. But they'll find us soon enough. We need to find Walker and David and stay together."

While Alan talked, Skye shimmied back into her skirt. She didn't want to be captured. She certainly didn't want to be captured in her underwear. When it was finally zipped—though the zipper was in the front instead of the side where it belonged—she made eye contact with Charlie. "Stay down. Stay quiet. Stay with me."

She would surely lose her lunch before the day was over. But when Alan hunched down and moved forward, she grabbed Charlie's arm and followed. Alan led them deeper into the thick woods before pausing long enough to scoop Charlie onto his back. "Run!" he hissed.

Briars slapped her arms, ripped her skirt. Twigs scraped her face, pulled her hair. Finally, she spotted two men. Four horses. Alan set Charlie down.

David moved forward, arms outstretched, and hugged Skye so tight she could barely breathe. "I thought you were dead. You are the bravest person I know."

Alan rasped out a command. "Get down! Someone is coming."

Horses' hooves approached from behind and surrounded them. Skye cocked her gun, aimed, and —

It was the men from the train! They made enough noise to wake a sleeping bear. If the bandits hadn't found them before, they surely would now.

One of the men let out a low "Hmph." Almost as if he'd bet against her and lost. Behind them, the bandits shouted directions and orders. The sounds got muddled in Skye's mind.

A single bullet whizzed past her and stopped with a sickening thud, followed by a groan. David!

He sank to the ground, blood gushing. Where from, she couldn't tell. His shoulder? His chest? She dropped to her knees. "Where are you hurt?"

He gritted his teeth. "I'm okay. Take care of...yourself...and the boy."

Somewhere in the distance, a voice shouted. "Over here!" She couldn't tell who'd said it.

The dark-haired man—Walker, was it?—scooped up Charlie onto his horse. "There's a ravine about a hundred paces north. Get there, fast. We'll soon be surrounded." He took off.

Skye hesitated. David!

"Go! I'll get him." Alan hoisted David up and supported his weight, helping him walk.

Skye would've shot, but she couldn't see where the bullets came from or whom she might be shooting at. She mounted the paint she'd ridden and followed Walker, trusting that Alan and David would come, hoping with all her might no one would die today.

CHAPTER 13

$\mathcal{A}$lan watched as if time had gotten caught in a sludge, as if the wheels creaked and strained to move forward.

This man, David. Who was he to Skye?

Bullets…so close to Skye.

When David went down, the look of horror on her face, the way she dropped to her knees, searching him for wounds… Did she have feelings for this man? The thought entered and left in an instant as he tried to push through the confusion and make sense of the chaos around him.

Somewhere, like an echo, he heard Walker say something about a ravine. Alan looked that direction, saw Walker had the boy.

He called out to Skye. "Go! I'll get him."

Men shouted. But right now, he couldn't tell who from whom, bandit or not. He hefted David up. It looked like a shoulder wound. "Can you ride?"

"Yeah." David's voice was strained.

Alan helped him onto his horse, then mounted Fiona. They needed to run, but for David's sake, he went as slowly as he could. He hoped David hadn't lost too much blood. He looked as if he might pass out. "Try to stay with me."

Behind them, more voices. Bullets whizzed, thudded into trees, whistled past their heads. Up ahead, a red handkerchief, waving. He followed it into a deep, crowded ravine.

"I think they've spotted us." Walker moved to the side to make room. "Soon, they'll have us surrounded. We'll hold them off as best we can, but it doesn't look good."

Several of the men cursed.

"There's a lady present. And a child." Alan couldn't help himself. The cursing stopped, but the bullets drew closer. "Don't shoot until you can see a target. We can't afford to waste ammunition." He didn't know if anyone heard him or not.

The men positioned themselves around the moist, knotty ravine so they could shoot from all angles. A thick layer of pine needles provided a soft carpet and muted the sound of their movement. David rested against the ravine's wall. His wound needed attention. "Skye! Can you use that handkerchief to stop the bleeding?"

One of the other men spoke up. "I'll do it. That little lady's one of the best marksmen I've seen. We need her aiming that pistol." Alan's eyebrows lifted. He looked at Skye, who peeked over the ravine. The voices grew louder, from all sides...the bandits were close. Another shot pinged over their heads.

If they died, they died. But they wouldn't kill Skye. At least not until they'd used her up, defiled her. *Please God. Get us out of here. We need a miracle.* He positioned himself beside Skye, Walker on her other side. The bandits were in clear view now between the tall, narrow trees, about thirty yards from them and moving in. "On the count of three, start shooting."

*S*kye had only felt this consuming fear once before. It was the night her father died. The night of the fire. Her mother had been gone a year.

She'd prayed. Begged God to bring her father back. He wasn't himself, hadn't been since Mama died. But he was all she'd had left.

All these years, she'd blamed God. Blamed herself for not being good enough, white enough, for the white man's God to hear her. But in that moment, in her fear, she heard that voice in her head. *Fear not, for I am with you.* And, *I did not give you a spirit of fear.*

On her left, Alan counted. The man on her right counted, too, in a different language."Chaffá:kan, Tóklon, Toccí:nan."

The Coushatta numbers her mother taught her as a child… One, Two, Three. She stared at Walker, who paid her no mind.

She was too stunned to move. Like a statue she knelt, while everyone around her defended them from the onslaught.

Behind her, Charlie's whimpers jolted her spirit. Something inside her woke up. She aimed at one of the riders. The red-haired man…

Got him in her sights.

Cocked the hammer.

Finger on the trigger.

The man clutched his chest, fell off his horse. Had she pulled the trigger?

Suddenly, the bandits turned and started shooting away from them. What was happening?

The men around her stopped shooting. One by one, the bandits either fell off their horses or took off into the woods.

The noise died down. The forest grew quiet. What just happened?

Then, the most beautiful words she'd ever heard pierced the silence. "This is the Texas Rangers. We have you surrounded. Drop your weapons and come out with your hands raised."

A man stepped into the clearing, gun aimed at the ravine. He wore a cowboy hat, white shirt, and vest. Pinned to his vest, clear as day, was the star-shaped Ranger badge.

$\sim$

One by one, members of their group placed guns on the ground and lifted hands in the air. Alan didn't know how this happened. He didn't care. All he knew was they were safe.

Skye was safe.

Charlie was safe.

He craned his neck around to find David.

The man watched Skye, his skin white as paper. He gave her a slight grin, as if it took all his energy to lift the corner of his mouth.

She smiled back. Turned, and caught Alan watching her.

He wanted to say something comforting, something wise and brilliant, that would make everything okay for her, but he couldn't think of a single word. They stood there, hands up, looking at each other. He wondered what she was thinking.

She looked away first.

Soon, four Rangers stood around the ravine, guns pointed at them.

Charlie sobbed behind them. "Don't shoot, misters! Please don't shoot us."

The Rangers lowered their guns. "Is anyone hurt?"

Alan let the other men take over. Let them see to David, to Charlie. Even the horses. As far as he was concerned, he had one responsibility right now, and she was right next to him.

Walker had already climbed out of the ravine. He reached a hand to Skye and helped her ascend the steep bank. When she stood at the top, she spoke to him in a language Alan didn't understand. Walker answered in his own language and moved away. Skye stared after him, transfixed.

Alan felt like an outsider.

And when it came to Skye Stratton, that was the last thing he wanted to be.

~

Skye felt like a tree...wooden. Heavy. She tried to clear the fog in her brain. What next?

Charlie.

Alan lifted the boy out of the ravine and placed him just a few feet from her. He threw his little arms around her waist and squeezed tight, his head buried in her skirt.

She knelt and wrapped him in a hug. Mama's words echoed in her memory: *When you're afraid, look out instead of in. Find someone who is worse off than you, and give them your strength. It will help them and make you stronger in the process.*

Mama had gone on to tell her that, while introspection is good, it's easy to get lost there. Skye wasn't sure what she felt right now, but holding Charlie, soothing his tears, did help her keep her head. There'd be time enough later to consider the feelings brought on by those three simple Coushatta counting words.

Other words flooded her memory, like they'd been held back by a damn that suddenly burst. Standing next to the man, she'd whispered, "*A lii la mo.*" Thank you.

He'd answered back in the same language. "You're welcome."

Charlie tugged at her skirt, tugged her back to the present.

Alan, to her left, checked her horse. He looked at her, as if to make sure she was all right. Across the ravine, the Rangers questioned several men. She looked down and met Charlie's eyes.

"You saved my life," the boy said.

She squeezed him tighter. "Let's get you back to your mother. She's very worried about you."

"I love you, Miss Stratton."

Liquid heat pressed her eyes. She fought it, but a few tears spilled over. "I love you too, Charlie."

A Ranger approached. "You're a brave woman. Normally I'd say you're also foolish, but since it all turned out okay for you and the boy here, I won't scold you." He drew out his words in that way Texas cowboys had, part charm, part grit. "If you weren't a woman, I might ask you to join the force."

That pulled a chuckle from deep in her gut, even through the tears. "I might say yes. So you'd better not ask."

He laughed too. "Most of my men are rounding up the scoundrels who did this. A couple of my officers will accompany you and the others back to the train. If you need anything, contact me at my Houston office. My name is Rett Smith." He handed her a card with his contact information.

"Thank you, Mr. Smith."

He knelt to speak to Charlie. "You're brave too. I'm proud of you for surviving that ordeal."

Charlie's forehead wrinkled. "What's an or-deal?"

"It's another word for what you just went through. Try to avoid them, whenever possible."

"Yes, sir."

With a tip of his hat, the man walked away.

Alan moved closer, leading her horse. "Should Charlie ride with you, or would you rather I take him?"

"I've got him. Thanks." She reached to lift Charlie into the saddle of the paint she'd borrowed at the same time Alan did, and their hands brushed. Something like an electrical charge passed between them at that touch. She met his eyes, and knew by his expression that he was attracted to her. But would a white man who knew her heritage ever view her as more than a plaything?

She straightened her hair and her skirt. Looked around to make sure none of the other men watched, then eyed Alan. "Turn around."

His ears turned a deep shade of red, but he complied.

She hiked her skirt and climbed up behind Charlie. "You may look now."

He turned, that lopsided grin in place.

"You have a piece of grass in your hair." She couldn't resist pointing it out.

"You have an entire meadow in yours." His eyes sparked, and he held her gaze while he mounted his horse. Then his eyes fell on Walker, who waited about a hundred yards ahead. "After you, Miss Stratton."

"What's the horse's name?" Charlie asked as she led the horse into a trot.

It may not be her horse. But considering all they'd been through, it needed a name. She eyed Walker ahead of her. So straight and tall. So proud. "Coushatta. Her name is Coushatta."

CHAPTER 14

$\mathcal{A}$lan looked across the hazy gray sky, the last streaks of pink on the horizon. A waxing gibbous moon peeped out, promising just enough light to guide their way. At the train, passengers cheered as if they were long lost heroes come home from the war.

A woman broke from the crowd and ran to Skye and Charlie, tears unchecked. "You're safe! Oh, Charlie. You're safe. My baby is safe." Several women followed, dabbing their eyes with handkerchiefs.

Charlie practically fell off the horse into his mother's arms.

Skye said something to Charlie's mother, then directed her horse to the rear car. Alan followed her.

Several men moved to assist her. She climbed down, stroked the horse's muzzle and whispered something in its ear. Then she moved back, letting the men take over.

Alan climbed down and stood next to her.

Walker waited just inside the wood line, out of sight of the crowd. Alan felt both relief and irritation at that. Relief that Walker was smart enough to avoid confrontation. Irritation that avoidance was necessary.

The conductor approached. "I'm so glad you folks are safe. Where are the rest of the men? Was anyone hurt?"

When Skye didn't answer, Alan said, "They're on their way, sir. One man was shot in the shoulder, so he'll need medical attention. Other than a few scrapes and bruises, I believe everyone else is all right."

"There's a doctor on board," the conductor said. "I'll make sure he's ready. We can't cross the bridge, so a train from Houston's coming to rescue us. We'll have to go back there and make other arrangements for you folks to get to Silsbee."

"If Miss Stratton is agreeable, I can take her with me. We'll need to have her trunks sent later, though."

"Oh, that'll be no problem, sir. I hate that this happened on my watch. We'll do whatever we need to take care of things."

Skye looked drained. "I'll need to get my bag off the train. Is it possible to remove a few things from my trunk to take with me now?"

"Certainly, Miss Stratton. Let me notify the doctor while you retrieve your bag. Meet me at the baggage car, third from the end." He held his lantern high and left them in search of the physician.

Skye looked at Alan, and dark circles shadowed her eyes. "I'm sorry to be so much trouble."

"You're no trouble. You're a hero."

Her shoulders slumped just for a moment before she straightened again. "I hope I don't need to be a heroine, ever again. At least not any time soon." She headed for the train and stopped outside a car with the number seven painted on the side.

Alan looped Fiona's reins through a handle bar near the door, then followed Skye onto her car. Gas lanterns provided plenty of light for the few passengers who'd chosen to remain on board.

A white-haired woman stood when Skye entered. "You're

back! Praise God, you're back. Where is David? Is the little boy okay?"

Skye hugged the woman like she was her grandmother. "Charlie is fine. David...he'll be here soon. He's going to be all right, but he did take a bullet in the shoulder. The conductor has already alerted the doctor.

"Oh, my." The woman dropped to her seat.

Skye sat beside her, and Alan lowered himself to the bench across from them.

"I don't know what I would have done without your son, Mrs. Kelly. He is truly one of the bravest, kindest men I've ever had the pleasure of knowing."

Alan didn't like feeling jealous. It was a nasty trait, yet he felt it all the same. He tried to push it away. "Ma'am, I'm Alan McNaughten, and I witnessed your son's valor first hand. You have every right to be proud of him."

"But..." The woman's gaze flicked from him to Skye and back. "He'll be all right? You're sure?"

Skye placed both hands on top of the woman's. "He lost some blood. He'll need a lot of rest. Maybe a few stitches. I'm no doctor, but I do believe he will recover from his wound. And he'll have quite a story to tell!"

The woman chuckled, though her eyes glistened. "I suppose I'll wait for him outside, then. Would you like to come with me?"

"I'm afraid I won't be staying. Mr. McNaughten has offered to take me back to Silsbee tonight, along with our chaperone." She didn't mention that the chaperone was an Indian man. Probably best.

"Oh, dear. How can I stay in touch?"

Skye looked to Alan, uncertainty in her gaze.

"Miss Stratton will be staying with my parents for a time in Livingston. My father pastors the church there. If you write to her, care of James McNaughten, the letter should find her."

"I'll remember that. Thank you, sir." She squeezed Skye's hands, then held out her arms and pulled her into a tight embrace. "You take care of yourself, young lady. Do you hear me?"

"Yes, ma'am."

The woman left, and Skye pulled out an intricately woven bag, hoisted the strap over her shoulder, and stood. "I suppose it's time. A new adventure awaits."

Alan didn't know whether to hug her or muss her hair. Her hair was already mussed. "After today's adventure, I'd like to keep things on the dull side for a while."

She grinned, and one dimple showed. "Where's the fun in that?"

Something inside came a little more alive, like it did every time he'd had an encounter with Miss Skye Stratton. Outside, a crowd gathered around somebody. Must be David.

"Oh! Give me just one moment, please." He watched her exit the train and push her way through the crowd in the most lady-like way one can push.

Alan stayed back. David seemed like a nice enough fellow, and Alan wished the man no harm. But he had no desire to watch a tender good-bye between him and Skye. He squinted into the dusk and caught sight of Walker, just inside the treeline, still as a statue. What must it feel like, to be forced to remain invisible or suffer the consequences of a hateful, prejudiced world?

He shifted his gaze to where Skye had disappeared. What must it feel like, indeed.

CHAPTER 15

"Miss Stratton." David's pale face, his weak voice, squeezed Skye's heart.

"Mr. Kelly. Thank you. For all you did today." She placed her hand on his good arm.

"It is I who should thank you. I've never had such an adventure. Now all these people are calling me brave. I don't know that I've ever been called brave."

"You've always been who you are. Which means you've always been a hero."

"You are too kind."

Skye turned to Mrs. Kelly. "Please write and tell me how he's doing."

"I will, dear. You do the same, and be careful."

Soon, Skye threaded her way back to Alan.

He held onto Fiona's reins. "Ready?" he asked.

"Almost. Let me get a few things from my luggage, and I'll be right with you." She left Alan waiting for her; she could see the conductor waiting beside the baggage car.

"Thank you," she told him.

He nodded, and she followed him into the car and looked for

her things by the dim light of the lantern he held up. It took some doing, but soon the two of them located her belongings, and she scuffled through, grabbing what she could and cramming it in her valise. At least she had some money. Surely she could purchase what she needed until the rest of her things arrived. After thanking the conductor again, she made her way back to Alan.

"Ready now?"

She nodded, and he lifted her into the saddle before climbing up in front of her. She sat straight and stiff, not knowing where to grab hold.

Right now was as good a time to leave as any, with everyone focused on David. She stretched her neck to look around her. "Where is Walker?"

"He'll join us shortly." He clicked to Fiona, and the mare moved forward with an easy gait that said she might be as tired as her humans. When they approached a low valley, Walker and his horse appeared from the woods.

When they began down the steep decline, there was no place for propriety. Skye had no choice but to grab onto Alan's waist and hold tight. He smelled musky and sweaty, yet altogether pleasant. What would he think if he knew her thoughts? A half breed? He'd probably drop her where they were and let her find her own way. She thought of Walker, behind her. Would he feel the same? Would the Coushatta scorn her because she wasn't full-blooded?

She didn't want to think about that now. She pushed the worries to the back of her mind and tried to come up with more agreeable contemplations.

"How are you doing back there?"

She felt the rumble of Alan's voice through his back, and it sent a thrill. Aside from her father, she'd never been this close to a man, ever. "I'm all right." Her voice was soft, though it took all her effort to make the sound. She wondered if he'd heard her.

"Once we reach the other side of this ravine, if you're up for it, I'll give Fiona her head. She'll have us back to Silsbee in no time."

Right now, Skye was enjoying the slow, easy pace, though she was fighting not to lean her head on his back and close her eyes. Maybe a fast run was just what she needed to jar her mind back into place. "After today, I suppose I'm up for anything."

He laughed, that deep, rumbly laugh she remembered from before, from back home. Too soon, they rode onto flat, straight land, and Alan spurred Fiona onward. Skye hung on tighter, closer, and tried to soak in the thrill of this scandalous moonlit ride. After the day she'd had, she deserved a guilty pleasure, didn't she?

After the day she'd had, she felt as if life had once again taken her tender heart, battered and beaten it, and left it on the road to die a slow, painful death.

Her day with Charlie.

With the Indian at the station.

With David and Mrs. Kelly.

With Alan.

With Walker and his strange-familiar words, hearing the language she hadn't heard since she was a child.

This was a day of remembering the past, of stepping into the future.

And somehow, after a day like today, she still wasn't sure about anything. Anything, that is, but the knowledge that right now, she was so, so tired. And that she liked being close to Alan McNaughten entirely more than she should.

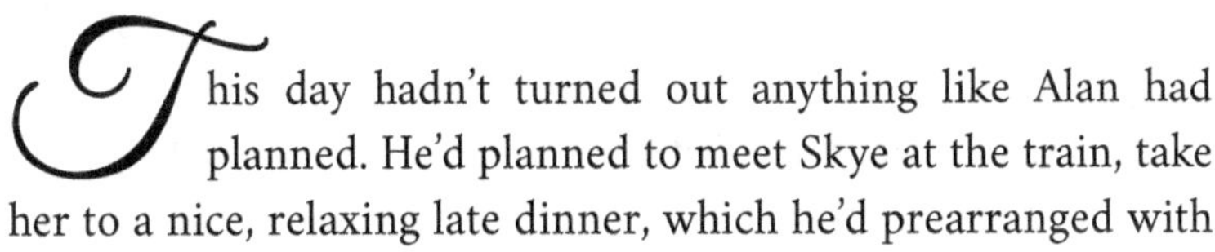

This day hadn't turned out anything like Alan had planned. He'd planned to meet Skye at the train, take her to a nice, relaxing late dinner, which he'd prearranged with the cook at the inn where they each had a room. He knew she'd be tired, yet they'd linger over dessert, perhaps take a turn around the starlit square before she retired for the evening. That prospect had excited him.

Nothing could have prepared him for the bizarre events that had occurred today. What was it they said about the best-laid plans of mice and men? Yet with all the things that went wrong today, he couldn't ignore what went *right*. Skye was here. She was *alive...* He could only credit that to answered prayer. When he thought about what could have happened, his insides twisted and knotted like roots on a cedar tree.

Her arms were wrapped around his waist, head leaning against his back. How did she still smell like sweet lemons and orange blossoms, when he was sure he smelled like a combination of sweat and horse manure?

Walker, who'd ridden ahead of them most of the way, slowed some to mind the thorny brush that grew close to the tracks. Alan followed the man's lead. The slowed pace would give him a chance to say a few things he wanted to say. If he held back any longer, he might bite his tongue off.

"Skye. Help me understand. Why in the world did you go after that boy? I could understand if no one else planned to go, but there were plenty of men there willing to handle things, as well as the Texas Rangers on their way. You could have gotten killed, or worse. Could have gotten Charlie killed. What were you thinking?"

The words came out harsher than he intended. He meant to communicate care and concern. He meant to let her know how devastated so many people would be if anything happened to her.

He felt her body stiffen. Felt her pull away from him, put as much physical distance as she could between her body and his. "Excuse me?"

"Now, don't get mad. But you must know how foolish your

actions were. If you'd been hurt, it would destroy your parents. A lot of people care about you. I can't imagine your father would approve of what you did."

She said nothing for a thick minute. Then she spoke, low and in control, like a queen ordering a servant. "Stop this horse. Now."

He pulled back on Fiona's reins, slowing more but not stopping, thinking she had some kind of emergency. "What do you need?" Maybe she needed to use the necessary. Good luck with that out here.

Despite the moving horse, she slid down, landing in the briars. That had to hurt. "Mr. Walker! Please stop." Her voice was tight, exhaustion mixed with anger.

Ahead of them, Walker drew up his horse and turned on the tracks. He approached Skye, who stood in the thorns, but said nothing.

"I would like to ride with you, sir, if that's all right."

Ride with Walker? "Now hold on. Don't be that way."

The slightest grin hinted on Walker's face before it disappeared. He hopped off his horse, placed his hands around her waist, and lifted her into his saddle. Then he climbed up behind her, instead of in front.

"Skye," Alan said. "Miss Stratton. You don't have to do that. I'm sorry. I...I just...I feel sick at the thought of something happening to you." Why couldn't he have just kept his mouth shut?

They were still close enough that he could see her glare at him in the moonlight. And they were still close enough that he could make eye contact with Walker, who still looked like he was trying very hard not to grin. Just before he clicked his horse into a jog, the Indian flashed a wide smile at Alan.

So, that's how it was.

Alan wanted to kick himself. Instead, he kicked the stirrups and followed the Indian and his *maiden* into the moonlight. A moonlight ride that was supposed to be his.

~

"I'm sorry you are...distraught." Walker held the reins, his arms wrapped around her, though nothing felt inappropriate about the way they sat.

Skye remembered so much when she was with this man. Riding just like this, nestled up to her mother. Or her father.

"I'll be all right. It's nothing new to me. When I try to do something good, it is viewed as bad."

Walker chuckled. "I take it the agent scolded you for your actions today."

"I know my actions seem foolish to most. But I can't explain it. I did what I knew I had to do. I know how to shoot, and I know how to track. I felt confident in my ability."

"Did you feel the same confidence when we were in that ravine, shooting to kill?"

She thought about his question for a time. "No. I didn't. I've never shot at a person before."

They rode in silence for a time before Walker spoke again. "Your actions were brave. In our culture, women must be...how do you say it? Rugged. Strong. Not like the white culture, where women are viewed as soft, as less capable than a man."

"I am Coushatta." She said it so softly, she wasn't sure he heard.

"I know. The agent told me."

"My father was white."

"Yes."

Should she tell him more? He was Coushatta. What would he think if he knew her whole identity? She was tired. Weary from the day. Weary from her life. Weary of pretending to be something she wasn't. "My mother... she was not full Coushatta. She was half Comanche."

She felt his muscles tighten. Other than that, he didn't respond.

"Do you have an opinion about that?"

"Does it matter?"

"I...I don't know. I guess I just want to know if your people will accept me."

More silence. She got the impression he was measuring his words. Something Alan could use practice doing.

"I cannot answer for others. Some will accept you. Some will not. That is the way of people, no matter the color of their skin."

He was right, she knew. Yet surely he, of all people, knew that the darker the skin, the darker the hair and eyes, the harder it was. Maybe she shouldn't have told him about the Comanche part. Even she knew the Comanche were among the most hated of tribes. She had secretly read everything she could find about both the Coushatta and the Comanche. While the Coushatta were a peaceful people, the Comanche were fighters. Warriors.

Maybe that's why she was so quick to go after Charlie. It was in her blood. She wished she knew more of her own story, of how she came to be such a mixture of bloods in a world where purity of blood was held in high esteem.

Walker slowed, held back until Alan was beside him. "This is where we part ways, Miss Stratton. If I am caught in Silsbee after dark, it will not go well for me. And you certainly don't want to get caught riding with me."

"I don't care what others think."

"Oh, but you should. A good name is rather to be chosen than great riches."

Her eyebrows lifted. Had he just quoted Proverbs? That was unexpected.

Walker climbed from the horse and helped her down. "Agent, do you need anything else from me?"

She caught the cat-ate-the-canary grin on Walker's face, the annoyed look on Alan's. Something bubbled inside her, and she giggled. Both men looked at her, and she strained to pull out some form of dignity, but given how tired she was, the whole scene was suddenly quite funny.

Alan looked at her like she'd lost her mind. He might be right. "We're fine, Walker. Thank you for your help today." Then he climbed down, as Walker had, and lifted Skye firmly into Fiona's saddle.

She waved at the Indian. "I look forward to seeing you again, Mr. Walker."

Walker smiled, nodded. "Miss Stratton. Agent." With a slight kick, he took off into the night, the moonlight reflecting off his white shirt until he disappeared into the dark.

Alan spurred Fiona into a trot. "Hang on just a little longer. We're not far."

She refused to acknowledge his words.

"I really am sorry. It wasn't the time or place. I just...when I found out you had left the group and gone after those men, my heart might as well have stopped. I was really frightened."

That block of ice that had formed in her heart at his earlier words melted, just a little.

"Forgive me? Please?"

He sounded so forlorn, so childlike. Oh, good gravy. "I forgive you. This time."

~

It took a minute, but he finally felt her relax against him. She'd only ridden with Walker for fifteen, maybe twenty minutes. Yet they talked the whole way, like old friends. He'd heard their voices drifting back through the wind, though he couldn't make out the words. As long as he lived, he'd never forget this wonderful, awful moonlit ride with the most beautiful, complex woman he'd ever known. Spirited, yet humble. Spunky, yet shy. Confident, yet uncertain.

"Will we ride to Livingston tomorrow?" Her words bounced with Fiona's trots.

"That was the original plan. Right now, I wonder if we shouldn't take an extra day for you to rest and recover."

"So I can sleep late in the morning?"

He laughed. This woman was an enigma. "Sleep as late as you want." Though conversation was difficult, he didn't want it to end. "Whenever we return, we'll stop by the reservation on the way. You can take a look around, perhaps meet some of your students."

"Really? I might want to leave tomorrow then."

"Let's wait and see how you feel in the morning."

"All right."

Soon the town's silhouette gained shape on the horizon. It was dark, but a few people still milled about. Likely, they'd heard about the train and awaited news. Alan and Skye earned a few curious glances as they rode through town, but no one addressed them. He'd get her settled at the inn, then return Fiona to the livery. Hopefully, the innkeeper would take pity on them and feed them, despite the late hour. Surely, under the circumstances.

He helped her down, then untied her carpet bag, stuffed and groaning with whatever extra things she'd squeezed in from her trunk. Then he dug in his pocket and handed her the key, which he'd already procured. "We're on the second floor. The key works for both the front door and your room."

She did the eyebrow thing again, lifting just one of them, looking at him as if he'd lost his ever-loving mind.

"Oh! Not the same room, I assure you. You're in room four. I'm in room one, at the other end of the hall."

Her eyebrows relaxed, and she nodded.

He wished she'd say something.

When she didn't, he cleared his throat. "It looks like the innkeeper's lights are out. I'll wake him and see if he can rustle us up something to eat."

"Oh, don't do that! I have sandwiches, if you don't mind eating those."

Day old sandwiches with Skye Stratton? "That sounds wonderful. I'll meet you in the parlor, to the right of the front door, in about ten minutes."

She agreed, then placed the key in the lock, wiggled the door open, and shut it behind her.

It looked like he'd get that dinner with Skye after all. If she'd offered him a piece of cardboard to eat, he'd have said yes with a smile.

He hurried to the livery, found Fiona's stall, and removed her saddle and tack. After a few brushes, an affectionate pat and a "good girl," he left her with a bucket of oats and water.

Across the way, he saw a lantern burning in the inn parlor. He couldn't hold back the grin he knew must make him look like a silly schoolboy. But when he entered the room, it was empty.

There, on the table under the lamp, wrapped in a blue checkered cloth, was a flattened sandwich, a few squished grapes, and some kind of smashed bakery item. Beside it was a note, written in perfect hand:

"I'm sorry for the presentation, but I assure you it tastes delicious. I'll see you in the morning. —S.S."

Disappointment cloaked him like a cold, wet blanket. But he was hungry, so he picked up the sandwich, looked at it from several different angles, and crammed half of it in his mouth. She was right. It was delicious.

CHAPTER 16

The sun was high when Skye awoke the next morning. She looked around, and for a minute she had no idea where she was. Like watercolor seeping through the lines on a page, yesterday's memories came back to her, slowly, randomly.

Was it really just yesterday morning that she woke up in her own bed, nervous and excited about what lay ahead? She felt like she'd lived a hundred years in the last twenty-four hours.

Charlie. She forgot to get his address. How would she learn what became of him and his mother? Panic overtook her, like that was the most important thing in her world.

Breathe.

Chaffá:kan. Tóklon. Toccí:nan. Just saying the Coushatta words calmed her, helped her think more clearly. Before they left Silsbee, she would send a wire to the train station in Houston, requesting information. If that didn't work, surely there would be a news story or something.

Then she remembered the Ranger in Houston. Rett Smith. She'd wire him and ask his assistance in finding the boy. She needed to wire her parents and let them know she arrived safely, too. But she'd save yesterday's story for when they came in person. The Houston paper would print a story about it, but maybe it wouldn't circulate all the way to Lampasas.

She stretched her arms over her head and squinted at the sun out the window. It was around ten a.m. She couldn't remember when she'd slept so late. She turned onto her side, pulled her knees up, and contemplated going back to sleep.

No. Too much to do. With a groan, she flopped her feet over the side of the bed and sat up. She'd missed breakfast, and she was starved. And all her clothes were wrinkled, to boot. After assessing each item in her limited wardrobe to see which was the least offensive, she chose a simple brown skirt and mustard yellow shirtwaist with brown buttons and trim. The shirt brought out the gold flecks in her eyes, and if they were to travel today, the brown color would hopefully hide the dust.

She used every bit of the water in the small pitcher to clean up, but she'd give anything for a bath. It took much longer than usual to work the knots out of her hair. She should have combed it out last night, but she'd done well to undress before she fell into bed. Once her hair was suitably tangle-free, she parted it in the middle and pulled most of it into a low, loose bun. The remaining section she braided and wrapped around her head in a crown, then secured it at the base. Finally, she pulled a few loose strands free around her face, the way the women in Godey's Lady's Book did, and wished for her brown floral hat. It was in her trunk, with the train. No telling when she'd receive it. She didn't even have a matching parasol. At least she still had her broach. She carefully pinned it at the neck of her blouse and looked at her watch. Ten thirty.

She straightened her things and placed them back in her bag as neatly as she could, pulled the covers up on her bed, and went downstairs in hopes that she wouldn't have to look very hard for Alan. She wasn't about to knock on his door, though she recalled he was in room one.

"There she is. Rise and shine, Miss Stratton." Alan rested

comfortably in one of the overstuffed chairs in the parlor, newspaper in hand. He wore a well-constructed cotton suit of blue plaid with a starched white shirt beneath the vest. His jacket—double breasted—lay beside him on the chair. The blue in his suit made his eyes pop even more than usual. What had he worn yesterday? She'd been too distracted to notice. But today...mercy. Those eyes would drive her to distraction all day long.

"Good morning, Mr. McNaughten. I didn't mean to sleep so late." A middle-aged woman on the other side of the room looked up from her book, and Skye nodded at her. The woman returned the nod and went back to her book.

"I hoped you'd sleep late. You must be hungry. There's a café up the boardwalk. Shall we?" He stood, offered his arm. She took it, though she was still miffed with him for his words to her last night. But she'd said she forgave him, so she needed to let it go.

"Oh! I almost forgot," Alan said. "I have a gift for you. A welcome-to-the-job gift, if you will." He held out a small, brown-paper-wrapped package.

"How thoughtful. You didn't need to get me a gift." She sat in the nearest chair and untied the string. Inside was a beautifully-beaded bag. She opened it, and inside was a smaller pouch with matching beadwork. The smaller pouch held pencils. "How lovely. Thank you."

"They were made by local Indians. I assume the Alabama-Coushatta, but I didn't ask when I purchased it. We can stop by the general store and ask the proprietor, if you'd like."

She traced the tulip pattern with her finger.

Pa kaa li. Flower.

Something stirred in her, that unexpected rush of heat to her face, and her heart sped up, and for a moment, she couldn't breathe. She forced back the tears that pressed against her eyes.

Would she feel this way every time something reminded her of her first family?

When she regained her composure, she took a deep, silent breath. "Thank you. This was very thoughtful."

"You don't have to carry it now, if you don't want. I'll wait while you put it in your room."

"It's all right. It kind of matches what I'm wearing." She placed her coin purse inside the larger bag with the pencil case and looped the long, leather strap around the button closure. "I'm ready."

It was a short walk to the café, and she noticed a general store and a ladies' dress shop along the way. She wondered if they'd have time to shop before leaving. She hadn't traveled much outside of Lampasas. Even though Silsbee was a small town, it was new and exciting to her.

A hostess seated them. Skye was half tempted to order the entire left side of the menu but settled on two eggs, a side of bacon, and a biscuit, along with a cup of coffee. "I'm glad they're still serving breakfast."

"I take it you slept well?"

"I can hardly remember when my head hit the pillow."

"Thank you for my dinner last night."

She laughed, nearly losing her coffee. "I forgot about that."

"You were right. It was delicious."

"I aim to please."

All around them, people greeted one another with small-town familiarity. The smell of frying bacon made Skye's stomach growl. She fidgeted with her new purse under the table and tried to think of something clever to say. After a few minutes of awkward weather talk, the waitress brought their plates. They both settled into their meals, and she tried to think of something else to talk about. In their few encounters, she'd bounced from feeling relaxed in his presence, feeling angry at his existence, and feeling like a tongue-tied schoolgirl watching her favorite beau.

Alan rescued her. "It takes between four and five hours to get to Livingston from here, if we don't stop. If we swing by the reservation, it will take another hour or more. Do you want to try and make it today, or would you rather rest and get an early start in the morning?"

She thought about the shops, as well as the wire she wanted to send to Houston. Tomorrow was Sunday. If she didn't send it today, she'd have to wait for Monday, and Charlie and his mother may be well on their way by then. "If we leave around one, will that give us enough time to make it before dark? I have a few quick stops I'd like to make."

"Yes, I think that will be ample time."

A shadow fell over the table. Skye looked up to see a tall, broad man with a handlebar mustache. He grinned at her, and his teeth were covered in disgusting tobacco juice. He pulled his gaze to Alan, as if his eyes didn't want to leave her face. She looked down at her food and tried to make herself invisible.

"If it ain't the Injun lover. Hello, *Agent.*"

Alan stood, placed his napkin on the table. "We don't want any trouble. Why don't you go on your way."

"Aw, don't be like that. I just want you to introduce me to yer *squaw* here. She's awful purdy."

Warmth soaked her chest, neck, cheeks. How did he know? She was stupid to think she could ever have a new start, anywhere. Stupid to think that in a strange town, people wouldn't know. That she could hide behind her education and good manners and fashionable clothes. She could never hide, because wherever she went, there *she'd* be.

She didn't look up from her plate until she heard a loud *crack!* When she lifted her head, the black-toothed man crashed into the table behind him, and Alan shook out his hand. All around them, restaurant patrons gasped and cried out. A couple of men approached, one of them wearing a sheriff's badge.

Fortunately, he addressed the injured man first. "Why do you have to cause trouble everywhere you go, Clem?"

The man rubbed his jaw, glared at Alan. "I ain't the one causin' trouble, Sheriff."

"I beg to differ," the sheriff said. "I heard the entire exchange."

"Then you know he hit me. I didn't do nothin'.'"

The sheriff held out a hand and helped Clem stand. "I said I *heard* everything. Unfortunately, my back was turned, so I didn't see anyone hit anybody. Why don't you go on home, sleep off whatever you've been drinkin'."

Clem snatched his hat off the floor, shot an evil look at Alan, then Skye, and left.

~

*A*lan reached across the table and placed his good hand on Skye's arm. "Are you all right?"

She nodded but didn't look up.

He turned, held out his aching right hand to the sheriff. "Alan McNaughten. New Indian Agent for this territory."

The man gripped his hand in a firm handshake that caused more pain, though Alan felt certain the man didn't intend that. "Nice to meet you. I'm sorry Clem interrupted your meal. I'll pay for it, if you don't mind."

"It's on the house." The woman who'd brought their meals refilled Skye's coffee. "Ridiculous. Anyone can see she's not an Injun."

Skye looked up, her eyes wide, but she said nothing. What must she feel right now? How had Alan lived his entire life unaware of his own privilege, simply because of the color of his skin?

The commotion settled, and soon the patrons went back to their meals. Alan's was only half eaten, but he wasn't hungry anymore. Skye's head was up, but her eyes were cast down, and she pushed her eggs around on her plate.

He pulled out his wallet, placed enough to cover the meal beside his plate. He didn't want to be beholden to anyone in this town. "You ready?"

She exhaled. Gave one quick nod, gathered her bag, and stood.

He allowed her to pass first, then mumbled another thanks to the sheriff and followed her onto the boardwalk. The sunny day, gentle breeze, and friendly boardwalk chatter belied the current mood. "I'm so sorry that happened."

"It's not your fault." She took his hand and inspected it. "That's gonna hurt for a while."

"You should see the other guy."

That brought a hint of a smile. "I did."

He shifted the conversation. "What did you want to do before we leave?"

She dropped his hand, chewed her bottom lip. "I need to send a wire to Houston and another to my parents. After that, I'll be ready to get my things and leave."

Somehow, he knew she'd removed a few things from her list. More than anything, he wished he could remove the heartache from her life.

CHAPTER 17

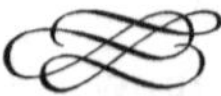

Skye sat straight and tall on the buckboard seat and took in the lush green landscape. The pine trees! They towered over her on either side of the road. Lampasas trees were short and scrubby. An occasional cluster of oaks provided shade when needed, but this… The pine forest was so thick, she couldn't see more than a few trees deep.

And the smell! It was glorious, as if she'd never truly been awake until now. Yes, she'd been in the middle of the piney woods yesterday, but she'd had other things on her mind. Right now, she lifted her face to the wind and took it all in. Was this the landscape of her ancestors? If her mother hadn't died, would she have grown up here?

"You all right?" Alan asked.

"I am. Really. I'm used to being singled out because of my heritage. It was a little worse today because I wasn't expecting it. I let my guard down because no one knew me. But believe me, it's nothing new."

She met his eyes, hating the pity she saw there. "Don't feel sorry for me. It's made me strong."

"Has it?"

She turned her gaze to the road. "I'd like to think so."

They hit a bump, and her shoulder grazed his. Even when they moved apart, the warm feeling lingered, and she longed for another bump so they could touch again.

What had come over her? She'd never had such scandalous thoughts. Considering she'd probably be working with him for a long time, she really needed to get this infatuation under control. Because she knew that's all this would ever be. An infatuation.

"We'll be at the reservation in about an hour. Do you have any questions before you arrive?"

"Do you have answers?"

He laughed. "Not many. But feel free to ask, anyway."

"How long since they've had a teacher?"

"They've been taught by one of their own. Until a few years ago, a missionary couple lived on the reservation and ran a school. They're not lacking in education."

A smile tickled her belly, crept through her heart, and landed on her face. "That's wonderful news. How many students?"

"Around forty."

The smile left, and her jaw dropped. "Forty? I can't teach forty students." Maybe she shouldn't have said that. This was the only job she had. "I mean, I'll do my best. That's a lot."

She caught a tight grin on his face, like he was trying to hide it.

"What? Why are you laughing? You're joking, right? I won't have that many students."

"No, you will. But hopefully not alone. I've requested that the current teacher stay on. You'll be the lead teacher, though."

Her muscles relaxed. She hadn't even realized they were tight until that moment. "Thank you." Lead teacher? She was a brand new teacher, and it sounded like the other person had been teaching for a while. Would she resent Skye?

They grew quiet, but it wasn't strained or awkward. After a

time, she thought of another question. "What are they like? The people on the reservation?"

He didn't answer right away, and she left him to his contemplation.

A gray brown squirrel skirted from branch to branch to her right, running beside them as if Skye and Alan were the spectacle and the squirrel was the audience. With each bounce, its tail curled and bobbed like plumes on a lady's hat. In many ways, Skye could relate to that squirrel. Its colors blended with the tree bark like it didn't want to be noticed, yet its elegant, fluffy tail said otherwise. For all Skye's love of fashion, she didn't want to be noticed either. Her experiences being the center of attention were mostly unpleasant, like the one in the café.

The squirrel scampered into the forest, out of sight.

Alan cleared his throat. "I suppose they're like anyone else. They work hard. They love their families. They like to laugh. From what I've seen, they seem like good people. Is that what you wanted to know?"

"I don't really know what to expect. But you're right. People are people, I suppose."

"Are you nervous?"

"Me? No. Of course not."

He looked right at her, as if testing the honesty of her answer. His brows rose.

"All right. That's a lie. I'm terrified."

He chuckled, and even though they weren't touching, the sound permeated her skin, filled her spirit. Such a great laugh.

"What are you most afraid of?" His words were soft, like he didn't want anyone to overhear, even though they were alone.

She breathed in. Breathed out. Considered her answer. "So many things. I want them to like me. I've never felt truly accepted. I hope...I don't know. I hope that will change, that they'll be okay with the fact that I'm a half-breed." She'd never spoken so bluntly with anyone. What was it about this man that loosened her tongue and made her admit things she'd hardly admitted to herself?

"I'm okay with it, if that makes any difference."

That heat, that was becoming all too familiar every time she was in Alan's presence, soaked through her skin. He was just being kind. Offering friendship. That was all. "That's kind of you."

"It's true." He clicked to Fiona and guided the reins to the right, where they left the main road and turned onto a narrow trail. "The reservation is just a few miles up this way."

Her stomach tightened. She was glad she hadn't eaten much. If she'd been with Mama and Daddy, she'd have dug in her case for her little hand mirror and checked her appearance. She wasn't about to do that in front of Alan. She hoped she looked okay. Hoped her dress wasn't too wrinkled. Hoped her hair was in place. With one hand, she felt around her hair line for flyaways, tightened a few hairpins, and hoped for the best.

Hope was a funny word...belief that something good was going to happen. In this case, she wasn't sure it was the right word. Because right now, she wasn't sure what she believed would happen. Good or bad, her new adventure was about to begin.

~

When Alan pulled up in the wagon, Walker stood from the chair he'd occupied beside Chief Scott and flashed a wide smile at Skye. His white teeth contrasted with his bronzed skin. Walker was a nice enough fellow, but at that moment, Alan wanted to wipe that smile right off his face.

Instead, he stopped the buckboard and hopped down so he could assist Skye from the seat. By the time he hit the ground, Walker was already on Skye's side of the wagon, extending his hand, and she got out that way. He led Skye to Chief Scott, barely giving Alan a cursory nod.

"This is the new teacher, Skye Stratton. Skye, this is our chief, John Scott."

Skye looked awed and unsure of herself. For a moment, Alan wondered if she might curtsy. "I'm very pleased to meet you, Chief Scott."

The chief stood, walked to within a few feet of Skye. He opened his mouth as if to say something, then closed it. His eyes glistened. After a moment, he said, "We are pleased to have you here."

The same young man who had assisted the other day brought out two more chairs, and the chief gestured for them to be seated. "Tell me about yourself, Miss Stratton."

She sat straight, stiff. Alan could tell she was trying to look dignified. She did look every inch a lady, but also terrified. It was there, in her eyes, as if she feared saying the wrong thing. Like she desperately wanted this man's approval. *Please, God. Calm her nerves.*

Alan didn't remember saying too many prayers for others in his life. His prayers were usually all about him. But right now, he wanted these people to like her as much as she wanted it for herself. Not because his job depended on her staying here, but because he genuinely cared for Skye.

"I understand you know some of my background," she said. "I am half white, half Indian. My mother was part Coushatta."

"And the other part?" Chief Scott's question was gentle.

Skye's face went pale, and she looked at her hands a moment before meeting the man's gaze again. "Comanche."

The chief, who had been sitting still, rocked in his chair. No one said anything for a moment, except the crickets, who apparently didn't understand the gravity of the situation.

Alan looked at Walker, who offered the slightest shake of his head. Alan said nothing.

After a long time—too long, in Alan's opinion—Chief Scott finally spoke. "When I was a young boy, a woman from our tribe was taken by Comanches. I remember her. She was quite beautiful. She looked very much like you."

Skye caught her breath, as if she might sob, but stopped herself before it fully formed. Other than that, she sat perfectly still, eyes fixed on the older man. In the middle of Skye's throat, in that delicate recess, Alan could see her pulse thrumming.

"Her name was Niłahasi. It means *moon* in English. The Comanche chief's son saw her and wanted her for his wife. The Comanche are warriors and were ready to fight for her, but Niłahasi volunteered to go. She did not want to go, but she did it to save her people, our people, from unnecessary fighting. We never saw her again."

Skye clenched and unclenched the fabric in her skirt, twisting it every which way, and Alan wondered if she'd tear a hole in it. But from the neck up, her face remained poised.

Chief Walker continued. "I believe that may have been your grandmother."

Skye said nothing for a time, and Alan knew she fought tears. Finally, she cleared her throat. "It sounds like it was."

"Is your mother still living?" Walker asked.

She shifted her gaze but didn't move her head. "No." Alan could barely hear the word. "She died when I was very young. As did my father. I was raised by my father's brother and his wife. They are my parents now."

Chief Walker motioned for the young man who'd brought the chairs and said something in his language. The boy took off running.

Alan hated that he could do nothing to make this easier for Skye. Despite the fact that he was the Indian agent, he felt like an outsider, like he didn't belong. He was the one responsible for this moment. So why did he feel so helpless? Why did he feel like an interloper in this deeply intimate family meeting?

The chief stood. "I suppose you'd like a tour of our village."

Skye rewarded him with a smile that could rival the sun. "I'd love that, sir."

The older man held out his arm to Skye, wrapped it around her shoulder, and nudged her toward the main street. "I will take you a little ways, and then someone else will take over. I don't get around so well anymore."

All of Skye's discomfort vanished. "You look like you get around just fine to me."

They walked ahead, Chief Scott pointing out different buildings and the purpose of each.

Walker stayed back with Alan. "Wow."

Alan nodded. "That was intense. What did he say to that young man?"

"He sent for Mary—the teacher."

"I guess we should follow them?" Alan wasn't sure of the proper etiquette when it came to the older chief. He didn't want to show disrespect or go where he wasn't invited. Then again, Skye was his responsibility. He began walking, Walker matching his steps.

By the time they caught up with Skye and Chief Scott, a group was forming just up the road. A woman approached them, lowering her head to the chief before giving Skye a tentative smile.

Walker stepped forward. "Miss Stratton, I'd like you to meet my distant cousin, Mary Johnson. She has been teaching for two years. Other women in our community take turns helping her, but she is the main teacher."

"I'm pleased to meet you, Miss Stratton." The woman didn't look exactly pleased, but she didn't look hostile either.

Chief Scott spoke up, sending Walker a look like he'd overstepped. "Mary, I'd like to introduce you to Niłahasi's granddaughter."

The woman, Mary, seemed confused. Stunned was a better

word. She looked from Chief Walker to Skye, then back to the chief. Then she let out a guttural sob, lunged at Skye, and threw her arms around her neck. She uttered words in her language, and again, Alan felt like an interloper.

Skye hugged the woman back. Searched the faces around her until she found Alan, and the look on her face was a mixture of terror and relief and something he couldn't identify. Had she found her home, at last? And if so, where did that leave him?

~

Surreal. That was the only word Skye could think to describe how this scene felt. These people, with their white shirts and course pants and brown dresses and bronze skin, seemed to actually want her there. This woman clung to her like a lifeline and said so many words, so fast, Skye could only make out every third or fourth one. One she knew...*home.*

It felt nice, and yet, overwhelming. These people...did they want to be her family? Mama's and Daddy's faces flashed through her mind. Cordell's and Anita's too. They were her family. What would they think about this scene...this place where she belonged but they didn't? She sought out Alan.... when her eyes locked with his, the look he gave her seemed to share her joy and understand her fear. It felt like he was sending her his courage.

The woman—Mary—stepped back, held Skye's face in her hands. Tears tracked her cheeks, but she wore a big smile. "I am your grandmother's niece. My mother, your grandmother's younger sister, is still living. I will take you to her. She has mourned her sister all these years, and now, here you are, proof that Niłahasi survived, that her legacy lives. Come with me."

Mary looked to Chief Scott, as if waiting to be dismissed, and he nodded to her. In the next moment, Skye was pulled by the hand through a small crowd who whispered and pointed and spoke in their language. Some wore smiles. Others looked at her like she was an intruder. Somewhere behind her, she heard the word *Comanche.*

Skye strained to look over her shoulder while she moved forward, Mary practically dragging her, to find Alan. There he was, next to Walker, both of them striving to keep up with the small woman who had taken control of Skye.

Soon, she was pulled through the doorway of a log cabin. It took a minute for her eyes to adjust. Mary spoke rapidly, too fast for Skye to follow what she was saying. When Skye could see, she noticed a tiny, silver-haired woman sitting in the corner on the dirt floor, a blanket pulled over her knees. Deep lines etched the woman's face like branches of a tree, and her eyes were sunken with age. When Mary finally stopped talking, the woman lifted a wrinkled, gnarled hand and motioned Skye forward.

She stepped toward the woman, knelt in front of her, and allowed her to stroke her hair. She said some words in her native tongue that Skye did not understand. She looked to Mary, who translated.

"She says you look like her."

How was she supposed to respond? "Thank you. I am Skye."

Mary said, "This is your great aunt, Tálwan. Most people call her Anna."

Tálwan. Song. "I'm very pleased to meet you."

The woman smiled. A single tear tracked her cheek and got lost in one of the wrinkles.

Skye looked around the room, now filled with strangers, hoping to find Alan. Or Walker. Anyone remotely familiar, but all she saw were people she didn't know, looking at her like a bug under a microscope. She was introduced to person after person—one of them she thought was Mary's husband. Sam, was it? She needed to breathe, but every breath she took was shallow. She fought to keep a pleasant, happy look on her face, because that was appropriate, right? She should feel happy that all these people were her family.

It was too much. She pasted on a smile and tried to look composed. Where was Alan? Had he left her there?

Before the thought fully formed, his voice came from near the entrance. "I hate to interrupt this reunion," he said, "but we still have a ways to go this evening. I'm afraid I need to take Miss Stratton for now, but we'll be back within a week's time. I promise."

Skye followed Alan's voice, though she couldn't see his face until...there! The crowded room parted like the Red Sea, and he stepped through like Moses on dry land. He reached a hand toward her, and she took it. Somehow, in a fog, her mouth formed gracious words. She thanked them. Told them it was lovely meeting them and that she looked forward to seeing them again.

And just like that, she walked beside Alan back up that long road, more people staring and pointing and whispering. Alan helped her into the buckboard, and they waved and left.

Her knuckles turned white as they clung to the wooden seat. She tried harder than she should have to breathe, but the air stayed on the surface, like her lungs were deflated and refused to open again. She felt... What did she feel?

Panic.

Alan placed one large hand on top of hers where she'd grabbed onto the seat. When they were back at the main road, he pulled Fiona to a stop. "You all right?"

She nodded but couldn't form words.

He lifted his hand, and she missed it right away. But then he placed that arm around her shoulder and pulled her to him. Reached his other hand across and gently guided her head to his shoulder, then stroked her hair back from her face. "That was a lot to deal with. I'm so sorry, Skye. I thought we'd make a quick stop so you could see your schoolroom. I had no idea it would turn into so much, so fast."

It was. So much, so fast. As she sat there, head on his shoulder, him stroking her hair, the air slowly filled back into her lungs. But with the air came a flood of tears, a torrent she tried to push back but couldn't. She sobbed and sobbed, soaking Alan's shirt. She sobbed until her nose was stopped up and her eyes felt puffy and she couldn't cry anymore. And the whole time, Alan just held her, stroked her hair, and rocked her gently.

She knew tomorrow she'd be mortified that she let him see her like this. But right now, he was the only comfort she had, and she clung to it like a life raft.

CHAPTER 18

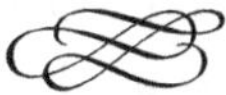

Alan pulled the buckboard into his parents' yard right at suppertime. It was a good thing, too, because the dried pemmican and fry bread Mary had sent with them was long gone. Skye had that look in her eyes again—quiet dignity with a good dose of fear beneath. How would she take to his parents? They'd do everything in their power to make her feel at home. But given what she'd endured today—what she'd endured her entire life—he imagined it was hard for her to trust people. She'd cried on his shoulder. She'd let him see her vulnerability. He vowed, right then and there, never to do anything to betray her trust.

"Here we are. I hope you're hungry, because I imagine Ma's prepared a feast."

She smiled, the mask up again. "I'm sure it will be wonderful."

The front door swung open, scraping the floorboards like it always did. It was Pa.

"Welcome! You must be Miss Stratton. I'm James McNaughten." He was at the wagon now, and helped Skye down like she was an old friend. "I hope you had a nice trip. Was the train ride pleasant?"

Skye caught Alan's eye and let out a little giggle.

He laughed, too, but more for the joy of seeing her laugh than for the irony of Pa's question. "We'll tell you all about it inside. I imagine Skye wants a few minutes to freshen up."

Pa took her carpetbag and looked around. "Is this all you have? I'm impressed. Most would have brought at least a trunk. I admire a person who knows how to pack light."

There was that giggle again. "There's a story behind my lack of luggage. I assure you, I have more coming. I hope you still admire me when you see the size of my trunk."

Ma appeared in the doorway, wiping her hands on her apron. For as long as Alan could remember, no matter how she felt, the prospect of company always got Ma moving a little faster, stepping a little higher. He hoped she hadn't worn herself out.

As Skye approached, Ma held out her arms and drew her into a tight embrace. "I hope you don't mind that I'm a hugger. I'm Sue. I want you to make yourself right at home."

Alan couldn't tell much about Skye's reaction, but she seemed fine with the hug. Her shoulders relaxed, and she reciprocated the embrace. He followed them all inside and took Skye's bag. The smell of chicken fried steak and onions filled the air and made his stomach growl in pleasure. "I'll show you to your room."

She followed him down the hallway to his room. Except, when he opened the door, it didn't look at all like his room. It was all flowers and lavender and lace. Ma had sure been busy the last few days.

Skye smiled. "It's beautiful!" That one eyebrow came up again. "I thought you said I was staying in your old room."

"Ma did some redecorating. She always wanted a daughter." As soon as the words were out, he realized that might sound like a hint of a marriage proposal. Heat rushed to his ears. "I mean, this is her way of saying she's glad you're here."

Skye laughed again, that low, husky, yet altogether-feminine laugh he'd come to know.

This woman had to be the most resilient person he'd ever met. From train bandit kidnappers to a bigoted bully to a day of revelations about her past...she seemed to bounce back from whatever life handed her.

He set her bag on the bed and brushed past her in the doorway, trying not to focus on the pleasure even the slightest touch brought. "Take all the time you need. But make it quick, because I'm starved."

~

Skye felt like she was in a truly safe place for the first time since she'd left her house early yesterday morning.

If she'd had any question about Alan's character, she didn't now. Anyone with parents as sweet as James and Sue McNaughten had to be genuine. How could he not be? Sue had fussed over her, making sure she knew where the privy was and showing her the small room at the back of the house where they took their baths in a wooden laundry tub. "It's all ready for you, whenever you want. I just have to heat another pot or two of water to add, and it'll warm right up." She'd leaned forward, lowered her voice. "I keep some dried lavender and rose petals in a jar in the cupboard there. Feel free to use whatever you want."

The house, though much smaller than the one Skye grew up in, had a peaceful homeyness to it. The front of the house was one big room that served as kitchen, dining room and parlor, but strategic placement of furniture and rugs defined each area so it seemed like a separate space. A hallway off the main room led to the two bedrooms.

Dinner felt very much like her own family dinners. James McNaughten began with such a simple, sincere prayer that Skye almost felt drawn in to the intimate conversation with God. What was wrong with her lately? In the last two days, her thoughts had turned to prayer more than they had in the last ten years.

Once the plates were passed and the food was served, James looked at her with smiling eyes. "I want to hear the story about your train ride. Something tells me it'll be quite entertaining." There was a presence about him, about Sue as well, that resonated...what was it?

Love. It was love. For the first time since she could remember, she felt absolutely safe in an environment that didn't include her immediate family.

"Well, it started out with my own father giving his ticket to a woman so she and her young son could see to a family emergency." Over the next hour, Skye spilled out the story, with Alan interjecting his parts here and there. There was an easy, relaxed rhythm to the conversation, with Alan's parents alternately laughing and gasping in shock.

"Oh, my dear." Alan's mother put her hand to her chest. "I knew you'd be exhausted after your journey, but I had no idea. Here, let me get you some apple pie with fresh whipped cream. After what you've been through, you deserve two slices."

Had Alan told his parents of her heritage? Would they treat her this way if they knew they had an Indian under their roof? The question, the uncertainty, flitted through her mind, yet it didn't have any weight. These people were different. Something told her they didn't care about her background or her heritage or the color of her hair and skin. Or anyone else's, for that matter. Deep down, she felt accepted in their presence. And that was new for her.

The pie rivaled anything the trained pastry chefs back home could make. And yes, each bite was a comfort. When she couldn't eat any more, she placed her fork across her plate. "That was the most delicious meal I've eaten in ages."

Alan snorted. "Ma, if you knew the kind of meals she eats every day, you'd understand what a compliment that is."

Mrs. McNaughten smiled, a question in her eyes.

Skye jabbed Alan with her elbow. "My parents own an inn. The cook they employ is quite talented, but I assure you, he has nothing on you. Here, let me help with these dishes."

"I'll hear nothing of it, young lady." Sue took Skye's plate and stacked on her own. "You've had a long journey. I have a rule, though. The first time someone eats here, they're a guest. After that, they're at home. So I'll take you up on your offer to help tomorrow."

"Yes, ma'am." Skye laughed at the woman's stern expression. Mama and Daddy would like these people. In a way, they reminded Skye of them, though the McNaughtens were older.

A few minutes later, Skye sorted through her things in anticipation of that promised bath. The small wooden tub was a far cry from her large cast-iron tub at home, but it looked every bit as inviting. A light knock sounded on the door. It was Alan.

"I'm sorry to bother you. I need to get a few of my things. I should have grabbed them before I left. It will only take a minute."

She swung the door wide. "Help yourself. It's your room, after all."

"*Was* my room." He lifted a corner of the lavender ruffled bedspread, a look of comic horror on his face. "I thought my parents would miss me. Clearly, they can't wait to replace me."

She forced back a smile. "Don't feel like you have to pretend with me, Alan. I won't tell anyone about your feminine side. It's nothing to be ashamed of."

He growled at her. *Growled.* It was so unexpected, she lost her composure in a new fit of giggles. What must he think of her? In the past twenty-four hours, he'd seen more of her emotions than she'd shown anyone since...she couldn't remember. She really did need to get control of herself.

She watched him gather some clothes out of the bureau. Then, almost as an afterthought, he pulled open the narrow drawer in the writing desk and removed some papers. "Good night."

A short time later, she relaxed in the most luxurious washtub bath she'd ever experienced. She even sprinkled a few rose petals in the water before she got in. As she lay back in the warmth, feet dangling over the side, she thought about dinner. About this place, and how unusual the experience was for her. Alan's parents had asked such thoughtful questions, and they'd listened as if she were the most interesting person they'd ever met. Most places she went, she preferred to remain quiet. Most times, she avoided making any type of social faux pas because people were always more critical of her than they were of others. But tonight, despite her past two days, she felt relaxed.

She compared dinner to the way she felt at the reservation. She'd certainly felt welcomed. Wanted. But she'd also felt like an outsider. Would that change with time? She hoped so.

She closed her eyes, and Alan's face swam in her mind. He'd flirted with her. Of that she was sure, just as she'd flirted with him. She knew she was pretty, and she was no stranger to men's attention. But most of the time, that attention had made her feel dirty and uneasy—the kind of attention men paid to a trollop, not a potential wife—and she'd avoided those interactions by remaining distant and proper. But with Alan, she could banter like she did with her brother. She felt Alan's appreciation of her feminine qualities, but she'd never once felt like his attentions were inappropriate.

But that didn't mean he would pursue her. No. No matter how nice he seemed, no matter how genuine his parents were, it could never be. She was setting herself up for heartache by allowing her thoughts to wander toward the romantic.

Starting tomorrow, she would rebuild the iron shield around her heart. Starting tomorrow, business as usual. If she didn't guard her emotions, she'd never survive.

$\mathcal{A}$lan barely slept. It wasn't because of the cotton blanket thrown over the bed of hay in the loft. He'd slept in worse conditions plenty of times. It wasn't worries over his new job or anxiety over Ma's health. It was the image of silky brown hair, honey brown eyes, and skin that looked softer than a kitten's belly, so soft he wanted to touch it just to see. What was it about Skye Stratton that turned his insides into a runaway sleigh ride?

He had a hard time controlling the grin that wanted to bust through as he crawled out of his makeshift bed, gave Fiona a rub on her muzzle, and finger-combed his hair. He'd have to get ready inside this morning. Later today, he'd find an old mirror and washbasin to bring out here, along with his razor and other toiletry items. It was still early, but he should probably see to his needs before everyone was up and about.

Sunday. Church day. He was excited for Skye to hear Pa preach. As much as Alan didn't always live up to the standards he was taught, he was proud of his father. He pulled on his boots and whistled the tune to "Blessed Assurance" as he made his way through the back door. The wash closet door was cracked open, so he knocked. No answer.

"Hello?"

Still no answer. Slowly, he inched it open, hoping he didn't walk into an embarrassing situation. He'd never had a sister, much less a beautiful woman who was very much *not* his sister, staying in his home.

Thankfully, no one was inside, so he set his clothes on the chair, closed the door behind him, and continued his hymn, this time singing the words softly.

Blessed assurance, Jesus is mine,
Oh what a foretaste of glory divine.
Heir of salvation, purchase of God,
Born of his spirit, washed in his blood.

He heard someone moving around in the kitchen and assumed it was Ma. He was glad she felt better. It was good for her to have another woman around. Once again, his thoughts turned to Skye's long-term living arrangement. Was it possible for her to make the one-hour drive, both ways, five days a week? Yes.

Was it practical? No. Nor was it safe for her to do alone. He'd have to take her, which could work, since he needed to be near the reservation, anyway. But his job also involved regular communication with D.C., which meant he needed to be near a telegraph operator. There was one in town, but if he took Skye to the reservation, he'd often have to come back during business hours. Then return before the school day ended, and back again. That was four hours a day in travel time.

And there was no way he'd let her ride alone. Not after what happened in Silsbee yesterday.

The smell of bacon beckoned him. He finished his shave, wiped his face, and put his hair in place. Pushed open the washroom door and headed for the kitchen. "Good morning, my beautiful moth—" But the woman standing at his stove was not his mother. It was Skye.

"Oh! Hello." He stopped short. "I didn't expect to see you here."

"I hope it's all right. I passed your father in the hallway, and he said your mother isn't feeling well. I thought I'd scratch around and see if I could make some breakfast for all of us."

Skye wore a simple white dress that was elegant, in spite of its simplicity. It was made of a gauzy fabric, with a high, lacy neckline and sleeves. A pale blue sash was tied around her waist. He hoped she didn't get anything on it, working in the kitchen. But she looked as at home in the kitchen as she did in the classroom. That surprised him, but he wasn't sure why.

"You don't have to do that. You're a guest."

"Last night, your mother said the first time a person eats at her table, he or she is a guest. After that, they're family. And since I'm to live here for a while, I might as well make use of myself. Do you want your eggs fried or scrambled?"

Her words were friendly enough, but something about her demeanor seemed distant. Had he done something wrong? "Either is fine."

She turned back to the counter and tied one of Ma's dish towels around her waist for an apron. Beautiful and practical. A deadly combination. At least, deadly for his heart. Her hair was different today, twisted away from her face on each side until it met at the nape of her neck. It was secured somehow with a blue silk flower, and the rest hung in loose waves down her back. He tucked his hands behind his back to keep himself from touching it.

"I...I'll go check on Ma." Why did he stammer around her? He'd stood in front of heads of state and not stammered at all.

She didn't respond.

He headed down the hall and knocked gently on his parents' door.

"Come in." His father stood at the mirror, straightening his tie. His mother was still in bed.

"Ma. I worried you'd overdone it last night. Can I do anything for you?"

"I'll be fine. I'm just a little tired. Y'all go on to church. I may join the service late if I feel better." She coughed, a deep, hacking cough.

Alan sat on the edge of her bed. "Thank you for working so hard to make Skye feel welcome. I know she appreciates it."

Ma placed a crepe-y hand on his arm. "She's delightful. You seem to think so too."

"I'm not sure what you mean by that."

Despite her weakened state, Ma's eyes sparked. "Deny it all you want. I have eyes."

He let that go without comment. "She's making breakfast. Would you like me to bring you anything?"

"I like a woman who can take charge. I'll have a cup of warm tea. Maybe a bite of toast."

Pa leaned past Alan and kissed Ma on the head. "I'll be back as soon as the service is over." He stroked her hair, and the wrinkles around his eyes sagged, like some of the joy had seeped out. Then he stood, clapped Alan on the back. "I'll see you at the church?"

"We'll be there." But the "we" felt kind of empty, without Ma included in it. He winked at his mother. "I'll be back with your order, madame."

Skye had placed a heaping plate of scrambled eggs, several pieces of toast, and a pile of bacon on the table, along with plates and utensils.

Alan smelled coffee and saw the kettle boiling on the stove.

Pa sat in his usual spot, and Skye studied him for a moment. "Mr. McNaughten, I'm happy to stay here and look after your wife while you preach. I don't mind at all." She served his plate as if she had experience as a waitress.

Pa offered a tender smile. "She'll be fine. She just needs rest. Thank you, though."

Alan moved past Skye and grabbed the mugs. He filled three with the coffee and set a pot of water to boil for Ma's tea. When Skye was seated next to Pa, Alan stood behind his father and placed a hand on his shoulder. "Don't wait on me. Go ahead and pray, and I'll take Ma her tray."

The man's prayer was short and sincere. When he finished, Alan looked up and caught Skye watching him. A flush of pleasure seeped through his cheeks, and he smiled before she looked away.

He sat with Ma while she ate. By the time he returned, Pa was gone and Skye was clearing the dirty dishes from the table.

"Thank you for making breakfast," he said, scooping some now lukewarm eggs and bacon from his plate. Even tepid, they were pretty good. Soft and fluffy with just the right amounts of salt and pepper.

"I'm sorry your mother is unwell. I hope it's not my fault." She still had that stiff, formal air. Had he offended her somehow?

"If anything, your presence has helped. Did you sleep well?"

"Yes, thank you."

He took another bite. Chewed. Swallowed. "Is your bed comfortable?" Oh, man. Why did he ask that? Was that inappropriate?

"Quite."

One-word answer.

"You all right? You don't seem yourself this morning."

"I'm perfectly fine. Thank you, Mr. McNaughten."

Mr. McNaughten? He might understand that if they were in public, but it was just the two of them. What had he done? "All right. As soon as I clean my dishes, we'll leave. That is, if you're ready."

"Certainly. Thank you." She left him in the kitchen to finish his meal. And to scratch his head in confusion. For as long as he lived, he would never understand women. Why couldn't they all be like Ma? Now, *she* was a sensible woman.

Feminine voices drifted from the hallway, and he realized Skye had looked in on his mother. And despite her cool reception to him this morning, her compassion drew him to her all the more.

~

*S*kye stepped away from Alan's elbow when he offered it to her and pretended she didn't see it. Why did he have to be so nice? Did he know what he did to her insides? In such a short time, he'd rescued her, made her spitfire angry, defended her honor, comforted her when she turned into an emotional puddle, and made her melt every time he spoke to his mother with such tenderness. In the interest of self-preservation, she had to distance herself.

She saw the hurt in his eyes. The confusion. But he wouldn't understand. He was just being kind, and now that she knew his parents, she understood why. He didn't mean to toy with her emotions. He didn't mean to capture her heart. He was just showing good old southern-boy charm, the way he'd been taught to. But oh, what that charm did to her. She breathed deeply, letting the scent of the towering pines on either side of the road fill her lungs.

"I'm sorry to press the issue, Skye, but did I do something to offend you?"

"Of course not. Why would you think that?"

"You just seem…different. Upset."

"Not at all."

"Oh. All right." They walked in silence for a time, and she was careful to keep at least three feet between them.

"Here we are." He gestured to a narrow path that led to a

delightful, white-painted church with a tall steeple that, though clearly homespun, looked elegant against the blue sky.

She led the way, and he followed rather than walk beside her. At least he'd figured out she didn't want to walk close to him.

"Alan. Over here, Alan!" An attractive woman with strawberry-blonde curls and enormous blue eyes waved a pink lace handkerchief in the air. Despite her calling him over, she came to him.

Alan stepped close to Skye and placed his hand on her back before she could react.

The woman eyed Alan's arm placement, then moved her eyes up and down Skye's person in a long, slow gaze before settling on Skye's face. "Oh. Hello."

"Margaret Tusselhoff, I'd like you to meet Skye Stratton. She's to be a new teacher in our area."

In our *area?* Was he embarrassed by her tie to the reservation? She offered the woman her bravest smile, but it didn't feel very convincing.

"A new teacher. How charming." The woman didn't sound charmed at all. "I thought Miss Sparks was still our teacher. There she is, right over there."

Skye stepped away from Alan. "I'll teach at the Alabama-Coushatta Reservation, about an hour from here."

The woman's face turned from cynical to horrified. "At the reservation? You're joking! Who would want to teach those beasts?"

Heat scalded Skye's cheeks, and she didn't know if she should run away or slap the woman. She didn't consider her next actions, just reacted. "I *am* one of those beasts. It's been lovely meeting you, Miss Tusselhoff." She lifted her skirts and ascended the stairs to the church building. She didn't know a soul. Only knew she had to get away from that awful, pink person.

Inside the sanctuary, she nearly ran headlong into James. Should she call him Reverend? She wasn't sure.

"Miss Stratton. You're early. Most people visit outdoors until I ring the bell. What's wrong, dear? What has you so flustered?"

"I-I shouldn't be here. I'm sorry. I should go." She turned, but the man gently took hold of her arm and gestured to a pew.

"Sit down. Tell me what's on your mind."

She sat, and he took the place next to her, watching her with those patient, kind eyes.

"I'm...Indian. Did you know that? Did your son tell you that? Because if you didn't know, and you were so kind to me, and... I'm tired of trying to be something I'm not. I don't belong among white people. I-I should just go. I'm sorry."

"Wait! Don't go. No, Alan didn't mention your background. But I'm sure that's because he didn't see it as an issue. You are as welcome in our home as ever, and that's all I'm going to say about that. I'm Scotch-Irish, and Sue is full-blooded Irish. Proud of it, too. I've lived a lot of years, and I've had plenty of insults hurled my way because of my heritage. But do you know what?"

He waited for her to lift her eyes to his.

"What?"

"The only heritage that matters is the heritage we have in Christ. God loves me, bless my dirty Scotch-Irish soul, and he accepts me just as I am. And he loves you, too, more than you know."

Skye was not going to explain to this man, a preacher, that she knew perfectly well God did not love her that way. He would only argue with her, and the last thing in the world she wanted to do was argue with this sweet man.

"I'm not sure what happened outside that sent you flying in here like a bat out of Hades, but I have a pretty good idea. You look at me, young lady, and you listen to me. Hold your head high. Look people in the eyes. And when it comes to your ancestors, or the color of your skin, or anything else about your family heritage, you apologize for nothing. Because without Christ, we're all on level ground. We're all nothing. Do you hear me?"

She nodded, too stunned to do anything else. No one had ever spoken so plainly to her.

"But that's not the end of the story. *With* Christ, we become children of God. Co-heirs with Christ. He loves us. He wants us. And He accepts us as we are. We belong to Him, and that's the only heritage that matters."

A shadow moved in the vestibule. Alan. He stepped forward and sat in the pew behind her and his father. "Skye, I'm sorry. Margaret has always been annoying, but I've never known her to be *mean*." He paused a moment. "Actually, that's not true. She's mean as a hornet."

Skye snorted a laugh through her tears and realized she'd forgotten her handkerchief. James handed her a clean one. "Come on. Have you ever rung a church bell? I could use an assistant this morning."

The fact that he spoke to her like she was a child didn't even bother her. She knew he was trying to help. She didn't want to stay here, in this awful place with these awful, holier-than-thou church people. But they weren't all awful, and the proof was right in front of her. She stood, took his offered hand, and followed him into a little stairway. She may not want to stay. But she might as well start owning up to who she was. If these people didn't like it, well, that was too bad.

She told herself that all the way up the stairs. But deep inside, she knew she'd never really belong anywhere. She'd never be accepted, even if the McNaughtens were kind enough to pretend.

～

*I*n all his days, Alan had never wanted to wallop a lady. Until today. Granted, Margaret hadn't known about Skye's background, but did that matter? She shouldn't have said what she did.

But he also felt a shame, deep in his spirit. He'd never been one to call names or bully others, but how many times had he listened as others insulted an entire race of people and done nothing? How many times had he been guilty of not even noticing, simply because hatred of the Indians was so common it felt normal?

Even those who wouldn't come out and say blatantly unkind things, even those with a little more class—many of them still spoke about the Indian people with an air of superiority, like the Indians were less than. Like they weren't intelligent. Like they were dirty, uncultured, uneducated. He'd seen in his limited encounters with Walker and Chief Scott, none of that was true. The Indians he'd dealt with were intelligent, kind, and wise.

What had Alan done? And more importantly, what was he willing to do to make things right? The task before him loomed heavy. When he accepted his post, he thought he'd just make sure the Indians had enough food and clothing and shelter. But they seemed to be doing fine with those things without him. What they really needed, it seemed, was respect. Acceptance. Love.

And he was at a loss for how to provide such things.

The church bells rang. Alan remained frozen in the pew as people filed in. Margaret passed by, with several other young women, and he knew she'd given them an earful about the new schoolteacher for the reservation.

How could he fix this? How could he make it right?

And that was the problem. He couldn't.

The bells stopped. A few minutes later, his father passed down the center aisle, greeting people, shaking hands. Skye never reappeared. When the first chords of the opening hymn began, Alan exited the sanctuary. Maybe she'd gone home. If so, he needed to find her and somehow make her understand that he didn't feel about her the way some others might.

He didn't have far to go. She sat in a corner of the vestibule. "If you don't want to stay," he said, "I'm happy to escort you home. I won't blame you."

"I don't want to be here. But I do want to hear your father preach. Something tells me it will mean a lot to him. I'll sit out here and listen, and slip out during the invitation."

"Mind if I join you?"

"Suit yourself." She moved over to give him room on the bench.

He'd experienced the service from the vestibule a few times when he was a boy. Mostly when he misbehaved and Ma dragged him out here to give him a whispered scolding. Then they'd stay in the vestibule so as not to interrupt the service again by reentering.

He listened to Pa preach from the first chapter of John. "'But as many as received him, to them gave he power to become the sons of God, even to them that believe on his name: Which were born, not of blood, nor of the will of the flesh, nor of the will of man, but of God.'"

Pa's voice rang clear and strong, echoing through the ventilation grates in the brick. In some ways, it was easier to listen from out here, without all the distractions of ladies' fans and men coughing and children shifting in their seats.

"In the Greco-Roman culture, if a couple had no children, they would find a young adult, usually a young man, and adopt him. By doing so, they gave the adoptee all the rights and privileges of an adult child, including status, inheritance, and full acceptance into their family. That's what God does for us. He longs for us to come to Him, and when we do, He adopts us. We have His full acceptance and love. We have the full range of His inheritance. We become His in every way."

Alan wanted to look at Skye, to see if she was listening, but he didn't want to make her self-conscious.

Pa continued. "Think about it this way. If you're in England, and Queen Victoria accepts you into her inner circle, you're in. At that point, it won't matter who in the outer circle snubs you. Their acceptance or lack thereof is of little consequence. The only person who matters is the queen.

"The same is true for every one of us in this room. It doesn't matter who you are, where you come from, or the color of your skin. Other people may not accept you, but God does. And if God is for us, who can be against us? We're not only accepted, but we are *wanted*. God *desires* us. He *loves* us."

Alan knew God loved him. He did wonder about the acceptance part, considering all the underhanded things he'd done in Washington. And the result of his most recent deal sat next to him, her heart fractured. Would God forgive Alan for things he'd done, things he couldn't make right?

Skye shifted, and she rested her head against the side wall. Pa continued, and Alan hoped the words soaked into her spirit.

"If anyone here is trying to find acceptance from other people, you can give up. Some people will never accept us, no matter what. That's usually because they can't accept themselves. In their own insecurity, they try to belittle others. Find your identity in God, and you'll never be left wanting."

The invitation began. Skye stood and, quiet as a rabbit seeking escape from a hawk, she exited the church. Alan followed, coming up beside her as they took the little path that led back to the main road, back to home.

It was a lovely sermon. Skye wondered if that had been James's planned message, or if he spontaneously preached it for her. Either way, he was an eloquent speaker. The words were well-spoken, the ideas lofty.

But they weren't for her. Just as Alan wasn't for her. This life, this white world, wasn't for her.

She looked down at the flounces of her skirt, kicking forward with each step. Even her pretty dresses weren't for her. They made her look like something she wasn't.

They approached the McNaughten home, and she wondered how Sue had fared. Before they reached the door, she paused and faced Alan. "Thank you for offering your friendship. You're very kind."

"It's not entirely out of kindness, Skye. Your company is a gift to me."

Such a charmer. "I don't think we should mention what happened with Miss Tusselhoff to your mother. I don't want to add to her burden by causing her undue concern. I'm used to being treated that way. It's fine."

She turned away at the compassion she saw in his eyes. She didn't want his pity.

A delicious smell wafted through the partially open window, and she pushed open the door.

Sue sat at the table, head in her hands. She looked up when the light fell on the table. "Oh! You're home early. Was your father's sermon short? I'm not quite finished with lunch."

Skye moved into the kitchen area, wrapping the same dishtowel around her waist. "It smells delicious. You stay right there and tell me what I can do to help."

CHAPTER 20

Monday, they rested. Alan gently refused Skye's request to visit the reservation again. "We'll go tomorrow, I promise. But after the last few days, I think we both need a day to do nothing."

Skye's "nothing" turned into weeding Ma's garden, dusting the furniture, and beating the parlor rug while Ma rested.

Tuesday through Friday, he drove her each day to the reservation. They determined she'd begin her teaching duties in earnest the following Monday. For now, Alan tried to keep the visits short, each with a purpose. One day, Skye made a wish list for supplies. Another day, she toured the grounds. Each day, she spent a little time with her students, reading them a chapter from a book or telling them a story about her family and where she grew up. They had many questions, and Alan was in awe not only at her confidence, but at her diplomacy. He stayed in the back of the room under the guise of making sure everything went smoothly for the new teacher. The truth was, everything about her captivated him.

Walker sat with him each day, under the same guise. But Alan knew Skye Stratton captivated the young chief as well. At least for now, Alan had the advantage. He got to take her home each day.

Thursday afternoon, when Skye closed *Children and Household Tales* by The Brothers Grimm, a young girl raised her hand.

"Yes, Anna?" Skye leaned on the edge of the teacher's desk.

"Are you Comanche?"

"My mother was part Comanche and part Coushatta. My grandmother was full Coushatta. I believe she grew up on this reservation."

A little boy raised his hand.

"Yes, Jacob?"

"Comanche are bad."

Mary scolded the boy in Coushatta.

"It's all right." Skye pushed away from the desk, walked down the aisle to where Jacob sat, and knelt so she was at his eye level. "Do you think I'm bad?"

At least the boy had the decency to look embarrassed. "I don't know."

She rested a hand on his arm and smiled when he looked up at her through thick, dark bangs. "I believe everyone has some good and some bad. Even Comanche. Even Coushatta." She stood, looked at all the students. "What do you all think?"

Many nodded in agreement. Some looked at her with fear, others with distrust.

Alan stood and pointed to his pocket watch. They could have stayed longer, but he wanted to spare her further pain. Once they knew her more, they'd love her. He was sure of it.

He eyed Walker, who grinned at Skye like a hound grins at a rib bone. Yep. To know Skye Stratton was to love her.

Alan looked forward each day to the hour-long journeys to the reservation and back. He tried to gently tease and coax Skye into conversation, but it seemed he'd lost his touch. Where she'd once shown him warmth, she now showed consistent, cool distance. On Friday afternoon, they stopped at the post office. She received three letters, though she didn't share who they were from, and he didn't ask.

When she settled back into the wagon, he took a deep breath. "You know, there's a dance tomorrow night in the town square. I was wondering if you'd like to go with me." There. He'd asked. He'd tried to work up the courage all week, but her attitude was thicker than the Great Wall of China.

"That's a thoughtful offer, but I'm sure you'll have more fun without me."

"Why would you think that?"

"I think that's obvious, Mr. McNaughten."

"Oh, yeah. Because you're uglier than a buck-toothed bull-frog with a glass eye."

The shock on her face was worth a thousand more silly insults. She looked for a minute like she might slap him. Then she snorted. Soon, her shoulders shook with laughter. She laughed so hard she lost her breath, and he thought she might fall off the buckboard. It was the first time she'd let her guard down in a week.

By the time he pulled into their yard, she'd regained her composure. "Yes, Mr. McNaughten. That's exactly why. I'm sure you can do better."

The spark in her eye told him she wasn't offended, so he pressed harder. "Please go with me."

"I'm afraid that's out of the question."

"I need you to protect me."

There was that perfectly arched eyebrow again. "Protect you?"

He tried to return the same look, but he was pretty sure he ended up looking like he had something in his eye. "From the hornet."

"Oh. Her. I'm sure you can defend yourself from her sting just fine. I don't think she aims to hurt *you*."

"*Au contraire, mon ami.* She wants to capture me, and that's worse than being stung."

"I didn't know you spoke French. *Combien de langues parlez-vous?*"

"Uh…you lost me there."

Her deep, husky laugh sounded like rain in the desert to his parched heart.

"I asked how many languages you speak. Never mind. I don't think it's a good idea for me to attend a public dance with you. Thank you for asking."

He should leave it be. A gentleman would take no for an answer and move on. But he knew the reason for her decline, and he also knew things would never get better for her if she didn't do some uncomfortable things, and just get on with living life, in spite of what people thought. "Look, Skye. If you *act* like you have something to be ashamed of, people will *think* you have something to be ashamed of, and they'll keep trying to shame you. The dance might be awkward at first, but you have as much right to go and enjoy yourself as anybody else. And I *won't* enjoy myself unless you go." He hopped out of the buckboard and jogged to her side of the vehicle, dropped to his knee, and removed his hat. "Skye Stratton, I'm begging you. I will be forever in your debt if you will accept my invitation and go to the dance with me."

Behind him, the screen door banged shut. "Better say yes, Miss Stratton, or you'll break the boy's heart plum in two. I've never seen a more pitiful sight in all my days." Pa's voice held levity. Alan hoped Skye would agree to please his father, if not for his own sake.

Her cheeks turned the prettiest shade of pink. Alan stayed where he was, one knee in the grass, hat at his chest, and gave her his best sad-puppy look.

"Oh, all right. Against my better judgment. For the record, I think this is a very bad idea. But since you're obviously not going to take no for an answer, I reluctantly accept." Her dimples fighting not to make an appearance assured Alan that somewhere deep inside, she was pleased.

He'd take it. He stood, swept his hat into a bow, then held out his hand. "I humbly offer my deepest gratitude."

She giggled again, took his hand, and stepped down. Without a backward glance, she left him in the yard, nodded to Pa as she scooted past, and disappeared into the house with her letters.

~

Skye tried to wipe the silly grin off her face. She did not want to go to that dance with all those people who didn't want her there.

But she did want to go. With Alan.

She didn't want to fool herself into believing he actually cared about her as more than a friend.

But she did want to believe that. She really did.

But—and this was a big but—she didn't have a thing to wear. She'd already worn each of the dresses she'd stuffed into her carpet bag last week. And those dresses were among her simplest. If it weren't so torn and stained, she might have worn her travel dress.

She'd look over her other dresses later. Right now, she had letters to read. Three, to be exact. She opened the one from her parents.

Dearest Skye,

We're so happy to hear you arrived safely. We heard about a train robbery on the same day and worried you were involved.

Oh, dear. She'd have some explaining to do when they came. But she still felt confident in her decision not to share that

information in a wire or a letter. They'd have questions, and she
wanted to be there to answer them. She kept reading:

*Home doesn't feel like home without you. Though our many guests
keep us busy, this place feels empty without our beautiful Skye.
Tourist season ends soon, so we'd like to visit you mid-September, if
that's all right. We'll secure a hotel room in Livingston, so don't worry
about our housing.*

*Please write soon and often. We hope you're still happy with your
decision. If not, you know you can always come home.*

All our love,

Mom and Dad, Cordell and Anita

*P.S. Anita wants to know if you're married yet. We assured her you'd
at least invite us to the wedding, but she insisted we ask, anyway.*

Skye could picture her family sitting at the dining room
table, shouting out words and phrases for Mama to add to the
letter. She could see Anita pouting when her question didn't get
included, and Mama, with a reluctant smile, adding it at the end.
She could envision Daddy folding and sealing it, and adding the
stamp after Mama wrote the address.

In spite of all the wretched things that had happened since
she'd left, she felt like she'd made the right choice. But goodness,
she missed home.

She refolded the letter and placed it in its envelope, then
held up the next one, postmarked Beaumont, Texas, from a
Bertie Calhoun. *Charlie's mother!* She tore into the envelope,
taking care not to damage the letter inside.

Dear Miss Stratton,
    I can't thank you enough for all you did for me and for Charlie

last week. You are a remarkable woman, and I don't know what I would have done without you, both on the journey and after. We made it home to my mother's, and she's frail but fighting. Please keep her in your prayers.

Charlie has asked if you'd like to become writing buddies. He's included a drawing with this letter.

Skye unfolded a picture of a giraffe. Or was it a bear? Whatever it was, it made her smile. She found a hair clip with a spring in it and used that to secure the picture to the curtains, so she could see it from anywhere in the room. She'd have to check at the general store for a frame.

So far, today was bringing more smiles than she'd had in a week. Her heart light, she picked up the third letter. From David Kelly. She held the missive to her chest, savoring the moment of having people show an interest in her in a positive way.

Never had she had so much attention from people outside her family. Though not all of it was good, even the negative attention of the past week seemed to build, rather than shatter, her confidence. She didn't know what was happening to her. All her life, she'd tried to be perfect. Perfect, so she could be invisible. If she didn't make mistakes, she could avoid too much notice, and people might forget she didn't belong.

With an audible sigh, she worked open the envelope and pulled out the letter.

Dear Miss Stratton,

First, I want to thank you for being such a remarkable, brave person. Though I didn't particularly enjoy the bullet in my shoulder, I have never in my life had such an adventure as the one I took with you last week. Because of you, everyone now sees me as rugged and brave, like some kind of hero. In my heart, I know that you are the true hero, but I do enjoy the attention. I am healing nicely, though the doctor says I may always have pains in that shoulder.

What a sweet man. She loved that he credited her for making him brave.

My father's bank is to handle the financial aspects of rebuilding the bridge. Because of that, I will travel to Silsbee sometime this fall. I know Livingston is only a short drive from there, and I'd like your permission to visit. My family owns some land near there, and I need to check on it anyway. Mother will be with me. She sends her love.

I look forward to hearing from you soon.

Most devotedly yours,

David Kelly

More smiles. Smiles and smiles and smiles. This afternoon was turning out to be more pleasant than she had a right to, but right now, she would savor it. She set the stack of letters on her bedside table and opened the small wardrobe that held her things. At least she'd packed skirts and blouses instead of dresses. Maybe if she mixed them up, she could come up with an entirely new-looking outfit for the dance. For a moment, a wave of panic threatened. Now that Margaret Tusselhoff knew of her heritage, she felt certain the whole town knew. They wouldn't want her there. They'd be rude. Some might be confrontational.

But Alan was right. She had nothing to be ashamed of, and the sooner she faced her adversaries, the sooner they'd decide she wasn't worth the trouble and leave her alone. That was the best she could hope for, she knew. But maybe...maybe there were more people like her parents, like the McNaughtens, who might actually befriend her. And if not...well, she wouldn't think about that right now. Right now, she let herself relish in the thought that tomorrow, she'd go to a public dance on the arm of the most handsome man in town.

Saturday morning, Skye had cleaned up the breakfast dishes and set out a few things for lunch when she heard a loud thud on the porch.

Wiping her hands on her apron, she crossed the dining room and opened the door. Alan was there, a grin smeared across his face. In front of him was her trunk!

She squealed. Jumped up and down and clapped her hands like a kid in an ice cream parlor. She didn't even care what he thought of her. "It came! Oh, I'm so glad it came. Can you drag it to my room?"

"I can carry it if you'll hold the door open. Ma will kill me if I scuff her floors." He hefted the trunk into his arms, and his muscles stretched and bulged in his shirtsleeves. She looked down and away as she let him pass, but got her eyeful as she followed him down the hall. Fortunately, the door to her room was cracked, so all he had to do was push on it and it swung open. "Where would you like it?"

"The foot of the bed will be great."

He set it down and scanned her room like he was looking for

something. The room felt so much smaller with him in it; his presence both stifled and thrilled her. She stood, one foot in the hallway. She wanted to tear into that trunk, but she didn't feel right about being in her bedroom alone with him. James had gone over to the church after breakfast, and Sue was still in bed.

Having him here, where she slept, felt intimate. He wiped his hands on his denim pants and smiled, and his teeth were white against his tan skin, and his blue eyes seemed to look right through her, read her mind. Did he know what she was thinking?

"If there's nothing else I can do for you, I guess I'll mosey along." He scooted past her in the doorway, and for just a moment, they were close enough to touch. To breathe the same air.

Close enough to kiss.

He paused for just a fraction of a second, and she did too, and in this moment, it felt like their hearts beat as one. And then the moment was gone, and he was gone. She scurried into her room, squeaking out an odd-sounding, "Thank you" before she shut the door. Oh, mercy and heaven! She was making a fool of herself.

After taking a minute to set her scrambled thoughts back in order, she opened her trunk and began removing items, placing them on her bed. Her books. Her pretty underthings. Oh, her cotton and eyelet nightgown! She'd been sleeping in one of her shifts. This would feel like heaven. And there, still folded nicely on the bottom and wrapped in tissue paper, was her favorite dress. The under layer was made of beige silk, with a sweeping A-line skirt that ended in a pleated ruffle all around the hem and up to a point at the bustle. But it was the over layer that turned the dress from simple to spectacular. A gauzy, see-through lace featured trails of green leafy vines, giving it an almost fairy-like quality. She'd shown Mama a picture in *The*

Delineator, and they'd immediately gone to town and combed through bolts of fabrics and samples. Normally, Mama would have made her dress—Mama loved to sew—but this one, she commissioned to Mrs. Wesson, Lampasas' local-seamstress-turned-designer, and one of Mama's dear friends.

Skye had only worn it at an extended family dinner at Uncle Colt's house. Aunt Allison had made a comment about the lovely dress in that tone that Skye never knew how to interpret. The words were flattering, but the tone was insulting. But that was Aunt Allison, full of contradictions, and fortunately Skye only had to deal with her a couple times a year. She didn't bother Skye as much as Uncle Colt did.

She pushed those thoughts to the side. She wouldn't let Uncle Colt or Aunt Allison ruin her joy at wearing this dress to a dance. With *Alan.* People could whisper and point and call her a dirty Injun all they wanted. This dress gave her confidence. This dress made her feel beautiful.

She checked the lock on her door, then stripped down to her shift. Tried the dress on and stood in front of the full-length oval mirror in the corner, one she felt certain Sue had placed there for her benefit. For some reason, she couldn't picture Alan caring about his full-length appearance. She turned to one side, then the other, studying herself from every angle. Yes. This dress would do nicely. She hadn't realized how much she'd missed wearing her nicer things.

Digging through the remaining items in her trunk, she found the green satin hair ribbon they'd bought to go with the dress along with several pink rose-head hairpins with green leaves. She lifted her hair and placed it in several different ways on her head, turning this way and that in the mirror, planning just how she'd wear it.

It wasn't even ten o'clock. She could hardly get dressed now, though that's exactly what she wanted to do. Gently, oh so carefully, she removed the dress and hung it up. Hopefully, some of the wrinkles would fall out by tonight. She felt like Cinderella going to the ball. Only she didn't have to wait until she got there to meet her handsome prince. She'd arrive on his arm.

When she returned to the front room, Sue was finishing up the dishes.

"I'm so sorry. That's my job. I got distracted when my trunk arrived."

"Alan told me. I'm sure you're happy to have the rest of your things."

"Very much so."

"Sit down and talk to me, dear." The older woman set two teacups on the table and filled each from the kettle. "I've always wanted a daughter, so I hope you'll let me live out my dream a little, through you. I understand you're going to the dance tonight. What are you wearing?"

Each day with this family, a little more of the ice Skye had placed around her heart melted away. In this home, she felt like she fit. She felt accepted. Wanted. She felt here the same way she felt around Mama and Daddy—and pretty much nobody else for her entire life. Cinderella indeed. At this moment, she really did feel like the heroine of her own fairy story.

~

*A*lan moved the lantern closer and retied his tie for the fourth time. Tonight had to be perfect. Tonight, he'd show Skye how he felt. Tonight.

He undid his tie and tried again.

He checked his watch. Grabbed the small bouquet of flowers he'd picked earlier today. Ma had helped him arrange them and tie them with a pretty lace ribbon. Then she wrapped the stems in a wet handkerchief to keep them fresh. Was he supposed to remove that before he gave them to Skye?

He wasn't sure. He thought yes.

It felt funny walking across the yard, knocking on his own front door to pick up his lady for the evening. After peeling the wet fabric off the bouquet, he laid it on the back of the porch rocker to dry and held the bouquet behind his back.

The doorknob moved, and he caught his breath. The door opened—it was Pa. "Come on in, son. Skye will be out in a minute. While we wait, I want to know, what are your intentions with this young lady?" The spark in his eye showed Pa was enjoying this far too much.

"My intentions are completely honorable, I assure you."

Then there was Ma, stepping around Pa. "Oh, my. Don't you look"—she coughed, that desperate, bottomless cough— "handsome! Here. Let me fix your tie."

A shadow moved in the hallway, and it took all his focus to remain still while Ma fussed over him. Over her head, he watched Skye step into the front room, all dewy and fresh and green like a mountain meadow. His breath caught, and Ma stepped aside.

Soft curls framed Skye's face and neck, and the rest of her hair was swept up in a bunch of soft, silky loops. A dozen or more tiny pink ribbon roses were tucked here and there, their leaves the same green as in her dress. A satin ribbon circled the crown of her head, and when she turned her face to say something to Mama—what, he had no idea—he saw it was tied in a bow at the nape of her neck.

"Hello," he said. It was the only word he could find.

"Hello."

They stood there for a minute like a couple of awkward teenagers.

"You look…beautiful."

"Thank you. You look very nice too."

Pa placed his arm around Ma, and they both stood there smiling, enjoying the show. Good gravy, this was embarrassing.

"Oh!" He brought the flowers from behind his back. "I brought you these." He held them out like a peace offering instead of a suave, romantic gesture.

She took them, brought them to her face. "They're beautiful, and they smell lovely. Did you pick them yourself?"

"I did."

She looked pleased. Good. "Let me put these in water. I don't want them to wilt."

Ma intercepted them. "I have just the vase. I'll take care of it. You two"—she coughed again—"go on, or you'll be late."

Skye handed Ma the flowers, took Alan's offered arm, and he led her to the buckboard. The way she looked tonight, the buckboard wasn't nearly nice enough. She didn't seem to mind, though. The dance was close enough for a leisurely stroll, but it was hot, and he didn't want her to have to walk.

The sun was low in the sky. Twilight was still an hour away, but all around them, fireflies skittered and played. Once they were settled, he drove Fiona at an easy pace. "In all my days, I have never seen anyone look as beautiful as you do right now. I'm honored to be your escort."

She smiled, her lips still together, her dimples winking through a soft blush. "Thank you."

He had a speech prepared, about holding her head high and ignoring any snide remarks people might make about her presence, but he didn't want to taint this perfect moment with thoughts of what might be. *God, give her this night. You shut the mouths of lions. Can you please shut the mouths of anyone who might ruin her evening?*

Their shoulders brushed, and Alan leaned a little in her direction in hopes it might happen again. She was quiet and kept her eyes focused on the scenery. Before they arrived at the square, the sounds of fiddles and banjos tuning and people laughing and talking met their ears. All too soon, he parked Fiona next to the other wagons.

"My lady." He rounded the wagon and swept into a low bow, as if they were going to court instead of a town jamboree.

She took his hand, and her tiny one was nearly swallowed up in his grasp. When she was settled on the ground, he didn't let go. Instead, he tucked her palm around his arm and held onto it with his other hand. She didn't pull away. For a moment, their eyes met and held, and the sunlight behind her formed a halo of light around her dark, swept-up curls, and he felt like he was in a dream. But this was very real.

He'd worked out in his mind all the safe people he knew, who would be there tonight. Even sought some of them out in town today, made some discreet comments, just to put them on alert. People with kindness of character, with class. Often those people were the quiet ones, standing in the background, out of the way of louder, mean-spirited people. But he'd seen kind people become fierce warriors for the right cause, and Skye was certainly a worthy reason for them to put on their armor. Tonight, Alan determined to keep Skye away from the Margaret Tusselhoffs of town and surrounded by those who would treat her with respect. *Help me protect her, Lord. Fill in the gaps, and protect her when I can't.*

He realized he was still staring at her, and her arched eyebrow pulled him out of his trance. "Uh...sorry. I got lost in thought there for a minute."

"I'm not sure I want to know where your thoughts had wandered." Her eyes held mischief, and he had the strongest urge to kiss her.

Instead, he laughed, and his cheeks felt warm. "I was just thinking about people I'd like you to meet. There are plenty here who would love to know more about the new school-teacher for the reservation."

"Is that so." It wasn't a question. More a statement of doubt. But she lifted her chin and looked at the crowd already gathering. "In that case, let's not delay any further."

Her eyes glinted with a spirit of determination and...
almost...pleasure? Like she'd made up her mind to enjoy this
evening, come what may.

CHAPTER 22

Thanks to all the guests at the Big Skye Inn, Skye had seen plenty of handsome, well-dressed men in her time. But never in all her days had any of them stolen her breath like Alan did, on this night. He wore his navy pinstriped suit—did he wear blue to bring out his eyes?—with a pale blue satin tie that was a little bit crooked. Just crooked enough to look charming and roguish, not stiff. She was so glad when he handed her that bouquet of flowers, because it gave her something else to look at. Without them, she might have dropped her jaw and gawped at him like some banana-craving gorilla.

Instead, somehow, she'd managed to keep her composure long enough to get in the buckboard. On the short journey, she trained her eyes forward, watching the trees and the fireflies, trying to ignore the electricity that flowed between her shoulder and his. Gracious and mercy. How would she make it through the evening when she couldn't even find her tongue on their short ride?

But when he said he wanted to introduce her to some people, she pulled herself out of her lovesick stupor, squared her shoulders, and prepared for battle. Because a battle it would be. But one of the beautiful things about making a new start was the possibility of reinvention. She'd stayed in the shadows and played perfect all her life. She was done with that, ready to shed her cocoon and spread her wings.

That was what she hoped for, anyway. And she hoped, in spreading those wings, she didn't get too close to the flame and singe them. She lifted her chin—instead of lowering it like she'd done at these types of community events all her life—looked people in the eye, and smiled. Looked around at the tables laden with home-baked goods and lemonade, at the little girls spinning in their dresses and the little boys, miserable in their ties. At the old men gathered in groups, probably talking about the weather, and the old women gathered in groups, probably talking about the old men. She listened as the fiddle players tuned their instruments, playing a few lines of one song, then another. A wave of homesickness washed over her, and then it was gone. Tonight, she would hold her head high and enjoy herself.

Alan led her to a young couple with three little girls, none of whom looked like they'd reached school age. My, their parents had their hands full. They sat at a wooden picnic table, and the mother held the youngest in her lap while the other two vied for their father's attention. "Lori and Patrick Freeland, I'd like you to meet Miss Skye Stratton. She'll be teaching at the Alabama-Coushatta reservation."

The woman offered a warm smile. "How fascinating! I have a beaded bag they made. It's one of the loveliest things I own. How did you come to be the new teacher?"

Skye wasn't sure how to respond. She didn't expect anything positive to be said about her position. "I was offered the job partly because of my heritage, I think." She might as well tell all. She was certain Margaret Tusselhoff had already told everyone, anyway. "My mother was part Coushatta."

"How fascinating," Patrick said. "Do you speak the language? What a silly question. Of course you do, if your mother did."

A thousand pounds lifted off her shoulders in that moment. "My mother died when I was quite young, but I do remember a few words."

One of the girls, the oldest, Skye thought, reached her chubby hand and touched Skye's dress. "You're pretty."

Skye knelt down to the girl's level. "Thank you. So are you."

Alan knelt then too. "I agree with you one hundred percent, Miss Emma. Miss Stratton is lovely."

The girl nodded, and Alan touched Skye's elbow. "I have some others I'd like to introduce you to."

She nodded and stood. "It was a pleasure, Mr. and Mrs. Freeland."

"The pleasure was ours. And please, call us Lori and Patrick." Lori waved the little one's hand for her, teaching her to say good-bye. "Do come back and sit with us when you have a chance. I miss having a woman near my age to converse with."

Alan led Skye through the crowd to a middle-aged couple. "Mayor Ide, Mrs. Ide, may I present Skye Stratton, the new teacher for the Alabama-Coushatta Reservation."

They both smiled and greeted her, and neither of them looked shocked or offended. The woman said, "Call me Kathy, please. I love your dress."

"Thank you. Yours is quite lovely as well. And you may call me Skye."

On it went for the next half hour as Alan led her from person to person, presenting her as if she were the queen of England. And each person treated her with kindness and respect. Could this be real? Slowly, gradually, she lowered that iron fence around her heart.

"Are you thirsty?" Alan gestured in front of them, and she realized he'd led her to the refreshment table.

"I am, actually."

He gave her a cup of punch and took one for himself, then led her back toward the Freeland's table. They stood there in the grass, watching the festivities, not saying much, sipping their punch. Why could she talk to all these strangers, but she couldn't find a single interesting thing to say to Alan?

Across the square, she spotted Margaret Tusselhoff with a group of other young ladies. They looked her way, and Margaret's expression reminded Skye of a puppy she'd once seen who'd been stung when he tried to eat a bee. His face had puffed up and his eyes turned to miserable little slits.

When Margaret saw Skye looking at her, she picked up her skirts and marched in their direction like a general advancing on the enemy.

The music changed from a waltz to a reel.

"Would you like to dance?" Alan looked across the crowd as he spoke, and Skye assumed he saw Margaret coming.

"I'd love to."

He took her cup, placed it beside his on the Freeland's table, and led her onto the dance floor—part of the packed-dirt road sectioned off by hay bales. They each took their place in the line just as the caller instructed them to get ready. Then it was, "Forward, bow, back in place. Swing your partner, dosey doe. Two hands and swing around…" and on and on.

Skye enjoyed the Virginia reel, especially since she didn't have to remember what to do next, as the caller commanded their moves. When it came their turn to slide the length of the line with their hands joined, that electricity sparked stronger than ever, and she wondered if he felt it too.

Far too soon, the dance ended, and she had a hard time catching her breath. She patted her hair to see if it was still in place, but even if it wasn't, she didn't mind.

"That wore me out!" Sweat dripped from Alan's forehead, and he loosened his tie and unbuttoned the top button.

"I wish I'd brought my fan." She laughed, not from anything

funny, but from the exhilaration of the music, the dance, the twilight sky with its pink and yellow and purple swirls streaked across the horizon in a one-of-a-kind work of art.

Alan led her back to the Freeland table, toward their cups. It wasn't until they were at the edge of the dance area that she noticed Margaret standing there, arms akimbo, blocking their way.

Alan gently took Skye's elbow and pulled her behind him while stepping in front of her. "Hello, Miss Tusselhoff. Are you enjoying the dance?"

"How could I? I don't feel safe, what with you bringing that savage here. Next thing you know, her kinfolk will arrive with knives and bows and scalp us all."

Patrick moved beside Alan, while Lori stood up, baby on her hip, and walked behind the two men to stand beside Skye.

Patrick chuckled, though he didn't sound amused. "Margaret, you always come up with the funniest jokes. Imagine. Miss Stratton a savage. From what I can see, she looks as civilized as anyone else in this town. Here. Come with me, and I'll get you a drink to cool off that wild imagination of yours." The man took Margaret's arm and led her—some might have called it dragging, though it was a tad more refined than that—to the refreshment table. Poor Margaret kept looking over her shoulder, opening and closing her mouth like a wounded codfish.

Lori placed her free hand at the small of Skye's back. "I watched you dance, and you must be exhausted. Patrick refilled your cups for you already."

Skye allowed Lori to lead her to their table.

Alan sat beside her and handed her a cup. "I'm not sure which is yours and which is mine. I hope you're not afraid of my germs."

With a laugh, Skye took a sip, set it down, then sipped from the other cup. "Now who's afraid?"

Surprise filled his expression before he leaned his head back and laughed. Several people looked over at them, then went back to their conversations.

Soon Patrick returned, sans Margaret, and joined them with three more cups. He offered one to his wife and one each to his two older daughters before taking his seat.

"Why aren't you two dancing?" Alan nudged his friend.

Patrick chuckled. "It would be a little crowded with five of us on the dance floor."

"Let us sit with the girls for a minute. You two should have some fun." Skye reached to take the baby from Lori. "I don't mind, really. I love children."

Lori looked at her husband, and a wide smile filled her face. "I won't refuse an offer like that."

The music was a slow waltz, and Skye watched as the young couple disappeared into the crowd.

"That was kind of you. I've noticed that about you. You're always looking for ways to help others. Always putting others' comfort above your own. I like that." Alan's voice was low, and though a hundred people or more crushed around them, it felt like they were the only two people there.

That is, until the baby reached up and pulled at one of Skye's pearl drop earrings. "Oh...ouch." She gently removed the infant's hand.

The oldest girl leaned on Skye's lap. "You have to be careful. She grabs everything."

"Tell me your names." Skye made sure to speak to the girl like she was an adult.

"I'm Emma, that's Ella, and you're holding Eva."

"What beautiful names! My mother's name is Emma."

The girl smiled like she'd just been given a special gift. The music died down, and soon the girls' parents returned.

The rest of the evening flew by. Skye laughed more than she ever had, and after leaving the Freelands, she and Alan danced almost every dance, both group dances and couple dances. Two other men asked her to dance, too—an awkward teen named Ben and a thirty-something widow named Bill. To her relief, Alan cut in on both dances.

Margaret didn't approach them again, though Skye saw her whispering with her posse several times. Even that couldn't lower Skye's soaring spirit. Tonight she felt...normal. Better than normal. Tonight she felt wanted. Accepted outside her immediate family, for the first time since...ever.

～

The waning gibbous moon still allowed plenty of light, even if the numerous lanterns hanging from tree limbs and street signs hadn't been there. Families with young children were leaving, and even the musicians seemed ready to call it a night. But Alan didn't want the evening to end.

The fiddle swooned into a slow waltz. The moon bathed Skye's shoulders and hair, and she looked ethereal, strong yet feminine, her dark hair and high cheekbones hinting more of an Indian legend than a real person. "I believe this is the last dance. Would you do me the honor?"

She took his hand, and he led her onto the floor one final time. Pulled her closer than the other dances had allowed, and she didn't resist. His cheek rested on her hair, and he felt her breath on his neck. He wrapped his arm a little tighter around her waist, and she did the same. Something magnetic pulled them together, and in that moment he knew. He'd suspected, but now he knew this was more than a passing flirtation. For him, at least, this was the real thing. He couldn't think of another living soul he wanted to spend his life with.

Considering how skittish she'd been with him the last few days, though, he must take it slow. No marriage proposals tonight. Or even in the next month. Though the way she made his head swim, that was going to be difficult.

"I hope you've enjoyed your evening." His words came out husky.

She pulled back, looked up at him, and at that angle, her eyes reminded him of a doe's, all golden brown and trusting. "It's been the most wonderful night of my life. I don't want it to end."

He could think of a thousand things to say, every one of them honorable, but none of them appropriate at the moment. He didn't want to scare her away.

Instead, he pulled her closer again, and she rested her head on his shoulder.

He did not deserve her. She was good and pure and strong and he was… Well, he tried to be all those things. But he'd failed so many times. She made him want to be a better man.

The music ended. Reluctantly, he let her go. She stepped back, slowly, as if she felt the same way, and their eyes held. Everything felt thick and slow and heavy and sweet, like warm honey straight from the comb, like hot syrup on fresh pancakes, like creamy butter on biscuits.

He wanted to kiss her. Oh, he wanted to kiss her. As much as he tried to look at her eyes, his gaze was pulled to her lips, full and plump, the color of summer raspberries. But there were people around, so he shook himself out of his stupor and moved back. Goodness, he was addlepated. "I guess we have to go home now."

She sighed, and he didn't know what that meant, but he thought it was good. "I suppose we do."

He offered his arm, and she took it, and they strolled back to the buckboard, where he helped her up before joining her on the other side. Fiona snorted at them as if to say, "It's about time."

Before clicking to Fiona, he looked at Skye again, drank in her presence. "It's a beautiful night. Would you like to go for a little drive, or do you want to go straight home?"

"A drive would be lovely, thank you."

So he took her the long way through town, around by the old millpond, across the bridge, past the schoolhouse, and back by the church, where he pulled to a stop. The white painted steeple fairly glowed in the moonlight, the stars shining like angels in the choir. "Skye, I'm really glad you said yes. I'm really glad you came."

She smiled, and he smiled, and she leaned forward just a breath, and that was all the invitation he needed. He bent toward her, and their lips met, just barely, in the softest of kisses. He pulled back, waiting to see if she welcomed another. She didn't retreat, so he placed one arm gently around her back and kissed her again. This time, he lingered, longer, more intense, and she responded with one, then both arms around his neck, her fingers grazing the hair at his collar.

Then they both pulled back. Bowed their heads, forehead to forehead, and just held each other for a long, thick, fragrant moment.

"I feel like God brought you here, like He brought us together." Alan didn't know where the words came from. They just spilled out, and he knew they were right.

She braced her back, just slightly, and then pulled away. "We'd best get going. Your parents will wonder where we are." Were her walls back up? Alan didn't recognize her tone. He decided not to question it.

All the way home, she kept one hand looped through the crook of his elbow, and he wanted to sing. Wanted to shout. Instead, he whistled "Oh! Susannah" and she hummed along, even sang a couple verses. It was hands down the best night of his life. And he decided in his mind, in his heart, that if she'd have him, he'd spend the rest of his days trying to keep that beautiful smile on her face.

The next morning, Skye stretched, wanting to prolong her pleasant dreams just a little longer. She lay in bed for hours before falling asleep, recalling every moment, every word, every laugh.

Recalling that kiss. She'd never been kissed before, and she wondered if all kisses were that perfect. Yesterday was flawless, from getting her trunk to her time visiting with Sue to every single moment of the dance. Even Margaret's part in it added to the simple perfection of the moment, when two people she barely knew came to her defense. It restored her faith in humankind.

Today was Sunday, and though she'd vowed not to go back to church, last night changed her mind. She would go and sit by Alan and smile like she belonged, because she did. She belonged with Alan.

He'd be at breakfast. Her skin burned at the thought of him, and her heart nearly pulled her out of bed. She selected a solid peach-colored dress with a scoop neck, with tiny ruffles at the neck, sleeves, and hem and cream-colored rosettes tucked into the ruffles. Today, she had a parasol! She chose her creamy lace one along with her creamy lace gloves, which she lay on the desk to put on after she made breakfast.

She made pancakes, thick and fluffy like Mama had taught her. Mama made those pancakes for Daddy every time she wanted to butter him up for something. Well, Alan didn't need buttering up, but Skye sure wanted to please him. She smiled as she stirred the batter and hummed "Oh! Susannah" and thought about that kiss, and she could almost taste his lips on hers.

Between pancake batches she mixed together the sugar and water for the syrup and set it to boil. She'd just added the final pancake to the stack when a soft knock sounded at the back door before it pushed open. Alan poked his head around the corner.

She couldn't hold her smile in. "Good morning."

His smile rivaled her own. "Good morning to you." He looked around, then stepped through the kitchen and peered around the corner, down the hallway. When he saw that no one else was around, he put an arm around her waist. "I really want to kiss you again."

She could feel the blush all the way to her toes. She laughed, scooped a finger in the batter bowl, and smeared it on his nose. Then she gave him a peck on the cheek. She wasn't sure why she played coy. She wanted another kiss as much as he did. But she couldn't let *him* know that.

He looked like a wolf—albeit a very friendly one—ready to eat her for supper when James came around the corner.

"Good morning, Skye. Oh! Good morning, son. You've got a little something on your nose, there."

Alan grabbed a rag off the counter and wiped his face. When his father's back was turned, he shook his finger at her, and she stuck her tongue out at him. When James turned back around, they both miraculously grew halos and presented their best behavior.

The whole scene felt mischievous and delightful, and Skye

wondered if some of last night's fireflies had somehow gotten loose in her stomach.

~

*A*lan had slept great and awoke with a smile on his face that wouldn't leave even if he tried. When he showed up for breakfast and saw Skye looking like a basketful of fresh peaches, he was glad she was dressed for church. After last week, he didn't know if she'd darken the door of that building again.

They worked together to clean the breakfast dishes and check on Ma, whose cough seemed worse. But she offered a knowing smile when Alan followed Skye into his parents' room to bring her toast and tea.

"Did you have fun last night?"

Skye grinned, revealing her dimples, and nodded, and Ma looked at Alan and winked.

They took their time walking through the thicket of pine trees, their boughs reaching across the road to touch and create a tunnel.

Alan wanted to hold her hand, but she clasped hers in front of her, so he wasn't sure how to gracefully execute the move. "Did you sleep well?"

"I didn't sleep much, but the sleep I did get was sound."

"Maybe you can rest this afternoon."

"I need to write some letters, but that shouldn't take long."

"Are you excited to start teaching tomorrow?" He scooped up her hand, and she intertwined her fingers with his. Did sparks of electricity run up her arm as well, or was it just him?

"I've had my lesson plans ready since last Wednesday."

"I know they're happy to have you there. Especially Mary."

"I do feel close to her, as if we're connected. Kindred spirits or something." Skye played with one of the tiny roses on her dress. Then, as if realizing what she was doing, dropped her hands to her side.

"I'm glad you found each other. I knew you had Coushatta heritage, but I wasn't sure if anyone there would be able to connect you with your past. That all happened with your grandmother so long ago."

"Yes."

Alan paused to face her. On one of their trips to the reservation, he'd shared details of his adoption. "I envy you, in a way. I mean, I'm happy for you. But I also understand what it's like to not know a lot about your biological roots. In that way, I feel like *we're* kindred spirits."

"That's true. Not many understand what it feels like. But we're both fortunate to have had adoptive families who loved us so well."

Alan reached for her hand and squeezed it, and they began to walk again. "Will we sit in the sanctuary today, or are you set on your place in the vestibule?" He tried to keep his voice light, teasing, but he knew it was a sensitive topic.

She lifted her head slightly and squared her shoulders, and that mischief he loved so much lit her expression. "Oh, I think I'd like to move into the sanctuary today. Maybe the back row? I'll make it a goal to move up one row each week."

"Back row, huh? You'll have to fight the Carpenters. They've claimed that row for generations."

"Then we'd better walk faster. I don't want them to beat us."

"All right then." He dropped her hand and took off at a jog. Her husky laugh echoed through the trees as she followed. Just before the turn-off to the church, they stopped, caught their breaths—both from the impromptu jog and from laughing—and put on their dignified masks.

A few parishioners stood in the yard, making Sunday

morning small talk. Most waved and nodded at Alan as he passed. A few lowered their voices to whisper, but no one was overtly rude. Just as they made the bottom step, Patrick Freeland called out from where he'd parked his vehicle. After helping his wife and daughters down, he scooped up the youngest and trotted to Alan and Skye. "Good morning, you two!" He reached his free hand to shake Alan's. "Miss Stratton, I can't believe you're still keeping company with this fellow. I'd think you'd be tired of him by now."

Skye cut her eyes at Alan. "He does try one's nerves at times, but all in all, he's not too bad."

Lori approached, one daughter holding each hand. "I think men in general are known to try one's nerves, but I suppose the same can be said for women."

Skye looked relaxed, comfortable. Alan realized that, though she always appeared composed in public, she didn't often seem as comfortable as she did right now. Like public interactions were normally a chore, but not this time.

They continued their chitchat, and before long, the church bell rang. People swarmed around them, including Margaret, who didn't acknowledge them at all. Skye and Alan accompanied the Freelands in.

"Oh, pity. The back row is taken." Alan whispered to Skye in a voice no one else could hear.

Lori placed a hand on Skye's shoulder. "Sit with us. The pew may be a little crowded, but I think there's room."

"All right." Skye beamed, and Alan's heart cracked a little more with compassion for this beautiful woman, who was all kindness and good will, who had struggled so much to find her place in this world. Hopefully, she'd be happy with the place she'd now found, right at his side. He sure knew he was.

~

he only thing that dampened Skye's spirits was the knowledge that she was a fraud. At least, when it came to attending church services. She did so for the same reason she'd always done so. It was expected. She thought of the list of teacher rules she learned in college, and all the rules she'd already broken:

You may ride in a buggy with a man, if the man is your father or your brother.

Women teachers who engage in unseemly conduct will be dismissed.

Men teachers who attend church regularly may set aside two evenings a week for courtship. Women teachers who marry or court shall be dismissed.

After ten hours in school, teachers should spend their remaining time reading the Bible or other good books.

She'd ignored so many of those rules. Fortunately, Alan was her supervisor, and he didn't seem remotely aware of any such list. Still, the least she could do was attend church regularly.

But, despite her resistance, despite her innate feeling that the God of these people could never be interested in *her*, she enjoyed the service. James seemed more genuine and sincere than any pastor she'd encountered. Lori Freeland showed promise as a real friend. Had Skye ever had a true friend her own age? She didn't think so. Sure, she'd had a few acquaintances back in Lampasas, but she'd never felt as comfortable with them as she did Lori. And of course, Alan sitting so close to her in the crowded pew filled the hour with thrilling brushes and accidental touches that she felt certain were not accidents at all. When the service was over, she was glad no one asked her about the sermon. She hadn't heard a word of it.

Later that afternoon, after she helped clean up the dishes from the delicious stew Sue had waiting when they got home, Skye sat on her bed and released the deep sigh that was part lovesickness, part exhaustion. She needed a nap. But first, she needed to answer those letters.

She scooped Friday's mail off her bedside table, found her pencil and notepad in her trunk, and sat at the small writing desk. First, she wrote to her family.

Dear Mama and Daddy, Cordell and Anita,

I am here in my temporary room with the McNaughtens. They are the sweetest couple. They remind me of you, Mama and Daddy, and I know you'll love them as much as I do. They've gone to great lengths to make me feel at home.

~~Alan has~~

~~Mr. McNaughten has been very kind, as well. I find myself drawn to him, and I think there may be more than friendship growing between us.~~

I can't wait for you to visit. Please make it sooner rather than later. I have much to tell you.

She set that letter aside. She'd need to give that one more thought, and copy it over once she knew what she wanted to say. On another sheet of paper she wrote:

Dear Mrs. Calhoun and Charlie,

I'm so glad to hear of the good news. I too have arrived safely at my destination, and I officially begin my new teaching job tomorrow. Charlie, I wish you were to be one of my students. Thank you so much for the beautiful picture. I have it displayed where I can see it every day.

Please write again soon.

Sincerely,

Skye Stratton

To David and Mrs. Kelly she wrote:

My dear friends,

I am so happy to hear that you're well and that the damage to your shoulder, David, is minimal. I wish it hadn't happened at all, but I'm glad you're enjoying your new celebrity status. I am settled nicely and will begin my official teaching duties tomorrow. Please let me know when you will be in Silsbee, and we can arrange a meeting. I would love to see you both again.

Sincerely,

Skye Stratton

She folded each of her two completed letters, placed them in envelopes, and addressed them. She'd have to get stamps at the post office. She scooped up the original letters along with the draft to her parents and looked around for a place to put them. She really needed to unpack her trunk and organize her things better. She pulled open the small drawer in the writing desk, thinking to place her papers there, but the drawer caught on something.

She gently tugged until it opened enough for her to slide her hand in. She felt around and—there. A piece of paper was caught in the back. She worked the paper back and forth, trying not to tear it, until it was loose enough to pull out.

It was a letter. To Alan. Normally she would have folded it and set it aside, but the name at the bottom caught her eye.

Colt Stratton.

Why was Uncle Colt writing him a letter?

Her other papers slid from her lap to the floor. She left them there, held the letter between clenched fingers, and devoured the words:

Mr. McNaughten,

I enjoyed our conversation at dinner last week. It's always nice to meet people who are likeminded, who understand how to get things done. As promised, I have arranged for your appointment as Indian Agent for the Alabama-Coushatta Tribe. The appointment is contingent upon you fulfilling your end of the bargain: removing my brother's half-breed child from Lampasas. Her existence is an embarrassment to my family and a constant reminder of my dead brother's mistakes, and I'd like to let his name rest in peace. Her removal must be permanent. If she returns to Lampasas, I will see to it that you are dismissed from your appointment. I hope you understand.

Colt Stratton

The truth seeped like acid into Skye's skin, her bones, her heart. Alan had looked her in the eyes and implied Colt had nothing to do with his appointment. Said he already had his position when Colt had recommended her to teach.

But this…it was all a lie. Skye taking this job was a condition of his appointment.

All of this…Alan's flirting, the dance, the kiss. It wasn't real. He was using her. He only wanted a job, and…what? Did he think he had to woo her and win her so she wouldn't go running home?

How could she be so stupid?

He'd kissed her. And she'd let him. She felt dirty and violated, like she needed a bath. Except, no amount of soap could rid her of the filth that now penetrated her spirit.

Fighting back the wave of nausea that threatened to bring up her lunch, she scooped her papers off the floor and shoved them in the small drawer. Crumpled up Uncle Colt's letter, then thought better of it. She smoothed it out as best she could, folded it neatly, and placed it inside the Bible on her bedside table. An appropriate place, since both works represented her inability to ever, ever truly belong.

CHAPTER 24

After his traditional Sunday afternoon nap, Alan hung around in his parents' parlor the rest of the day, hoping for a glimpse of Skye. And that's all he got of her—a glimpse. She wandered out to the kitchen just before dinner and offered to help Ma with reheating the stew from lunch.

"No, dear, you've done enough, and I need to be up and moving around as much as I can. Right now, my cough isn't too bad, though I'm sure it will return later tonight. I feel so lazy, sleeping in every morning, but I haven't been able to rest until the wee hours."

"I'm happy to help."

Ma shooed her away. "Go. Sit down. Relax."

"In that case, I think I'll turn in early. I'm really not hungry, and I have a big day tomorrow." Skye didn't even acknowledge him before disappearing back into her room.

An uneasy feeling soaked through Alan's pores, and he grew cold in spite of the warm day. Something had happened. Something was going on in that brain of hers, and he didn't know what it was or how to fix it.

He felt Ma's eyes on him. "Let her be. She's anxious about tomorrow. Anyone would be."

Maybe. But after last night, after this morning, after all the smiles and flirtations and connection of spirits—at least that was what he'd believed was happening—he thought she'd at least give him a smile. A nod. Something.

He pawed through each memory, each conversation of the last twenty-four hours. Had he said something? Done something? Not said something? Not done something? He knew romantic relationships could lead to all kinds of misunderstandings, but Skye didn't seem the petty type. Straightforward and sensible, he didn't think she would hold some minor infraction of word or phrase against him. Yet, she clearly held *something* against him. Because, despite what Ma said, he knew. He *knew* this was more than anxiety over her first day at a new job.

He ate his leftover stew, helped with the dishes, and returned to his makeshift room in the barn. *God, show me what's going on. So I can fix it. And if I can't fix it, I need You to fix it. Because I can't lose her, God. She's the best thing that's happened to me in a long, long time.*

The next morning, he rose and dressed while it was still dark. If they were to make it to the reservation by seven-thirty so Skye could have a few minutes to prepare herself before her students arrived at eight, they needed to get started early. It would be a long day. Especially if she chose to ignore him like she did yesterday.

When he entered the back door, a single lantern lit the room. A pan of still-warm biscuits sat on the stove, along with a crock of butter and another of honey on the counter. Four pieces of bacon rested on a plate. He knew his pa wouldn't be awake for another half hour at least, Ma, probably not until much later. He scooped up two pieces of the bacon and popped them in his mouth, then spread some honey and butter on one of the biscuits. For all her wealth, no one could accuse Skye Stratton of being a spoiled princess. Everything she did, she did well... including cook.

A scuffle behind him drew his eyes around. There she was, looking pretty as a picture, except for her missing smile. She kept her eyes focused on her case as she shuffled around making sure she had everything she needed. He'd hoped she'd carry the beaded purse he got her, but he didn't see it anywhere.

"Are you ready?" *Please look at me.*

"Mmm-hmmm." She closed her bag and walked out the front door without even a glance his direction.

He grabbed a couple more biscuits and wrapped them in a cloth, then used his free hand to pour milk from the pitcher into a cup and gulped it down. Placed the cup in the dishpan, covered the milk and the biscuits. Had she eaten? He grabbed the remaining bacon, wrapped it with the biscuits, and followed her out the door. If she wouldn't eat it, he would. As for the biscuits, he'd share with Fiona.

She was already in her seat when he arrived. He climbed in, flicked the reins, and moved forward, grateful for the gray dawn that allowed him to see where he was going. Winter would come soon enough, and they'd have a hard time making it home in the evening before dark. He really needed to find her a place closer to the reservation.

He pulled his thoughts back to the present, to the woman beside him, the woman who wasn't speaking to him. "You want to tell me what's going on?"

She didn't respond.

"Hello?"

She drew her bag, which rested on her lap, closer to her like a shield. "I think it's best we keep our relationship more businesslike and professional than we have the past few days, Mr. McNaughten. It will make things easier on everyone. Don't worry. I'm not planning to bolt."

"Bolt?"

"I won't be returning to Lampasas any time soon. I've made a commitment to these people, the Alabama-Coushatta people. *My* people. Now that I've found them, I want to stay and learn more about my heritage. So don't feel the need to coerce me into staying. Your job is safe."

What was she talking about? What in the big, wide world was she…? Oh. Oh no. The letter. From Colt.

He'd gotten all those papers out of his desk, hadn't he? He scanned his mind, mentally searching through the papers in the wooden box next to his bed of hay. Wasn't it in there? He couldn't remember seeing it, but he hadn't looked through them since placing them in the box so they wouldn't get bent.

He didn't argue with her. Didn't play dumb, which would be pointless, as she clearly had read the letter.

Every blasted word of it.

He had no idea how to respond. Right then, anything he said would be misunderstood. It was a long, painfully silent ride to the reservation. He'd planned to stay and see how her first full day went, but her words had brought a change in plans. He'd drop her off and head back home. He needed to find that letter. Reread it and refresh his memory on what Colt had said. Maybe that would help him make sense of just how deep her hurt went. Because he'd lost her. And it was all his fault for not being honest with her from the beginning. And he wasn't sure there was any way to ever win her back.

~

It should have been a perfect day. Would have been, except for the gaping, ragged tear in Skye's spirit. But she'd faked a smile all her life, so faking wasn't hard.

"Miss Stratton, will you read us another story from your book?" The children had been on their best behavior all day, as was often the case when children had a new teacher. She wasn't sure how long it would last, and she wished she were more herself so she could enjoy the day.

"Our time is up, but I'll read you another one tomorrow. I promise."

Low groans blended from around the room, and she couldn't help a small smile, even if she didn't feel it all the way through. Any time children groaned because the school day was *ending* was a good day for a teacher.

Mary directed the students from their seats, one row at a time, and placed an older girl in charge before sending them into the schoolyard. Mary stayed behind. "Well done, teacher. They love you."

"I'm just new and interesting. It will wear off soon enough."

Mary sat in one of the student desks. "Do you have time to stop by and see Mama before you head back?"

She didn't know if Alan would be waiting for her, but she didn't care. "Certainly."

"I need to stop and gather some blackberry root. Mama has a bad cough."

"Blackberry root?"

"Yes. We mix it with honey or maple syrup."

"Mrs. McNaughten has a cough as well. Can we gather some for her too? Maybe you can show me how to make it."

"Of course! Leave your things. We'll come back here for them before you leave."

Skye followed Mary into the nearly-empty schoolyard. Mary said something to the remaining students in Coushatta before heading into a thick copse of pines behind the school-house. Soon, they came to some thick, thorny blackberry brambles. Mary dropped to her knees, grabbed a twig, and started to dig.

Skye did the same, though she wasn't nearly as efficient as her aunt. Or was Mary her cousin? She couldn't remember how the family tree branched. As they dug, she tried to figure out how to ask the question that was on her mind, but she didn't know how to word it.

When they had a nice pile, Mary grabbed the bunch in both hands. "This is plenty. Let's go."

"Wait." Skye set aside her digging stick and sat back on her heels. Hopefully the pine-needle carpet would keep her skirt from getting too dirty.

Mary returned to her knees and sat back to mirror Skye. "You have something on your mind?"

"I-I was wondering…"

"Just speak. You have a safe audience with me."

Skye took a deep breath. Exhaled. "I was wondering if I might stay here. With you, Sam, and Tálwan. On the reservation."

Mary's eyes widened. "You want to stay here?"

"Yes."

There was a long pause. Skye's heart thudded, and heat burned her eyes. Would these people, this family, reject her too?

"We welcome you. It would be an honor for you to stay with us. But you must consider the consequences of such an action. The white world and the Indian world don't easily mix. You are able to live in both, but the fact that you seem more…white… probably makes it easier for you. If you stay here, with us, the white people in your world may not see you as one of them ever again."

"I'm not one of them now."

Mary picked up the twig and began drawing little pictures in the dirt below the pine needles. "Go home to your white village tonight and get your things. Bring them with you tomorrow. Stay with me, in my home, until Friday. Ask the agent not to tell anyone that is what you're doing. That will give you a few days to see if you want to make this a more permanent arrangement."

Skye considered the suggestion. Though she was eager to leave Alan's home for good, Mary made sense. "Thank you."

Mary placed her hand on Skye's. "We are family. No need to thank me. You always have a home here, if that is what you desire. I just want you to be sure."

The women stood and dusted off, and Skye followed Mary back to her home. She watched as Mary made the herbal syrup and gave it to her mother. Soon, there was a knock at the door. It was Alan.

"Are you ready?"

She embraced her new aunt and cousin, grabbed the bundle of blackberry root, and walked the short way back to the schoolhouse, Alan behind. She gathered her things and climbed into the buckboard.

Neither of them said a word. Skye wanted to scream at him. Spit on him. Hit him. She wanted him to hurt the way he'd hurt her. But that would only make her look like the savage he and her uncle thought she was. No. She wouldn't give him the satisfaction.

~

They'd ridden a good quarter hour without a word between them when Alan decided to break the silence. "I know what you're angry about. And I don't blame you."

She said nothing. Just looked into the pine thicket.

"I know you read this, Skye." He pulled the wrinkled letter from his shirt pocket, held it where she could see it.

She whipped her neck around. "You went through my things? How dare you."

"How dare you read my letter!" He wanted to suck the words back. He wouldn't get anywhere by hurling accusations. If he'd been in her place, he'd have read it too. "I'm sorry. I shouldn't have said that. You did nothing wrong."

"Alan McNaughten, you are no gentleman. I can't believe you went in my room."

"My mother was there the whole time. Telling me to get out. But she can attest to the fact that I didn't go through any of your…girl things."

Skye clenched her fists, and for a minute he thought she'd hit him. Maybe that had been the wrong thing to say too. She let out a low growl and turned away from him again.

"Skye, I'm sorry. I didn't know you when I agreed to your uncle's terms. And even if I had…I was wrong to ever make a deal with your uncle in the first place. He's not an honorable man. I just wanted to come home."

It felt more like January than September, with her icy response to his words.

He continued. "I don't know how to make you understand. But it's true. I didn't know you then. Once I met you, once I spent time with you… Skye, you've come to mean a great deal to me."

"Please stop speaking. Your voice pollutes this lovely drive."

"Skye, I—"

"If you are any kind of gentleman, you will leave me alone. After tomorrow, you won't have to deal with me any more."

"What does that mean?"

"Tomorrow, I'll take my things with me. Mary has invited me to stay with her. It will give me a chance to know my people better."

"Skye, no. You can't."

"I can't? What do you mean, *I can't?* I'd think you'd be happy to be rid of me. I know I'll certainly be happy to not have to look at your lying face every day. I asked you to stop speaking, and I meant it."

"But I—"

Whap! Her open palm met his face. His whole cheek burned,

a stinging pain he was sure left a mark. Probably in the exact shape of her palm. It might even leave a bruise.

Still, he was glad she did it. That slap hurt less than her words.

~

After she slapped him, they rode the rest of the way in silence, if she didn't count the crickets taunting her from the trees. It was as if they laughed at her pain, at the very idea that she'd thought she could ever be truly accepted. With each turn of the wheel, she added another brick to the fortress around her heart. From here on out, she'd guard it more closely.

Alan didn't come in for the dinner Sue had fixed. The woman cast a curious gaze at Skye but didn't ask questions, and Skye didn't offer answers.

When dinner was over, Skye pulled out the blackberry root. "I brought you something to help with your cough. It's an Indian remedy. Mary, one of my relatives at the reservation, insists it will help." Skye added the root to a pot, stirred in some maple syrup, and, brought it to a boil.

When Sue tried it, she smiled and smacked her lips together. "Whether it works or not, it tastes delicious."

Skye poured the rest into a container with a lid and handed it to her. "Keep this by your bed. When you start to cough, take a spoonful. Hopefully, it will help you rest."

"Thank you, Skye. That's very thoughtful of you."

She stood awkwardly in the living area. "I'd like to talk to you and James, if you don't mind."

Alan's father sat by the window, lantern turned up high, trying to read the newspaper. He folded the paper and set it aside. They looked at her expectantly, anxiety tingeing their features.

"Tomorrow, I plan to take my things to the reservation. I'm

going to stay with my family there. My grandmother's younger sister is still living, and her daughter works with me at the school. It will save Alan from having to make that long drive every day."

Sue cocked her head to the side. "Alan will make that drive anyway. That's his job."

"It will be easier if he doesn't have me along. He can simply ride Fiona and not worry about the buckboard, and he won't have to go every day."

James gestured to the love seat. "Sit down, Skye. Why don't you tell us what this is really about?"

Skye hated withholding information from these two dear people, but it wasn't her place to tell them that their son was a scalawag. A miscreant. A scoundrel. "I appreciate all you've done for me. Really, I can't thank you enough for your hospitality. But this is something I need to do."

CHAPTER 25

lan couldn't find a comfortable spot, no matter how hard he tried. His face was bruised, and one look in the mirror told him anyone would be able to tell he'd been slapped. He was hungry, but he hadn't wanted to invite questions by showing up at dinner.

After several hours of tossing and fretting, he sat up, lit the oil lamp, and pulled out his Bible. It was still in pretty good shape. He'd taken it to Washington and back, but, he'd never read it much.

Pa had given it to him when he was a teenager and had underlined several key verses throughout. Alan flipped through, looking for the underlined parts, in hopes of finding an answer to this mess he'd created.

A lot of verses were underlined in Proverbs. He found chapter fourteen, verse twelve: *There is a way which seemeth right to a man, but its end is the way of death.*

Or a broken heart.

He turned back a few pages to the beginning of the Psalms. *Blessed is the man that walketh not in the counsel of the ungodly, nor standeth in the way of sinners, nor sitteth in the seat of the scornful.*

But his delight is in the law of the Lord; and in his law doth he meditate day and night.

He leaned his head back. A single tear slipped down his cheek and stung the tender skin there. *God, I've tried to do things my way, never stopping to consult You. When Colt offered me a way to come home, I took it. It seemed like a good deal at the time. But I walked with an ungodly man. I sat with him. I ate with him. I shook his hand and made a contract with him. And it's turned into disaster.*

I don't know how to fix this. I hurt Skye. Even if she can never love me after this, I want to make things right. I want to take away the pain I caused, but I don't know how.

Show me what to do, God. I've made a mess, and I'm sorry. Please help me.

He wanted to read more, but his eyes drooped. He set the book aside, blew out the lamp, and rested. Morning came too soon, but he awoke with a calm assurance that, even if things were never the way he wanted them to be, somehow, they'd be all right in the end.

He entered the house, careful not to wake his parents. Skye stood at the stove, scrambling eggs. Her eyes widened when she saw his face, but she said nothing.

"You still planning to stay there?"

"I am."

"Is your trunk ready?"

"It is."

His legs felt heavy as he walked to her room. He grabbed the trunk on each side and hefted it to his waist. When he returned to the living area, he whispered, "Can you get the door?"

She held it open for him, shut it behind him. When he came back in the house, she was gone.

He helped himself to a few eggs, and though they tasted delicious, he had a hard time swallowing. After a short time, she walked through the house carrying her travel bag, out the front door and to the buckboard. He watched her out the window.

She pulled something out of her pocket and gave it to Fiona. Rubbed the mare's muzzle. Climbed on board and waited.

Halfway to the reservation, Alan took a deep, ragged breath. "I don't suppose there's anything I can say to change your mind."

"There is not."

They rode about ten more minutes. "For what it's worth, I really am sorry."

She said nothing. Silence had never been so loud.

He drove her right into the schoolyard. "I'll drop your things at Mary and Sam's place."

"Thank you." Her voice was ragged, as if she fought back a sob. She didn't look at him. Just turned her back and walked into the school.

By the time he got back to Livingston, the town was awake. He parked the buckboard, pulled his hat low, hoping no one would stop for conversation, and entered the post office. When Shelby saw him, he smiled, but the smile fell almost instantly. "Oh, my. That's quite a bruise."

Alan ignored the comment. "I need to send a wire to Lampasas. Right away."

~

It was one thing to teach school here every day and leave. But it didn't take Skye long to see that she didn't fit in. Not that she wasn't welcomed. She was enough of a novelty among these people that they were at least polite. But her clothes, her hair… If she wanted to belong, she needed to make more of an effort to do as the Romans do. Or in this case, the Indians.

The women here dressed differently than she did. Their clothes were nothing like her colorful, flouncy dresses. For the most part, they wore plain, simple dark skirts and dresses. They accessorized with colorful, beaded jewelry and brightly woven shawls. Skye had nothing to compare to their attire. On Wednesday, after sleeping on a pallet on the floor next to her great aunt's bed, she donned her simplest dark skirt and a white blouse. Instead of pulling her hair up in loops and curls, she fixed it in two simple braids and left them hanging over either shoulder. She paused before pulling the beaded purse Alan had given her out of her trunk. The sweet memory caused an ache inside. But the long strap could crisscross over her shoulder like a sash, and it would complete the outfit.

When Mary saw her, she didn't even try to hide her shock. "You look…different."

"If I'm going to be one of you, I should dress like you."

Mary laughed. Paused. Then laughed some more, so hard she had to sit down. Skye didn't see what was so funny.

After a long minute, Mary calmed down. "I'm sorry. I'm not laughing at your clothes. You look beautiful. But…you are such a delight. I love that you want to fit in. The truth is, most of our women would love to have some of your dresses. That's why I laughed." She looked at Skye, head to toe, as if appraising her. "You want to dress like us, do you? You haven't seen us in our best clothes. Mostly, we wear the clothes the government gives us. But this Friday night is our powwow. Today, when we get home from school, you can try on some of my *special* dresses. I'll let you choose the one you want to wear."

The students were getting used to her presence. She knew because today, for the first time, they seemed more relaxed. Antsy, even, as if they couldn't wait for recess. Which, for school-aged children, was far more normal than the stiff, perfect behavior they'd shown up to now. But with only a few stern looks from their new teacher, they got through the day just fine. Truth be told, Skye was just as anxious as they were for the school day to end. Offering a chance to try on new clothes was like dangling a sugar beet in front of her nose. She couldn't wait!

That evening, Mary and Tálwan treated Skye like a live doll. With each dress she donned, they offered this necklace, these earrings, or that hairpiece. In one corner of the room was a small mirror. She wished for her full-length one from her room at James and Sue's house.

She felt like an Indian princess. This was how she would have dressed if she'd grown up here. The clothes made her feel feminine, but a different kind of feminine than her own wardrobe. Instead of delicate and dainty, these clothes made her feel strong and powerful and beautiful.

She wore a dark blue cotton tunic with fringed, beaded hem and sleeves and intricate beadwork around the neck and waist. Tied around one braid was a string of leather adorned with a single black-and-white feather, along with several dangling rows of beads. The women were oohing and ahhing over her when a knock sounded at the door.

Walker entered the home, looked past Skye like he didn't recognize her, then hitched his neck back, realization filling his expression. "Miss Stratton. You look…different."

The other women laughed as if they knew a secret.

"What can we do for you, Chief Walker?" Mary gestured to the table, and Walker took a seat. Sam appeared from the back room and sat next to him.

"I just wanted to make sure our new teacher is settling in. I can see that she is." Appreciation lit Walker's eyes as he took her in.

She smiled, but something inside felt uneasy. Not threatened at all. But…did his eyes show interest? After what happened with Alan, she wasn't ready to flirt with another man. Not for a long time.

Then again, Walker was a good man. She could sense that in her spirit. If she was going to embrace her Indian heritage, if she was truly going to be one of them, what better way to belong than to marry the second chief?

Alan's face flashed through her mind, and all the hurt and anger returned.

Mary spoke to Walker in their native tongue, and Skye only caught a few words. With a nod, she dismissed herself to the bedroom to change out of Mary's clothes and back into her own. That had been fun, but she was starting to feel overwhelmed.

~

Thursday mid-morning, Alan leaned back in his chair and pushed the half-empty cup of coffee away from him. "That's everything there is to tell."

Ma and Pa sat with their elbows on the table, drinking in his every word. The tick-tick-ticking of the grandfather clock filled in the silence that stretched to eternity.

After a time, Pa let out a low whistle. "I wish you'd confided in me sooner."

Ma dabbed at her eyes with the corner of her apron. "You know we love you no matter what. Nothing will change that."

"I know. I just didn't want you to be ashamed of me." He thought about that statement. "I know I gave you cause to be ashamed. I didn't want you to find out."

"We all make mistakes." Pa held Alan's eyes in his gaze. "We all find ourselves in situations where we don't know what to do, how to respond. When that happens to me, I pray, and sometimes, the Holy Spirit gives me clear guidance. Other times, I feel like I'm left in the dark even after praying. That's when I seek advice from people I respect, people I know to be wise and honorable and trustworthy."

"Yeah. I didn't do any of that. I've dug myself into as deep a hole as I've ever been in, and I don't know how to get out."

Ma covered his hand with her own. "From what you've said, I think you're off to a good start. You've asked for forgiveness. You've given Skye some space. And you've taken the first steps to see that her needs are taken care of. The rest is up to Skye. And God."

Alan felt pretty sure, if it were all up to Skye, he wouldn't be pursuing any kind of romantic relationship with her, ever again. That was his fault, and he'd have to live with it.

He might live. He might keep breathing. But he wasn't sure if his heart would ever fully recover. "I haven't been at the reservation in two days. I should head out there this afternoon. I'll keep my distance from Skye, but I do need to talk to the chief and find out if there's anything I can help with."

He pushed his chair back, and Pa stood at the same time. He reached over and clasped Alan's hand in a firm handshake, then pulled him in for a hug. "I'm proud of you, son."

"There's not much to be proud of."

"Oh, that's where you're wrong." Pa leaned back but held Alan at arms' length. "It takes a big man to own up to his mistakes. It takes humility and a willingness to turn around and start over. A lot of men your age wouldn't do that."

Alan swallowed. In private, he thought he'd cried his tear ducts dry. Pa's words nearly set them off again. "Thank you."

The ride to the reservation did go faster with just Alan and Fiona. He let her run. The wind on his face felt good, and for just a little while, he let himself just be. Just exist. And tried to ignore the ache that stretched through every ligament, flowed through every vein.

CHAPTER 26

About an hour before the school day ended, Mary stood up. "I'm sorry, Miss Stratton, but there's been a change in plans. Our next lesson will take place in the school yard."

The students cheered. Skye had no idea what was happening, but she agreed to go along with Mary's mischief. She'd gladly step back and let Mary take the lead for this last hour. She could use the break.

But she wouldn't get a break. As soon as they were outside, Mary instructed the children to stand in a circle and told Skye to get in the middle. "Students, today I need you to change places with your teacher. Tomorrow night is our powwow, and Miss Stratton has never been to one. She doesn't know our dances, and we're going to teach her."

Skye's hands came to her face. She didn't know whether to laugh or feel terrified. She did both. Mary disappeared back into the schoolhouse and returned with some small drums, jingle bells, and a pair of long sticks. After passing out the instruments to several students and giving a command in their native language, the music began.

All around her in the circle, the children danced, moving from one foot to the other in a pattern Skye couldn't quite decipher. Several little girls moved into the circle, lifted their skirts so their ankles showed, and slowed their movements so Skye could learn.

She copied them, and they smiled and nodded their approval. When that song ended, they showed her a different dance and before long, for just a few moments, Skye forgot how sad she was and just let herself have fun. Let herself be right here, right now in this moment, instead of mourning the past or worrying over the future. It felt good to have this small relief. Dancing. Children's laughter. A beautiful fall day.

After a time, they pulled her into the circle with them, and she joined them in their clockwise dance. And even though the sadness was still there in the background, right now, she felt like she was home. And that felt really, really good.

$\approx$

After talking with Chief Scott, Alan roamed the reservation with Walker, watching as the man pointed out improvements they'd like to see, problems with access, and new ways they'd like to increase the reservation's revenue. They crossed the woods behind the schoolhouse. At one point, they could see through a small break in the trees. The children were outside practicing their tribal dances.

Walker stood there, watching, so Alan had no choice but to stay and watch, too. They looked like they were having fun, and he remembered when he was young and learned to square dance in the schoolyard. About that time the circle of children parted, and a woman became visible.

It didn't take him long to realize the woman with long braids, dressed in standard Indian garb, was Skye. She looked stunning. She took his breath away, and he had a hard time pulling his eyes from her, even after Walker headed back the way they came. The two men said nothing for a few minutes, but Alan knew they were both captivated.

"We are fortunate to have her here. She is a good teacher." Walker slowed his pace to match Alan's.

"Yup."

"She seems to have taken to our way of life."

Alan didn't want to discuss this with Walker. "Seems so."

"You're concerned."

Alan shot the man a shut-up look, but Walker didn't see. Alan sucked in a deep breath, prayed a silent prayer. How much should he say? "I want her to be happy. This is all a big change from what she's known most of her life."

"You don't think she could be happy here?"

"I don't know. But she was brought up by loving parents… loving *white* parents, in a very *white* community. I don't doubt her ability to adapt to your way of life, and I know there is much to love about your people. But to embrace this, she will have to say good-bye to a lot of other things she loves. But Miss Stratton strikes me as someone who knows her own mind, and it's not my place to influence her decisions."

"But you wish it were your place."

Alan shot him another look, and this time the man caught it.

"Come. Let me show you our plans for next year's crops."

The two men didn't speak of Skye again that afternoon. But she was heavy on Alan's mind. Come to think of it, he wasn't sure he'd ever rid his thoughts of her, for as long as he lived.

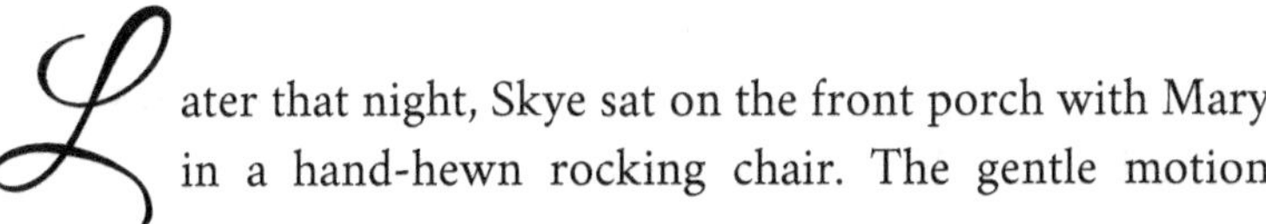

*L*ater that night, Skye sat on the front porch with Mary in a hand-hewn rocking chair. The gentle motion calmed Skye's troubled spirit somewhat. But the explosion of fireflies brought to mind last Saturday night, that wonderful, perfect evening before her innocence was shattered, her trust stolen.

"You have much on your mind. Would you like to share?" Mary's words were soft, probing but not harsh.

Skye took a moment to gather her thoughts. It would be nice to talk to someone about her troubles, and Mary seemed like a safe enough person. She missed her mother. But she wasn't sure she'd ever share those particular struggles with Mama, anyway. "I've never felt like I belonged anywhere. My parents love me. I couldn't ask for better parents. But they're white, and I'm not. And everyone in my community knew I wasn't white, and I never felt accepted there."

"Hmm..." Mary ceased her rocking for a moment, then started up again. "But Skye. You *are* white. You are as much white as you are Indian."

"Maybe so. But most white people don't see it that way."

Their rocking chairs made a steady creak-creak on the wood porch planks. "Do you think the people here see you as Indian?"

Skye stopped rocking and pulled her knees to her chest. "I suppose not." Crickets chirp-chirped in time with her shallow breaths. Would she never be accepted? In her peripheral vision, she saw Mary look at her, but Skye didn't meet her eyes.

After a time, Mary spoke, her voice barely a whisper. "Does it matter how they see you?"

"Yes. It matters to me."

"Why?"

Skye hadn't expected so many questions in return. "Because I'll never feel accepted anywhere. I'll never be one of you, because some of your people see me as half white, part Comanche. I'll never really be white, because in that world, I'm just an Indian half-breed. It's a lonely way to live."

"I imagine it is."

The fireflies grew brighter as the sky grew darker. Skye wrapped her arms around her legs and rested her chin on her knees.

"There's something you're forgetting, though." Mary took a sip from her mug. "As long as you're accepted by God, that's all that matters. He created you exactly as He wanted you, to fulfill His purpose. There is not another Skye Stratton, anywhere in the world, and you are fearfully and wonderfully made. God thinks you're special. That's the only stamp of approval any of us needs."

Mary's words sounded nice, but she didn't understand. She had a tribe. She had people and a place where she belonged.

"Skye, you do understand that none of us ever really feels accepted in this world, don't you?"

"What do you mean?"

"For you, it's your mixed heritage. For someone else, it might be their height. They're too short or too tall. Or maybe they don't think they're smart enough or skilled enough. Every single person doubts his or her place in this world. Every person, at some time or other, feels like they don't fit in, like they don't belong."

Was that true? That idea had never entered Skye's mind. She'd always assumed everyone else had access to a special club that she could never be a part of. "I'm not sure I agree with you."

Mary chuckled, the sound low and warm. "That doesn't make it any less true. But Skye, that voice that's telling you you'll never belong, you'll never be good enough, you'll never be accepted…that's not God's voice. That's Satan."

Skye tried to absorb Mary's words. "I think it's God who doesn't accept me."

"Why would you say that?"

The memories came back. Her heart pounded a drumbeat in

her ears. "I barely remember my first mother. I know she was beautiful. Laughing, smiling, singing. She and my first father loved each other. The memories I have of them together are happy." She lifted one palm and smeared her tears into her hair. "Then she was gone, and so was my father. Except, he was still alive. But he changed. He drank too much alcohol—I remember the smell. He was as sad as I was, and I wanted to help him, wanted him to help me, to love me again, but he was so lost. But I thought he would come back to me one day, and love me like he did before my mother died. I was wrong."

"What happened?" Mary's voice was barely more than a whisper.

"Emma—my second mother—came and got me, and at first I was excited because she was pretty and sweet like my mother. I loved Emma. But then she told me my pa was at her house, and when we got there, I could see there had been a fire in one of the buildings. I was so young, but I knew. I knew something was wrong. And I prayed. I begged God not to take my pa like he took my mother. I prayed, Mary, but God didn't listen. My pa was killed in the fire that night. So what you're saying sounds nice, but it's not true. I'm not accepted. I'm not His child, because why would God do that to one of His own? Take both my parents away and leave me an orphan?"

Mary left her chair and knelt in front of Skye. Reached up and wiped her tears. Then rested her hands on Skye's legs. "Sweet child. Don't you see? He didn't leave you an orphan. Didn't you say you already loved Emma? That she became your second mother? You told me before that your adoptive father is your biological uncle. God loves you, child. He didn't cause your first mother or father to die. We all die. Death is a result of sin in this world. But when you lost both of them, God made sure you had a safe, loving place to go. Even when you couldn't see it, He was working on your behalf. Though your story is filled with pain, it is also filled with love. God has not rejected you, child. He has poured out His love on you."

Could that be true? Could Mary's words be right? Something stirred deep in Skye's spirit, and she heard that voice that she'd pushed away so often.

I love you.

I've chosen you.

Please choose Me back.

Please love Me.

And somehow, it was like her eyes were opened, like she'd been walking in darkness all this time, and here was a light to show her the way. For the first time, she knew. She *knew.* Mary was right in what she said. Why had Skye never seen it that way before?

The tears came, a torrent she couldn't suppress. Skye sobbed, gasping for breath, crying fifteen years' worth of tears she'd kept bottled up. God loved her! She thought back over all the sweet, tender times with Mama and Daddy, with Cordell and Anita, and she knew God had placed her there, in a family who truly didn't recognize that she wasn't their own biological daughter and sibling. What was that verse? *God sets the lonely in families.* God had forged the relationship between Skye and Emma *before* Emma became her mother. He opened the path for Skye to have a safe haven even before she lost her father.

Mary held Skye tight, in a mother's embrace, and a new realization flooded her. Now she had not one family, but two. She wasn't a misfit or an outcast. She was loved and wanted more than she'd ever let herself believe.

Mary spoke soft words in Coushatta, but Skye somehow knew she was praying. Praying for *her.* And though she didn't recognize all the words, she felt something change within her, like she'd been viewing things through a fog, and now the fog had lifted.

In that moment, all the years of Sunday School stories and

Bible readings about God's amazing love, about Jesus and all He did, fell into place in her heart. When Mary grew quiet, Skye lifted her own prayer. "God, I'm sorry. I was wrong." And somehow, even though she didn't say any more, she knew God heard the words of her heart.

Forgive me, Lord. I love You, too.

CHAPTER 27

Friday afternoon, Alan clutched the paper in his hand. The wire said the stage would arrive around four, but that was always a rough estimate. It was now four forty-five, and he'd paced the boardwalk for more than an hour.

"Hello, Alan."

He tried not to cringe at the voice, schooling his features before he turned. "Hello, Miss Tusselhoff."

"I feel I need to apologize for my behavior."

"Oh?"

"I know I must have come across as rude to your Indian friend. I had no idea she was living with you."

"She's not living with me."

"Really? I heard…"

"She's been staying with my parents while we find her a more permanent place. I've been staying in the barn."

"The barn? How…humble of you."

"If there's nothing else, Miss Tusselhoff, I have some business I must see to."

While he spoke, he heard the rumbling blend of wagon

wheels and horse's hooves, and a cloud of dust appeared up the road a ways. The stage coach.

"I hope I haven't offended you," Margaret said. "I really do admire your work with those people. It shows how charitable you are."

That woman annoyed him like a mosquito at a box lunch. Only more, since he couldn't swat her away.

The stagecoach neared, and with the added noise, Alan pretended he didn't hear her. It was either that or say something he'd regret. He offered a polite nod and jogged to meet the coach at the station. He opened the door even before the driver could climb down.

"Hello, Mr. McNaughten."

Riley Stratton's words were friendly enough, but the look on his face told Alan to tread lightly.

"Hello, Mr. Stratton. Mrs. Stratton. I'm glad you're here."

"Where is our daughter?"

"She's at the reservation, about an hour from here. I have my buckboard ready. Would you like to unload your things and check into your hotel first?"

Riley Stratton motioned to the stagecoach driver. "I need you to take us to the Alabama-Coushatta reservation, about an hour from here, then wait for us until we're ready to come back."

The driver shook his head. "I'm sorry, sir. This is the drop-off point. I'm officially off the clock."

Riley pulled out his wallet while Emma fussed with her gloves. "Name your price."

Within a half hour, the driver had secured a new set of horses at the livery, and Alan was inside the high-dollar stage-coach with plush seats and velvet curtains. This was a whole lot nicer than the buckboard. He would have enjoyed it more if both Riley and Emma weren't looking at him like he'd stolen their firstborn. Which, in a way, he had.

"Mr. McNaughten, we have an hour to kill. Why don't you start at the beginning and fill us in on everything we need to know. And even the things you think we don't need to know."

~

"You look beautiful." Mary stepped back, her expression one of satisfaction and admiration. "Here. One final touch." She added a beaded clip to Skye's hair, which she'd left long, flowing down her back.

"Alí:la mõ. Thank you." Skye felt like a little girl playing dress-up. She wore a simple white blouse paired with a colorful skirt woven with pictures of trees and flowers and animals. Around her neck, she wore layers of colorful beads that matched her skirt. She even wore new moccasins that Tálwan had fashioned just for her. They were the most comfortable shoes she'd ever had on her feet. "I feel beautiful. *Inside,* I feel beautiful."

Mary beamed, and Tálwan's eyes glistened. Skye got the feeling the older woman understood a lot more English than she spoke.

Sam appeared in the doorway carrying a fat bouquet of wildflowers and wearing a smile. He presented his bride with the flowers, then pulled two single buds from the group. He handed one to Tálwan and one to Skye. Now *that* was diplomacy.

Skye took her flower and smiled. "Alí:la mõ."

Mary kissed her husband on the cheek and placed her bouquet in a crock of water. "It's time to go. Skye, you grab that pot of beans. Mama, can you carry this basket of bread in your lap while I push you?"

The wheeled chair provided a way for Tálwan to attend village events, since they took place in the center of the reservation, and it was too far for the woman to walk. The sounds of drums reached their ears even before they opened the front door.

Less than a week ago, Skye had gone to the dance with Alan. Tonight, she'd attend another dance with a different escort. This time, she knew God was with her, before and behind. He held her hand. Even more important, He held her heart.

They were barely at the road when Walker approached from the center of town. "*Cikáʼnó*. Hello. I came to escort our new teacher to her first powwow. I also brought you a gift." He held out a bracelet made from several colorful leather straps, all strung through a single stone bead. The stone wasn't one Skye recognized; it was red with some brown flecks in it.

"It's lovely. Alíːla mõ."

He helped her slip the bracelet onto her wrist, and she held out her arm to admire it.

"Did you make this?"

"Yes. I'm glad you like it." His expression was almost embarrassed, which looked odd on the confident young chief.

She rewarded him with a smile, then averted her eyes. Was this really a welcome-the-teacher gift? Or was he showing interest in her? If he was, did she want to encourage that?

In spite of her newly found joy, a pang of sadness pulsed through her. Walker didn't do the same thing to her heart that Alan did. Yet unlike Alan, Walker seemed good and decent and honest.

Do not judge, lest ye be judged.

Before she realized it, she let out a sigh. It was hard not to judge someone who broke your heart. They walked a little way in silence, and Skye realized Mary, Sam and Tálwan had fallen behind. She looked over her shoulder, but Mary waved her on.

"We're fine. Don't wait for us." She had a little grin on her face, and Skye blushed. Her new aunt was trying to play matchmaker, and she wasn't very subtle about it.

A crowd of people laughed and talked up ahead. Children

played tag while older adults placed chairs and blankets under shade trees. It felt like so many parties and picnics Skye had attended all her life. The only difference was the attire. And maybe the rhythmic drums playing in the background. Add a fiddle or two, and she'd feel right at home.

Walker led her to a secluded table and gestured for her to sit. "I have some official roles I must see to tonight, but I'll check in with you when I can."

"I'll be fine. Thank you."

Skye watched Walker disappear into the crowd. She looked around for Mary, but there were too many unfamiliar faces. *Breathe. Relax. Enjoy this. I'm with you.*

"It's our teacher! Look!" Skye heard the voice from behind before several small, dark-haired, dark-eyed people surrounded her. "Do you remember the dances we taught you? Come. Let's practice." Julie and Kelly dragged Skye from her chair and began dancing to the drums. No one seemed to pay them much mind, so Skye took the opportunity to brush up on her skills. She could square dance with the best of them, but this footwork was a bit of a challenge. Her students clapped and gave their approval, so she guessed she did okay.

"It's time. Let's get in line." Eva, a preteen girl, pulled on Skye's arm.

"Time for what?" Skye let Eva lead her, and several other students followed.

"It's called the Grand Entry! We'll all file in so everybody can see everyone else."

The music began in earnest, with several vocalists chanting songs in the Coushatta language. Would she ever understand the words? Would she ever be fluent? The people in front of her began to move in a circle, some dancing to the rhythm, others just walking. It was like a parade.

"Come on, Teacher! Do the dance."

Skye joined her young friends in the fast-fast-slow, fast-fast slow steps, noticing the way the fringe on her skirt bounced. Joy like she'd never known bubbled inside her, and she couldn't keep her cheeks from smiling. Right now, in this moment, she was home, and it had nothing to do with the clothes she wore or the people she was with. It had everything to do with a change that took place inside her less than twenty-four hours ago.

Bravery took over, and she tried some more difficult moves. She spread her arms out and turned in a circle while she kept up her foot rhythms. Her students clapped and cheered, and for that moment, for the first time in a long time, she realized she was at peace. No anxiety. No worries. No fear. Just...freedom.

She laughed and danced and turned and—wait.

What was that? *Who* was that?

She stopped spinning, and the girl behind her bumped into her. There, to one side of the circle, was a group of very fair people, and they were not in native dress.

"Mama? Daddy?" She lifted her skirts and ran, full speed, to her parents. By the time she got to them, both had their arms open wide, and she flung herself into their embrace, both of them at once, forming a tight circle of family love. Should she laugh? Cry? Her emotions were so mixed up, she couldn't name them. All she knew was, she had never been so glad to see anyone in her life. "What are you doing here?"

Mama pulled back, looked at her from head to toe. "I came to see my beautiful daughter. And I don't know that I've ever seen you look more radiant."

Daddy held out a small, wrapped gift. "You forgot something. I had to deliver it."

She tore open the tissue paper to find Rilene, her childhood doll. She hugged the doll close. "Thank you. I...I'm so confused. I don't understand. Where are Cordell and Anita?"

Mama put her arm around Skye's waist, pulled her close. "A little bird told us you might be having a hard time. We just wanted to lay eyes on you, make sure you're okay. Your brother and sister are with Uncle Lyndel."

That's when Skye noticed, standing in the shadow of some oak trees, Alan. Watching her. Her smile faded, and her chin lifted just a bit. She turned her attention back to her parents. "I do have a lot to tell you about my life during the last few weeks. But first, come. I have some people I'd like you to meet."

She pulled her parents through the crowd, just as her students had done to her earlier, searching faces for Mary, Sam, Walker, Chief Scott, or any of her students and their parents. She felt like her two worlds had just collided. Maybe she should feel awkward, but she didn't. All she felt was happy.

There. On the raised platform at the front was Chief Scott. Next to him, Walker. She hoped she wasn't breaking any rules by approaching them while they served in an official capacity. Chief Scott smiled and waved her forward.

"I'd like to introduce my parents, Riley and Emma Stratton." After names were said and hands shaken, Skye stood on her tiptoes to find Mary, Sam, and Tálwan. As she searched the faces, she saw Alan, still standing in the shadows, watching her, and her joy deflated a little. Her parents were engaged in conversation with Chief Scott. "I'll be right back."

She was still hurt. She didn't know if things would ever be the same with Alan. But she had to let him know…she forgave him. If he hadn't done what he did, if he hadn't made that deal with Uncle Colt, she would never have had the opportunity to meet these people. *Her* people. Her mother's people.

He removed his hat as she approached.

"Hello."

"Hello." His eyes were sad. "You look beautiful tonight."

She looked down at her Indian garb. "Thank you. I must admit, it's more comfortable than my usual clothes."

"You looked like you were enjoying yourself out there."

"I was. I am."

His eyes dropped to his boots. "I'm glad everything seems to be working out for you. I'm just sorry it had to be…that you had to learn…"

"It's all right. I don't like that you weren't honest and up front. But the end result is actually pretty amazing. I'm learning things about my heritage I never would have learned if I hadn't come here."

"I'm glad. I…I wish there were words to tell you how sorry I am."

She placed one hand on his arm. "I forgive you."

Alan's eyes flicked behind her, and she heard someone approaching.

"Agent," Walker said.

"Walker."

These two were friends, right? Skye couldn't understand why they eyed each other like two dogs guarding their territory.

"Miss Stratton," Walker held her eyes, "we'd like to introduce you to the village. Would you mind coming back to the podium?"

"Oh." She ran a hand over her hair. "I didn't know I'd be on display. All right."

Walker placed one hand on her back and led her toward the chief and her parents. She took some deep breaths and prepared to be the center of attention for a few moments. And she resisted the urge to turn and look at Alan as she walked away.

CHAPTER 28

Alan could kick himself for riding with the Strattons in the stagecoach. It was a comfortable ride, but now he was stuck. Unless he wanted to walk home, he'd have to wait here, watching Walker make eyes at Skye, watching her fit so perfectly into this world Alan wasn't a part of, until the bitter end.

Then again, he *had* been invited to this powwow. Walker told him about it earlier in the week, but with all the chaos with Skye leaving and trying to get her parents here to talk some sense into her, he'd forgotten about it. He might as well pull out some of his Washington D.C. skills and mingle.

Unfortunately, many of the Alabama-Coushatta tribe didn't seem at all interested in making his acquaintance. Less than half spoke English, and of those who did, only a few feigned politeness. Most just looked at him like he was a monkey on a dairy farm and went about their business. Awkward as his attempts were, they weren't as painful as watching Walker walk around, his hand on Skye's back or arm like he had some kind of right to her. Even more painful, watching Skye not flinch or pull away at the man's touch.

The question was, what was Alan going to do about it? He'd messed up. No doubt about that. Was he going to stand by while some other man stole the woman who'd stolen his heart? Or was he going to fight to win her back?

What should I do, Lord? Which is best for Skye? Because I love her. I want her to be happy. And if this life can make her happier than a life with me, I'd rather step back and leave her be.

Show me what to do, God. 'Cause I don't have a clue.

There were times he really wished God would take his finger and write the answer on a chalkboard in the sky. But he knew enough about God to realize that sometimes, God was silent. Sometimes, you just had to seek Him and do what you thought was best, and trust that God would guide you. Sometimes, even when you ask Him to light the path, He only lights one step at a time. And taking that step, even when you don't know what lies ahead…that's called faith.

This was one of those times. Alan didn't know what would happen, but in his heart, he knew he couldn't just roll over and let Walker steal her. Skye had Alan's heart, and fighting for her felt as natural as a drowning man fighting for air. It was a matter of self-preservation.

The question now was, where did he start?

Chief Scott lifted his hands to call everyone to attention. The noise died, and the man motioned to Skye. Spoke in Coushatta. The only words Alan recognized were "Skye Stratton." People clapped. Walker grinned like a possum eatin' a sweet potato.

Alan skirted the crowd until he stood at the edge of the podium. He didn't know what he'd do, but somehow, he wanted to be near Skye. If she was the fisherman, he was the large-mouth bass, hook in his mouth, reeled in by her every breath.

Chief Scott noticed Alan, motioned him onto the platform. "I want to introduce you, as well." Then he spoke some more words in that strange language. Alan understood his own name and that was it. Next thing on Alan's agenda: learn Coushatta. Right after winning Skye's heart.

~

Skye introduced her parents to the key people in her new world, then found a shady place for them to sit. She urged them to join the festivities.

"We're fine. We'd rather just watch." Mama wore a smile, but was her skin paler than normal? Why did her eyes seem tighter?

"All right. If you're sure." Skye felt strange about leaving them when they'd just arrived.

Daddy waved her away. "Go. It's important for you to get to know your students and their culture. We're not going anywhere."

Mary approached, holding two plates of food. She handed one each to Mama and Daddy. "I thought you might enjoy some of our traditional food." She named each of the dishes, and Skye's parents tasted the meal. Both of them were gracious as ever. Tálwan sat in her chair to one side, smiling her peaceful smile.

Skye felt a hand on her shoulder. It was Alan. "May I have this dance?"

"I don't think this is that kind of dance."

"Maybe not, but if I'm to be a successful Indian Agent, I should learn the culture. I was hoping you'd teach me some of the steps."

Walker's voice sounded from behind her. "Good idea, Agent. But Skye is still learning. You need a teacher with more experience." He called out to a heavyset, middle-aged woman and spoke to her in Coushatta. "This is Dancing Cloud. Her English name is Dana. She teaches the children our dances. I know she'll be happy to show you what you want to know."

The woman smiled. Her eyes crinkled at the corners, and she

249

was missing one front tooth. She pulled Alan's arm, and before he could respond, he was being led into the center of the crowd. She began with simple steps, demonstrating in half time how each was done. From Skye's vantage point, it looked as if he had no choice but to follow the woman's lead. She held in a giggle.

Walker touched Skye's elbow. "Would you like to go for a walk, or would you rather sit a while?"

"I think I'll join my parents. I'm not sure how long they plan to stay, and I'd like to spend as much time with them as possible. You're welcome to join us."

"I need to speak to a few people, but I'll join you in a while, if that's all right." He waved at her and her parents, and she took a seat between her mother and Mary.

"I still can't believe you're here," Skye said. "Where are you staying?"

"At the hotel in Livingston." Mama wiped the corner of her mouth with a napkin. "We're hoping you'll come back with us tonight, at least for the weekend."

Mary nudged Skye's shoulder. "I think that's a good idea. It's good to spend time with family. We're not going anywhere."

Mama smiled her appreciation before looking back at Skye. "We brought more of your things. I just guessed what else you might need."

"Thank you." For some reason, anxiety crept along Skye's skin, threatening her earlier joy. Why had they come? Did they disapprove of her staying here? Would they try to talk her into going home with them? Probably not, or they wouldn't have brought more of her things.

The evening passed with many people stopping by to speak to Skye in broken English or say a word of greeting in Coushatta. She couldn't help but notice, though, that not everyone seemed thrilled at their presence at the powwow. Or perhaps it was her parents' presence that bothered them. It seemed the racial prejudice existed on both sides of the bridge.

Her parents had been nothing but gracious, yet more than once, she saw groups of Coushatta whispering and shooting glances their way, and their expressions were far from friendly. But none of those people approached them directly. It probably helped that several times, Walker sat with them, making polite small talk.

But each time Alan tried to join them, Walker found something he wanted to show the new agent, or someone he wanted Alan to meet. Skye might not have had a lot of beaus—or any, really—but she was no fool. It felt nice to have two handsome men vying for her attention.

"Well, she's not lonely, that's for sure." Daddy winked at Mama, and Mama and Mary laughed. Skye blushed but didn't comment.

The stars were out, the moon was high, and the crickets were in full orchestra when a nervous-looking white man Skye hadn't seen before found them. He smelled conspicuously of alcohol. "Excuse me, Mr. Stratton, but I was wonderin' how long you want me to wait. I really need to get back."

Daddy stood up. "I understand. We'll be there shortly."

The man disappeared, making a wide arc around the crowd of Coushatta people. "We need to go, or I'm afraid our driver will leave us." Daddy helped Mama to her feet.

"From the smell of him, I'm not sure he ought to be driving," Mama said under her breath.

Skye got up and smoothed her skirt. "I should get my things."

Mary leaned close to Skye. "If you're going with them, you should wear your own clothes. You won't be welcomed in town dressed like that."

A feeling like paper ripping down the middle filled Skye's senses. To go there, she had to leave part of herself here. To stay here, she had to leave part of herself in the other world. It wasn't fair. But it was reality.

Mary left Tálwan in Sam's care and accompanied Skye back to the house. "You seem...what is the word? Pensive."

"My life is made of two worlds. I'm not sure how to blend them."

"You will figure it out. You are blessed to have so many who love you."

"True."

She changed out of Mary's powwow attire into her simplest dress. When she started to change her shoes, Mary shook her head.

"Keep the moccasins on and carry your others. They won't show under your skirt, and you'll be more comfortable. You can change them before you get to town."

"Good idea."

The sound of a carriage stopped in front of the house. When Skye opened the door, Alan and Daddy were on the porch.

"Are you ready?" Daddy asked.

Was Alan going with them? Where was Fiona? She may have forgiven the man, but that didn't mean she wanted to be confined in close quarters with him for an hour.

Alan met her eyes. Shrugged.

This would be awkward. She took Daddy's arm and let him help her into the carriage. She took the seat next to Mama. At least she could distance herself from Alan as much as possible.

Someone called out, and Daddy and Alan turned toward the voice. Walker. He appeared in the doorway. "You are leaving us, Miss Stratton?"

"I'll return Monday. I want to spend time with my family."

Walker looked at her clothes, then back at her face. Was that disappointment? "Enjoy your time. I look forward to seeing you soon." He shook hands with Daddy, then Alan. Only, when he gripped Alan's hand, the two seemed to clench tighter, longer than a normal handshake, almost like they were about to arm wrestle.

Then Alan smiled a toothy grin and said, "It was great seeing you, Chief Walker. I suppose I'll see you on Monday as well." He climbed into the stage with a cat-ate-the-canary smile that died as soon as he saw Skye's disapproving look.

Skye leaned forward. "Chief Walker, thank you for all your kindness. I'm very grateful for your help as I've adjusted to my new role here." Then she gave him her warmest smile, and Walker smiled back before he threw Alan a triumphant grin.

Walker told Mama good night, and they waved as the stagecoach pulled away, away from the reservation, away from Skye's new family, away from the part of her identity she'd lost for more than fifteen years. Now that she'd found it, she didn't want to leave it behind.

CHAPTER 29

The quarter moon gave just enough light for the driver to see where he was going. It was a good thing it was as dark as it was, because Alan felt as out of place as a coon dog at a cotillion. Skye clearly didn't want him there. She couldn't open up to her parents with him sitting across from her.

Mrs. Stratton placed one hand on her daughter's in a gentle, loving movement, but he could see what Skye couldn't. On Emma's other side, her hand rested on the seat, and she clenched and unclenched her lace handkerchief in what could only be anxiety. Was it over her daughter's choices? The driver's borderline inebriation? But Riley had questioned him, and the man had walked a straight line and sworn he was as sober as a Sunday School teacher.

Nobody said anything. Alan was grateful he hadn't received the blunt end of Riley Stratton's fist against his jaw after he'd spilled the details of the past weeks.

Emma Stratton had avoided eye contact with him all evening.

And now Skye, though she said she forgave him... Well, he was pretty sure that just meant she didn't hope he'd die a premature, unseemly death. It didn't mean she wanted to spend time with him. Time that, if he weren't here, he was certain she'd spend telling her parents what a louse he was.

Riley looked out his window, even though it was too dark to enjoy the scenery. Skye lay her head on her mother's shoulder and closed her eyes.

Alan might as well do the same. He leaned his head against his side of the carriage and prayed this trip would end soon. The quarter hour they'd been driving already stretched into oblivion.

They'd traveled maybe ten minutes more, no one saying a word, when the stage jerked them around, slamming Alan's head against the carriage wall and leaving him with a gash at his hairline. The jerking only lasted a moment before they were at a dead stop, tilted in a precarious position. Each of the four passengers clung to the seat and walls. At this angle, Emma Stratton pressed against Skye, while Riley strained not to slide into Alan's lap. A slurry of obscene words spilled from the driver's mouth and wafted, like a foul odor, through the open windows.

The man's face appeared in the window nearest Riley. "You folks all right? I musta ran in a hole. Looks like the wheel's broke. No worries. I have a spare strapped under the carriage. I'll need some help, though."

He held the lantern up, and they all squinted at the light.

"Alan! You're bleeding." Skye's voice held shock and concern and…was that compassion? Did she care?

For just a moment, Alan was glad for the gash. "I'm all right."

"No, you're not. Here." She grabbed her mother's handkerchief, reached across the carriage, and held it to his head. The action brought her face close to his, and he looked at her, hoping for some hint of their previous spark. She met his eyes, held them for only a moment, then looked at her mother.

"Mama, you see to Alan. I'll get out and hold the lantern so Daddy and the driver can change the wheel."

Alan wasn't about to play the ninny while two other men and Skye took care of the broken wheel. He took the handkerchief, dabbed the wound, and said, "Really, I'm fine. It's just a scratch." He climbed out of the vehicle behind Riley.

Both women scrambled out after him, and Skye grabbed the lantern and held it. Man, she was a hard-headed woman. Hard-headed and soft-hearted. And that combination was exactly what captured him, tied him up, and held him hostage. Probably for the rest of his days.

Riley was already on his back under the vehicle, loosening the spare wheel. The driver struggled to hold up the carriage. The last thing they needed was for it to fall and hurt someone. Alan knelt and tucked his shoulder under the floorboard, absorbing some of the weight.

"Not too much. Don't want to tip it the other way." The driver sounded fully sober now, but Alan questioned whether or not one two many sips from a flask hadn't contributed to their current situation.

The coach was heavier than a wagon, which surprised Alan. He could feel his muscles quiver under the weight. Would he and the other man be able to hold it? What was taking Riley so long?

Skye must have noticed his strain. "Mama, here. Hold the lantern."

Surely she wasn't going to try and help. Stubborn woman.

Instead, she disappeared into the dark. When she returned, she was lugging a large, flat rock. She set it on the ground behind Alan and disappeared again. One by one, she found rocks and stacked them until they reached the bottom of the rig. About that time, Riley got the wheel loose and crawled out. Her weight-bearing contraption would hold things in place while they changed the wheel.

When Alan was certain it was safe, he released his hold. Stood. Rolled his shoulders and neck, stretched his arms, trying to work out the kinks. Riley, Emma, and the driver discussed how best to remove the damaged wheel. Alan stretched his neck again and noticed Skye looking at him. He held her gaze, moved closer.

"Calamity seems to follow you around, you know that?" His words were soft, teasing, not accusing.

"It didn't until you came along, Mr. McNaughten."

"I suppose that's true." Could she read his thoughts? Did she know what she did to him?

She brushed a loose strand of hair away from her eyes, and something sparkled on her wrist.

"That's a pretty bracelet. Did one of your students give you that?"

Her eyes moved to her wrist. "Actually, Walker gave it to me."

He felt like he'd been gut-punched. Had she transferred her affections so quickly? Less than a week ago, they shared a kiss. He didn't know what to say, so he turned his back on her and joined the conversation about how to fix that dadgum wheel, in the middle of the dadgum woods, in the middle of the dadgum night.

CHAPTER 30

*S*unday afternoon, Skye sat on the bed in her room at the Livingston Hotel, facing her parents, wondering if she'd disappointed them somehow. Their expressions of concern left her not knowing what to say, what to do, to make things right.

"You know we support your decision to come here. And we know you're perfectly capable of handling your own affairs." Daddy leaned forward in the wooden, straight-backed desk chair. "But I hope you'll at least listen to us. It's one thing to teach on the reservation. But if you move there, live there, become one of them, it will be hard for you to come back. It's not right, but society won't be kind to you."

She should have known this talk was coming. This morning, they'd had breakfast in the hotel dining room before attending church. They'd sat with Alan and his mother, who thanked Skye for the cough remedy. Then they all dined together at the hotel, and the whole charade of trying to act *normal* in front of Alan, trying to be kind to him without dying inside every time she looked into those eyes the color of the clear Lampasas River in summer, trying not to notice how well he filled out his Sunday suit, trying not to be mad at him after she said she forgave him, well, she was exhausted. She needed a nap.

She held her father's gaze. "Daddy, society has never been kind to me."

The look of confusion, then hurt that passed her daddy's eyes stabbed Skye's conscience.

"I know you love me," she was quick to add. "I'm grateful for all you've done for me. But I'll never truly be accepted in your world. I might be accepted in that world."

"What do you mean, you were never accepted?" he asked. "That's ridiculous. You are our daughter."

"I can't go back to Lampasas. Not with Uncle Colt. He'll never get over the shame he feels that a half-Indian is his blood relative. He's too bitter, too powerful. He'll never rest until I'm gone. Permanently."

Mama moved next to her on the bed, pulled Skye's head to her shoulder. "He is a horrible man." Then, as if second-guessing her words, she said, "I'm sorry, Riley. I know he's your brother, but he is."

Daddy didn't deny it. "I'll deal with Colt when we get home. Right now, *you're* my concern. Alan told me his side of the story on the way to the reservation last night. Now I'd like to hear about everything that's happened since we put you on that train, from your point of view."

So, for the next hour, Skye told them everything. *Everything.* The train ride. The holdup. The kidnapping and her part in Charlie's rescue. She told them about the flirting and the dance and yes, even the kiss. And she sobbed her way through it until she was a big, blubbery mess and her nose was stuffy and her eyes were swollen and she could barely speak. The whole time, Mama held her and stroked her hair. When she finished, she blew her nose into Mama's lace hanky. At this rate, Mama wouldn't have any hankies left.

Finally, she curled up on her bed, Mama next to her, and

sobbed. She heard the door open and close, Looked to see Daddy had gone. Next thing she knew, she woke up, and her head throbbed like she'd been through a hailstorm without a bonnet.

~

"Mr. McNaughten, I need to talk to you. Now."

Alan opened his eyes at the harsh words. He was staying in the barn.

He hadn't brought himself to move back into his old room just yet. It still had Skye's fingerprints all over it. It even smelled like her. Besides, what if she decided to come back and stay with them again? He wanted to leave everything just the way she left it. He sat up and stretched his neck to see over the side of the loft.

Riley Stratton glared up at him.

"Yes, sir. I'll be right down." He ran his hands through his hair, pulled out a few strands of hay, and tried to shake himself awake from his nap. Climbed down, then turned to meet the man's openly hostile gaze. "What can I do for you?"

"I oughtta plant my fist right in your jaw. That'd make me feel a lot better, for a minute, anyway. Instead, I need you to do your job."

Alan braced himself. He wasn't sure if that punch might come at any moment. "What part of my job is that, sir?"

"The part where you find a safe place for my daughter to live while she teaches on the reservation."

"Yes, sir. I…uh… She was staying here."

"That's not an option anymore. Not unless you decide to move back to D.C. What I need from you, *Agent,* is for you to find a house within ten minutes of the reservation that I can buy. And if there's not one available, find me some property, and I'll build her a house."

"I'm not sure it's a good idea for Skye to…" The irritation in the other man's eyes made Alan rethink his familiarity. "I mean, for Miss Stratton to live alone out there."

"Then I'll stay here and live with her until she makes up her mind about whether or not she wants to remain on at the reservation. You grew up here. You know people. Ask around. Find us a place."

Alan tried to catch up with Riley's words.

Riley clenched and unclenched his fists.

"Yes, sir. Right away, sir." He lifted his saddle off its place on the wall and began to ready Fiona.

"Where are you going?"

"To the reservation. If there's a home anywhere near there, they'll know."

"I'm coming with you. I'll meet you at the livery." The man walked away without so much as a by-your-leave.

Alan knew Riley Stratton was a good man, unlike his brother. But they shared one quality. It was dangerous to be on the wrong side of a Stratton.

Just over an hour later, Alan and Riley spoke with Chief Scott. After hearing their predicament, Chief Scott directed them to a place about three miles on the opposite side of the reservation. "No one has lived there for years. I don't know what kind of shape it's in. But the young man whose family owns it has stopped by here a few times. I believe he would be open to selling it. I'm sorry to say, I don't recall his name." He summoned Walker, who led them to the remote cabin.

It wasn't the worst Alan had seen. Clearly, a family had once lived there. The log structure had two rooms on the main floor, a closed off bedroom and a common room with a place for cooking, eating, and living. Above the living room was a loft with enough room for another bed.

The main room held a table and four chairs. A rusty iron

skillet hung near the fireplace. The windows didn't have glass, but the wood shutters seemed sturdy.

"Someone keeps an eye on this place. If it were truly abandoned, there'd be evidence of animals." Riley opened up the cupboards and examined the walls for structure. "It seems pretty sound."

Alan's gut twisted to think Skye would be even further from him, even closer to Walker. But right now, there wasn't much he could do about that. "I'll see if I can find out who owns it."

Riley left him standing in the cabin. "You do that, Agent."

Alan looked at Walker, who'd stayed silent during the interaction.

Walker flashed him a smile, part superiority, part mischief, and followed Riley outside.

CHAPTER 31

Two weeks later, Skye finally felt her teaching job had settled into a nice routine. The students understood her expectations and were, for the most part, hard-working, well-behaved, and respectful. She'd ordered supplies from the general store in Livingston, and though Daddy wouldn't own up to it, she was pretty sure he'd paid for a lot of it.

The students were thrilled with their new slates, chalk, pencils, and paper. The inkwells were new to them, and Skye showed them how to shape the ends of feathers to use as pens. Mary recalled doing that as a girl, but they hadn't had easy access to ink or paper on the reservation for years, so they'd used their old, cracked slates with chalk rocks. Today, the students would write letters and draw pictures to send back to Lampasas, to Skye's first students. As promised.

What *wasn't* falling into place was Skye's living quarters. She grew weary of the hour-long drive to and from The Livingston Hotel every day. Daddy drove her in his rented carriage. She had no idea what he did during the hours between, but he was always there when school let out, ready to drive her home. She loved the time with him, but it did make for a long day.

She also missed being able to cook her own meals, sit on the front porch, and watch the fireflies play. Right now, her front porch was Livingston's Main Street.

On Friday afternoon, Daddy dropped her off at the hotel and said he'd meet her later, after he took care of some business. She found Mama in the hotel parlor, looking through the books in the limited library. "Mama, how long do you and Daddy plan to stay? I love it that you're here, but what about Cordell and Anita? And I know you miss having your own space."

Mama smiled that I-have-a-secret smile she always wore around birthdays and Christmas. "Cordell and Anita are having the time of their lives, being spoiled rotten by your uncle. He's taking them fishing every day after school. No doubt Anita will have unlearned all her manners by the time we return."

Skye smiled at the thought but said, "You didn't answer my question."

Mama returned the book she was holding and chose another one. "We're to have dinner with a new business associate of your father's. We'll meet him at seven-thirty. I know that's short notice, but it gives you time to rest and freshen up. I know you're tired from working all day." Apparently, Mama was full of mysteries, and she wasn't going to reveal her secrets.

"Any suggestions for what I should wear?"

"Wear what you want. You'd look beautiful in a potato sack."

"I think I have one. Maybe I'll wear it."

Mama shot her a don't-be-sassy look and went back to perusing the books. "I ordered a bath for you. It should be ready about now."

"Thanks. You're a peach." She kissed her mother on the cheek before heading to her room. She deposited her things on her desk and flopped onto her bed. Dinner with Daddy's business associate. Sounded like a stuffy, boring way to spend an evening. All she wanted to do was curl up with a book and read until she fell asleep. Plus, she had math papers to grade.

Well, there was nothing to do about it. She would not dishonor her parents by begging off this dinner. She pulled herself up, gathered her toiletries, and headed down the hall to the bathing room. That was one indulgence she would not deny herself.

A few minutes later she leaned back, closed her eyes, and let the warm suds wash over her. Questions sifted and swirled in her mind, and she couldn't fully relax. For weeks, Walker had paid her special attention. She knew his intentions were honorable. But could she really embrace the Indian way of life after the life she'd led? Could she be happy as a chief's wife, never wearing silk again or carrying a parasol, not able to stroll through town and window shop with her mother? She supposed none of that would matter if she really loved him. But when she pictured her life twenty years from now, it wasn't Walker's face she pictured sharing it with.

It was Alan's.

And that was a malady she wished she could rinse away as easily as she washed the day's grime from her body.

She dried and returned to her room to dig through the clothes Mama had brought—the ones Skye initially thought were a waste of space. Would she ever need to wear such fine things again?

She would tonight. She selected the dress Mama had commissioned from Mrs. Wesson for Skye's graduation from Centenary College. It was silvery-gray silk with vertical stripes of ivory lace and burgundy-and-mauve roses. The oversize, leg-of-mutton sleeves helped emphasize the cinched waist and peplum, and the simple, scooped neckline provided a lovely frame for her heart-shaped, rose quartz pendant necklace and earrings. This may be her last time in who-knew-how long that she'd get to fix herself up. Maybe ever.

She took extra time with her hair. How long had it been since she'd taken such trouble with her appearance?

Oh...the dance. With Alan. Three weeks ago.

She sat on the embroidery-cushioned stool and looked in the mirror. Turned this way and that, examining herself from every angle. Her hair was lighter brown than that of her Indian relatives. Her eyes, too. Golden flecks, with just a hint of green, gave a nod to her paternal heritage.

Dressing in pretty clothes...that was a big part of her identity. In public society, in a world where she felt she had to stay quiet and keep her thoughts hidden, her clothing had always been a silent form of self-expression.

And then it occurred to her... Did the Indians feel the same way? Like a part of their identity had been stripped when they were issued government-ordered clothing and encouraged to dress like white people? The thought made her sad, and tonight, she didn't want to be sad.

God, why does life have to be so complicated?

She pushed her musings to the side and made her way to the hotel parlor. Mama was already there, a big smile on her face.

A familiar masculine voice spoke from the corner of the room. "Miss Stratton, there are no words to describe how lovely you look."

She turned, and there was David in a black tuxedo and sling, looking quite dapper and comical at the same time.

"David!" Without thought to propriety, she flung her arms around his neck with as much care and caution as one could use while flinging, so as not to bump his shoulder.

He wrapped his one good arm around her waist and laughed. "And I was worried you wouldn't remember me."

"That's absurd." She drew back and gave him a teasing smile, then reached for his mother, who stood alongside. "Mrs. Kelly. What are you doing here? David wrote that you might visit sometime, but I thought I'd have some warning! This is such a pleasant surprise."

"I'm glad it's a pleasant one. Those are always the best kind." Mrs. Kelly's eyes sparked with humor.

Skye looked between the two, and she couldn't keep her cheeks from stretching in a delighted smile. "I thought you would write, or at least wire me, before you came."

David held out his good arm, and she tucked her hand in his elbow. "I'd planned to. When I received a business offer from a man named Stratton who happened to be in Livingston, I thought it might be your family, but I wasn't sure. I thought if it was, it might be a fun surprise. If the name turned out to be a coincidence, I thought I'd send a calling card and hoped you'd make time for me. We arrived this morning. Mother and I met with your parents this afternoon." His grin turned shy. "I brought you these." He motioned to a vase of yellow roses on the table.

"Oh, David! They're beautiful. Thank you."

Mama and Mrs. Kelly watched as if they were the audience at a romantic play.

The entry doors opened, and a wave of sunlight washed over the room. A silhouette of two tall, broad men was backwashed by the sun, but Skye didn't need to see their faces to recognize those shapes. Daddy and Alan.

What was Alan doing here?

Alan stepped inside and closed the door behind him. He looked at her, and she couldn't identify his expression. Discomfort? Sadness? She nodded to him and looked away.

"David." Alan's greeting was terse. Usually he was so diplomatic and charming.

"Agent." David's greeting was just as clipped. These men had practically been through battle together. You'd think they'd be happier to see one another.

Daddy shook David's good hand, then kissed Skye on top of her head. He looked at Mama and Mrs. Kelly. "Ladies, I believe we're ready if you are." Instead of leading them into the hotel dining room, he led them outside. Skye wasn't aware of another restaurant in town.

Alan held out his arm as if to escort Skye. Immediately David was on her opposite side, his good arm facing her, his elbow crooked for her to take.

Skye heard Mama giggle, then cough to cover it, and it dawned on Skye that the men were acting like two bucks after the same doe. She decided the only polite choice was to take each of them by their arms, herself in the middle.

The only problem was, they wouldn't all three fit through the door.

Mama snorted, then coughed again. Skye shot her a *be-quiet* look and dropped both their arms. "It looks like we'll have to take turns, gentlemen." She stepped outside and held the handrail to descend the short stairs to the sidewalk.

Another man stood with Daddy on the sidewalk.

Walker.

He smiled at her, his white teeth gleaming in the evening sun. He wore a brown suit and tie, and his hair was combed back, away from his face. He looked positively...white? No. Civilized? Whatever the adjective, she knew he looked *handsome.*

Walker's eyes flitted behind her to David and Alan, and the smile tightened and lost some of its luster. He spoke to both of them, but there was that same competitive buck look in his eyes.

Skye looked at Mama, eyebrows raised, in a silent plea for help.

Mama drew up beside her and linked arms. "Pardon me, gentlemen. May I steal my daughter while we walk?" She pulled Skye onto the sidewalk behind Daddy.

She glanced over her shoulder to see Walker fall in step with Alan. David brought up the rear with Mrs. Kelly.

Mama leaned close and whispered, "Your father wanted Mr.

Walker to be included in this dinner, but the hotel dining room does not allow Indians to dine there. Mr. and Mrs. McNaughten offered to host us."

Skye felt like she'd been punched. "Did Daddy tell them that I'm an Indian?"

Mama squeezed her arm. "No need to make more trouble for you here. But if you want him to, I'm sure he'll be happy to bring up the issue later."

Skye had tried to avoid that kind of "trouble" all her life. "Why are all these men here, Mama? Is Daddy trying to marry me off, or scare me witless so I'll come running back to Lampasas?"

Mama giggled again.

"It's not funny! What is happening?"

"It's all quite innocent, I assure you. Just wait until dinner, and your father will explain everything."

"You're really not going to tell me?"

"Skye, we have no control over the power you hold over the male species. Your father was quite unaware of Mr. Kelly's interest in you, I assure you. We both assumed he was a paunchy old bald man, and we had no idea the two of you had ever met. But I must say, this *will* make for an entertaining evening."

"For you, maybe."

Mama squeezed her arm. "Oh, stop being so stuffy. How many women can claim to have enjoyed three suitors in one night? Relax and enjoy it."

Mama might enjoy the show, but Skye had not auditioned for the lead in this particular drama. All she could see in her immediate future was one very long, very miserable night.

*A*lan sat at the long, picnic-style table in his back yard, drinking sweet tea from a mason jar. The sun setting in the distance turned the sky a golden amber, with wavy stripes of purple, orange, and blue. It was stunning. Like Skye.

She sat across from him, between David and Walker, looking very much like a Rembrandt painting. She was perfect. And though the table only spanned a few feet, he felt like there was a chasm between them.

David leaned over and whispered something in Skye's ear, and she smiled and blushed. Said something back.

Alan felt nauseated.

In all his days, Alan couldn't recall a single time when it was harder for him to be kind. To smile, show interest in other people, and pour on the charm. It was why so many people had encouraged him into politics. But right now, diplomacy was the last thing on his agenda.

Who did this David fellow think he was? Skye wasn't about to move to Houston to be some financier's wife. Was she? She wanted to teach. And she wanted to be near her Indian roots. But Alan could see this man had another agenda, and Alan didn't like it. Not one bit.

And Walker. Did he *really* think Skye could fit in with his life on the reservation?

Okay, she could probably fit in just fine in any setting. But would she be truly happy with Walker? Alan wanted to punch both men in the jaw and settle this once and for all. He could win against David. Walker would be harder...

But that would hardly be the way to win back Skye's affections. If Alan had only been honest with her from the start instead of trying to cover up his shady dealings with Colt...but he hadn't been. Would she ever trust him again?

Probably not. But he wouldn't go down without a fight.

Riley pushed his chair back from the table and stretched his legs out. "Mrs. McNaughten, that was the best meal I've had since I can recall."

Alan had sampled the food at The Big Skye Inn, but he had to agree that his mother's simple, homespun cooking could rival any fancy restaurant.

Ma beamed. "We're not done yet. I have peach cobbler."

Several of them groaned.

"We can wait a few minutes." Ma was in her element, and feeling better than Alan had seen her feel since he'd returned from D.C.

"I suppose now is a good time to discuss the business at hand." Riley looked at his daughter.

"Please do." Skye arched that one brow at her father, and everyone chuckled.

"Well, daughter. Since you're determined to leave your poor mother and father to waste away, all alone, in our golden years—"

"Speak for yourself, sir." Emma Stratton threw her husband a defensive look, bringing more laughter.

"All right. Since you're determined to leave your father to waste away while your youthful mother cares for him alone so you can pursue your passion of teaching, I figured you needed a more permanent place to stay. I found a cabin near the reservation, and after doing a little digging at the courthouse, Agent McNaughten and I learned that the Kelly family owns that land and have wanted to sell it. I had no idea, of course, that you were already acquainted with them, but when you have a famous daughter who is not only a world traveler but a child-saving, outlaw-fighting heroine, it's to be expected that everyone will already know her."

Skye appeared to be fighting a smile, and her dimples formed deep caverns in her perfectly-formed cheeks. Alan noticed Walker couldn't take his eyes off her either. David reached over and touched her arm with his good hand, and she smiled at him before looking back at her father.

"David sent a wire when I first contacted him that they'd be willing to sell me the property for a great price. They even gave me permission to begin making repairs on it. So with Chief Walker's help, and the help of several men from the reservation, the place is ready for you to move in."

A look of true gratitude, mixed with little-girl excitement, captured Skye's face. "My own place? Really?" She clapped her hands and bounced up and down in her chair. She looked all of twelve and absolutely adorable. Alan wanted so much to be the one to put that look on her face.

Riley continued. "Yes. But with a condition. I don't believe it's safe for you to live alone. So, while making repairs on the cottage, we built another cottage next door. Chief Walker and Agent McNaughten have arranged for Mary, Sam, and Tálwan to live there for the time being. That will leave you less vulnerable, yet still give you some privacy. It will also give you opportunity to develop your relationship with that branch of your family."

The table grew quiet. For the first time that evening, Alan took his focus off his own ailing heart and noticed Riley's glistening eyes.

Emma sniffed and wiped at her cheek. How difficult this must be, to release their daughter to people they don't even know. People who very well may claim her identity.

That, he realized, was what love did. It set aside one's own wants in favor of what was best for the other person.

He looked at Walker. At David. Both honorable men. Both would love her, care for her tenderly, for the rest of their days. That was what she needed, an honorable man. In that area, he had failed miserably.

God, help me be an honorable man. And if it's all right with you, let Skye love me again. His stomach muscles clenched. *But if that's not Your plan, then let whatever man she chooses love her well.*

"Your mother and I will stay here for two more weeks and help you get settled," Riley said. "And I know Chief Walker and Agent McNaughten will do all in their power to make sure you're safe and comfortable."

Walker nodded, and so did Alan. Skye stood up, made her way to her mother, and wrapped both arms around Emma's neck from behind. "Thank you. Thank you so much." Then she turned to Riley. "Daddy, thank you. I don't know what to say."

She hugged her father tight. When she let go, for a brief moment, her eyes locked with Alan's, and the joy there dimmed just a little before she looked away.

On second thought, God, I'm pretty sure she's the woman You have for me. It won't be easy to win her trust again. I'm gonna need Your help.

CHAPTER 32

Saturday morning, Skye was up before the sun, dressed in her green traveling suit and ready to go, pacing in the parlor before the dining room even opened. Today she would see her new house! Imagine. Her own place. How grown up.

She'd use her teaching money to buy fabric for curtains, maybe a sofa or a chaise lounge. So what if it was a rustic cabin in the woods? It was *hers.* She could decorate it however she wanted. After a time, she took a seat in the parlor and watched the grandfather clock tick the seconds by. Fifteen minutes until breakfast was served. She hoped no one was late.

Footsteps on the staircase drew her eyes up, and David turned the corner. His eyes crinkled at the corners when he saw her. "Skye. I thought I'd be the first one down." He sat in the chair next to hers. "You look lovely today."

"Thank you. I suppose I'm too excited for my own good. Tell me. How did you come to own this property?"

A wistful look passed through David's eyes. "My grandparents lived in that cabin when they were first married. My father was born there. Throughout my childhood, we'd visit every year or two, and I have such pleasant memories of playing in the woods, finding pinecones and using them as toy soldiers, and watching the squirrels hoard acorns in their fat little cheeks. There's a little stream that runs through the back of the property. Sometimes I fished. Mostly I just splashed around."

"Why are you selling it?"

David rested his head against the side of his chair. "As the years passed, life got busier, and we visited less and less. My father isn't in the best of health, and he doesn't want to see the place disintegrate for lack of use. We discussed it, and he decided if we could find a buyer who would actually live there and care for the place, he'd sell it. Most people lose interest as soon as they learn it borders the reservation. If they only knew the Alabama-Coushatta people, they'd know they make excellent neighbors and friends."

Skye warmed inside. "Thank you for saying that."

He looked surprised. "It's true. I love that you've chosen to work with their children, to provide them with an education. You're an admirable woman."

"Thank you. Did you know I'm part Coushatta?"

"I gathered that after your father's speech last night. He mentioned the Indian part of your family."

"That doesn't...offend you?"

"It does not. I suppose that must come as a surprise to you, given the popular opinion regarding Indians. But I have my own experience with being an outcast. I tend to sympathize with anyone with similar experience."

"Really? How?"

He chuckled. "I imagine you'll be shocked to learn that I was a sickly child, given my fine display of masculinity in recent days." He feigned flexing his muscles, but his thin arms didn't fill out his jacket at all.

She smiled. She liked a man who could laugh at himself.

"At school, I never did quite fit in. I was the smart, skinny kid who missed too many days due to a deep cough and who still made the highest marks in the class. Not the best way to win friends, I suppose."

Skye placed one hand on his arm. "You've won me as a friend."

He placed his other hand on top of hers. "I'm glad to hear that."

"Please know that you're a welcome guest at the cabin any time. Just send me a wire ahead of time so I can make arrangements for a chaperone."

His eyes warmed, and he leaned forward. "I don't suppose you'd allow me to—"

"Good morning, you two!" Mama stood, arm in arm with Mrs. Kelly, at the parlor entry. "It's time for breakfast. Eat up, because we have a big day ahead."

What had David been about to say? Was he going to ask if he could call on her? Oh, dear. She wouldn't hurt him for the world. But as much as she adored David Kelly, she didn't think she could ever see him that way.

What was she doing wrong? She tried not to flirt or be coy. The last thing she wanted to do was lead David to believe she had feelings she didn't have. It looked like today would be another very long day.

But she was wrong. The day passed in a flash. The cabin was adorable and clean and promised a gorgeous view of the sunrise in the east and the sunset in the west. Mama and Daddy told her they'd opened an account for her at the general store so she could order whatever she wanted.

"Thank you. I'll let you purchase a few basics for me to get started. But I want to pay for most of it myself."

Daddy looked hurt, but the look quickly shifted to pride.

Mama just shook her head. "You always were a stubborn, independent child. We'll leave the account open for you. Feel free to use it for what you need."

The rest of the group filed out of the cabin to examine the newer one, where Mary, Sam, and Tálwan would live. Skye lingered in her home, looking around, imagining where she'd put this or that. She felt like a little girl fixing up her dollhouse.

"You seem pleased." Alan stood just outside the doorway, waiting for her.

"It's lovely. It's a little scary to think of living out here by myself, but I'll have Mary right next door. It will be a lot more convenient."

"I'll be here every day. You can count on me for anything you need."

She held his eyes. How could he say such a thing after he'd already betrayed her in the worst way? *Judge not, and ye shall not be judged: condemn not, and ye shall not be condemned: forgive, and ye shall be forgiven.* "Thank you."

They walked to the new cabin together, and his nearness brought a gentle, miserable ache to Skye's heart. She wanted to trust him. *God, show me what to do. I love this man. I don't want to, but I do. If he's going to break my heart, then please. Change my heart.*

She caught sight of Walker, who'd met them at the cabin site, deep in conversation with her father. He saw her looking and flashed that perfect smile, and she returned it. *Show me whom to love, Lord. Or, if you want me to be an old maid, I guess that's okay too. It's how I always expected my life to turn out.* Except, she really, *really* didn't want to be an old maid.

~

*A*lan didn't know whether to be happy or disappointed that Riley and Emma were leaving today. He knew Riley didn't like him. Not that the man was ever rude, and Alan didn't blame him for his hostility. If some man ever broke *his* little girl's heart, he knew he'd feel the same way. But Riley and Emma's presence made it easier for Alan to stop by Skye's cabin each day before he went home. She was always chaperoned, and he could make up some reason for checking on the new teacher.

Several times in the last couple of weeks, he'd had wires to deliver. From Houston. From David, no doubt, but at least that man was far away, and Alan was here, which gave him an advantage.

Walker was another story. He was within a couple miles of Emma. And once her parents left, her only chaperones would be her Indian relatives, and Alan felt pretty sure they'd do all in their power to encourage a match with their young chief.

"What's on your mind, Agent?" Riley took a seat next to Alan on the station bench while Skye and her mother window-shopped across the street. The early October air had a snap to it, and here and there the ground was littered with pinecones.

"On my mind, sir?"

Riley laughed. "Don't play dumb with me. I know you're enamored with my daughter. Anyone with eyes can see that."

Not one for beating around the bush. Like father, like daughter. "I won't deny it. I made a terrible mistake, and I wish I knew how to make it right."

The older man straightened his legs and crossed them at the ankles. "Trust is a fragile thing, like a butterfly's wings. Once it's broken, you may be sorry, but the damage is done."

"A butterfly wing, once damaged, can never be restored. Are you saying trust is like that? Should I just give up?"

Riley remained silent for a minute. The only sign he was considering his answer was one foot tap-tap-tapping on the boardwalk, as if the motion helped his thinking. After a time, the tapping stopped. "Trust is fragile. But while butterflies live only a few weeks, maybe months, humans have more time to heal. One beautiful thing about life being so long is that there's always time for a new start. So you're not without hope." He uncrossed his ankles and angled his body toward Alan. "But I'd say you have a long road ahead. If you're not in it for the duration, I'd prefer you quit the race right now."

Alan met Riley's eyes. "I will do whatever it takes, however long it takes, to win Skye's trust back."

"I appreciate your tenacity. But understand this. You've hurt my daughter once. You do it again, and you'll wish it were Colt you were dealing with instead of me."

Skye and Emma approached, Skye carrying a large, brown-wrapped parcel tied with twine. She held it up with a triumphant smile. "I found the perfect fabric for my curtains, and a coordinating pattern for a tablecloth and some chair cushions."

Emma placed her arm around Skye's waist. "I can't wait to see it all come together. We'll plan another trip around... Thanksgiving?" She looked at her husband like she was asking a question, but Alan got the feeling it was more of a statement.

"Thanksgiving it is. We'll bring your brother and sister next time. That is, if we can get them re-acclimated to civilized behavior after spending a month being spoiled by your Uncle Lyndel." Riley pulled Skye in for a tight hug, and Emma joined the circle.

Alan felt like an intruder on the intimate good-bye. The stagecoach driver—a new one this time—signaled to Emma and Riley that it was time to go.

Riley offered his hand to Alan. "Agent. Take care." He squeezed Alan's hand a little too long, a little too tight for it to go unnoticed. What he really meant was, *Watch yourself, and take care of my daughter.*

Alan reached for Emma's hand, but she pulled him into a hug. She whispered in his ear, so low he was sure no one else could hear, "Be good to our girl. She's a special one."

"I know." He hugged her back, then stood with Skye as they boarded. They watched the stagecoach roll away, both parents leaning out the window, waving until they disappeared into the cloud of dust created by the massive wheels.

While Skye stared in the direction they'd gone as if they might miraculously reappear, Alan felt someone's gaze on him. He searched the streets. There, in front of the saloon, was Clem, the cowboy from Silsbee, not even trying to disguise the open look of hatred on his face. He held Alan's gaze, then turned his eyes to Skye, who was oblivious to the interaction. Clem's lips curled into a sinister grin before he looked back at Alan and disappeared into the building. Alan's blood turned to ice.

"We'd better get you home while it's still daylight. It looks like you have some sewing to do." Alan nudged Skye toward the livery to get her new horse, Chok-fi, meaning *rabbit*. Appropriate, since the Appaloosa was lightweight and fast.

Once she was settled in her saddle and Alan in Fiona's, he turned the opposite way from the reservation and motioned for Skye to follow. He didn't want to ride in front of the saloon. "This way. There's a pretty trail I want you to see."

Skye arched that eyebrow but didn't question him. When they were beyond chance of being sighted from anywhere on Main Street, he found a small path to get them back on track. "Look. Aren't those blue flowers pretty?"

"You mean the hydrangea? The same flowers that grow on the main path we take every day? Yes. They're very pretty." Her voice was teasing, not annoyed.

"Oh. I didn't know what they were called."

She and Chok-fi moved around him on the path, and she began a lesson in botany. "Those are *Black-eyed Susans*. That should be easy for you remember, because see? She has black eyes. That one is a *Bundleflower*, and the one, there, with the layers of color, is called *Indian Blanket*. That yellow one is a *Cat's Claw*, because its thorns curl around. That's how it attaches to trees and other vertical surfaces. It makes a great medicine for arthritis."

"I had no idea you were a botanist. I'm impressed."

"Mary's been teaching me. She's the real expert. All these things grow around the cabin, and we see them on our ride home from school each day."

"This will be your first night without your parents in the cabin with you. How do you feel about that?"

"It'll seem empty. But I'm looking forward to having my own space, too. I'm glad they'll be back in a few weeks, though."

"Lock all your doors and windows. You have a gun, right?"

"Paranoid, Agent? You're making me nervous. Yes, I have a gun, and I will be fine. Mary and Sam are right next door."

"I don't doubt your ability to take care of yourself. I just want you to be extra cautious."

"I've already had the lecture from my parents. Don't worry. I'll be careful."

Alan clamped his mouth shut. He didn't need to press further, or he'd scare her. But something in his spirit told him he needed to stay on high alert.

CHAPTER 33

For Skye, the next few weeks turned into a glorious routine of waking up, going to school, coming home, grading papers, and usually sharing a meal with Mary's family. They took turns cooking and sharing Indian and American recipes. Other than Alan, the only people she saw were Indians, and for the most part, she felt accepted. A few people gave her sideways looks and whispered words like *half-breed* and *Comanche*. But she'd ignored that kind of behavior all her life, so she was pretty good at it.

Each day, Alan waited after school and escorted her and Mary home. He never came inside, but sometimes he sat on her front porch, and she served him tea or lemonade, and they'd talk like old friends. Which in a way, they were. Yet something inside her waged war. She wanted more, but how long until he betrayed her again?

Each day, about a half hour after Alan left, Walker showed up, asking if she needed anything, offering to fix this or that. Sometimes he stayed for supper, and they ate around the fire pit.

But after Walker left and Mary, Sam, and Tálwan retired,

Skye often lay awake. Something felt off. She was sure it was because this was the first time since living with Mama and Daddy she'd been alone at night. She had memories of after her first mother died, when her first father still lived, when he would leave at night and stay gone until the wee hours and come home smelling of alcohol. She'd been scared then. Now, she reassured herself that she was fully capable of caring for herself, and that no one was coming home drunk.

She'd get used to it, with time.

Walker often lingered after Mary's family retired. Tonight, they sat on the porch. The fireflies had long since burrowed into their homes in the ground, and she offered Walker a blanket before wrapping one around herself. This was easy. Comfortable. Her feelings for Walker weren't the same as her feelings for Alan, but she could grow old with Walker. Maybe.

Maybe she could choose Walker.

"Who do you want to be, Skye?" Walker played with the fringe on the edge of his blanket.

"Who do I want to be?" It was a strange question. Yet she thought she understood.

"Do you want to be Indian? Or do you want to be white?"

She didn't answer him for a long time, and he seemed comfortable with the silence. The stars blinked at them from the heavens, and she searched them as she searched her heart for an honest answer. "I am both."

"Yes."

"I suppose I don't want to be one more than the other. Both races are part of who I am."

"I respect your answer. But you cannot live in both worlds any more than you can simultaneously swim and walk on dry land. If you try, you'll not do either one well."

"I-I don't know what to say. I am both. That's my answer."

The quiet stretched between them like threads on a loom. After a time, Walker shifted. Stood. Folded the blanket and placed it on the chair. "May I tell you what I have come to see, Skye?"

"Of course."

"I see a beautiful woman, both white and Indian. A woman who loves to dress in fancy dresses, who enjoys buying pretty fabrics and sewing curtains and cushions. A woman who knows how to be white more than she knows how to be Indian."

Skye sucked in a breath. That stung. Was he trying to insult her? To hurt her?

"Please do not be offended," he said. "You are beautiful and unique. Surely you must know how I've come to care for you. But one day, I will be chief. All my days, I will live on the reservation. Our women are not allowed to leave except under government orders. Only select men are allowed to even visit the town, and that only during daylight hours. Do you think you could live that way?"

Could she?

"You don't have to answer me," Walker said. "I just want you to think about it."

"If my grandmother hadn't been kidnapped, the reservation is the only life I would know." She couldn't help feeling defensive.

"If your grandmother hadn't been forced to marry a Comanche, you would not exist. If your mother had not married your white father, you would not exist. We cannot change what has happened, Skye. It has made you who you are."

"And part of who I am is Indian. It's not fair of you to judge me for things I have no control over."

"I am not judging you. I'm simply wondering what we are doing here. You and me."

She didn't know what to say.

He turned and gripped her porch rails, looking at the stars, like diamonds on velvet. "Do you remember that night when we first met, after the train disaster?"

She nodded but realized he couldn't see her. "Yes."

"You asked to ride with me. Remember? When we approached Silsbee, I told you I had to leave, that I wasn't allowed in town after dark."

"I remember."

He turned, found her eyes. "You didn't even question whether you would be allowed there after dark. It never occurred to you that you'd break a law by entering. By going to your hotel and spending the night and eating in their restaurants and shopping in their stores. It never occurred to you because, though you have Indian heritage, you identify with the white part of your heritage. It's you. It's your history. It's where God placed you in His divine scheme."

She knew Walker meant no harm. But his words hurt all the same. She couldn't choose half of herself and ignore the other half. It wasn't possible. "Maybe so. But right now, I'm here. Right now, *this* is where God has placed me."

"And I'm glad. But Skye, to choose a life with me is to choose a life without all the things that make you...*you*. And your spirit is too beautiful, filled with too many colors, for me to want to change you at all. I have thought much about this. My heart has ached over this decision. I will always be here for you, as a friend. If you need help, I will be here. I give you my word. But I will not visit you in the evenings any more or share private meals with you and your family. We are not a fit, and I must move on. And so should you."

After a moment, he descended the stairs, his moccasined feet silent on the steps. Then he turned, looked up at her, and the moon lit his face so he looked like a celestial being. "I don't believe you'll have to look far to find another who loves you very much."

Just like that, Walker left. And she sat on her porch and cried. Tried to sort through her emotions, to find the reason for the tears. They weren't so much for Walker's gentle rejection as for her realization that no matter what she did, she'd never truly belong anywhere.

~

It was a strange and cruel form of self-inflicted torture for Alan to sleep in the woods near Skye's cabin every night. Every night, a half hour after Alan left, Walker showed up and stayed the rest of the evening, sitting at the fire with Skye and her extended family like they were an old married couple or something. Alan really wanted to dislike Walker, and he hated that the guy was so dadgum *likable*.

But every night, Alan watched from a distance as Mary, Sam and Tálwan retired to their cabin and Walker and Skye lingered by the fire, talking in voices too low for him to understand. Tonight, they moved from the fire to Skye's porch, backlit by a kerosene lamp on a hook, and Alan waited for that painful moment when he'd watch them kiss.

Alan had tried to take it slow and easy. Tried to show her he was interested but that he respected her boundaries. Tried with every hello and good-bye, every glance, every breath he took in her presence, to send the message that he *loved* her. That he'd wait for her. Sometimes, he thought she understood. Other times, she acted indifferent, friendly in a polite-stranger kind of way. Every time that happened, his heart crushed in on itself a little more.

Twice during the last couple of weeks, he'd seen Clem in town, though he didn't think the man saw him. As long as that fellow was around, Alan had no choice. Not after the way the lowlife had looked at Skye. Alan would camp out, far enough away to go undetected, close enough to keep an eye on things. And each day, he got up, bathed in the creek, and showed up at the reservation as if nothing was amiss.

As much as he wanted to look away, his eyes were pulled to

Skye and Walker by an invisible, magnetic pole. When that kiss came, and he was sure it would come, he would die a little bit inside.

But Walker stood, placed his hands on the rail, and looked at the heavens. A couple times, he lowered his eyes, and Alan felt like the man was looking right at him. He held his breath, didn't move, until Walker looked away again.

But Skye remained seated. They talked some more, and then Walker descended the stairs. Alan let out a long, slow breath, sweet relief filling his veins. They hadn't kissed. Walker paused, looked right at Alan again—there was no possible way Walker could see him—then turned and said something else to Skye before leaving her yard.

That's when he heard her quiet sobs.

Anger bubbled and boiled like acid in Alan's chest. What had Walker said to her? Why, Alan ought to…what? He couldn't go after him, and he couldn't comfort her, not without revealing that he'd been creeping around in the shadows outside her house like some kind of reprobate. So he held his breath and held his temper and listened to her cries and inside, his heart imploded with each sniffle.

Then, he heard a twig snap. From the opposite direction of where Walker had gone. Alan sat up, felt for the gun in his holster, and slowly pulled back the hammer, hoping to avoid a loud click.

~

Skye stayed on the porch long after Walker left, her heart pounding, holding her breath until he was far enough away he wouldn't hear her. And then, she cried. And cried and cried, though she tried to keep her sobs to a mini-mum. The last thing she wanted was to wake Mary and Sam and have them ask all kinds of questions she wasn't ready to answer.

She wasn't sure why she cried. She wanted to love Walker, but deep inside, she knew she didn't. She *wanted* to want that life, but he was right. About everything. She didn't fit into his world. She didn't fit into her parents' world. She didn't fit into *anybody's* world. She was a stranger, a misfit, everywhere she went.

Her face was buried in her hands, and she didn't notice anyone approaching until footsteps hit her porch. "Walker?" When she looked up in the darkness, she saw two men's silhouettes against the night sky. Before she could cry out, one of them grabbed her and cupped his mammoth hand tightly over her mouth and nose,

She couldn't breathe, couldn't make a sound.

"Hello, little squaw. I was hopin' we'd meet again. You be real quiet and do everything I say, and you'll be just fine. You hear?"

She struggled, but the other man wrapped his arms around her in the chair, binding her arms to her sides. "Shh-shh-shh. You're a wild one. I like wild squaws, don't you, Clem? We're gonna have fun with this one." Then he tried to kiss her ear, since Clem's hand was still over her mouth. She kicked, but they just laughed, low, quiet laughs nobody would hear.

Oh, God! Help me. Please, save me!

One of the men picked her up—Clem, she thought—and the other held open her door. Clem threw her on the bed and was on top of her before she could catch her breath. He held her mouth again with one hand, clawed and pulled at her clothes with the other, trying to undress her. For a sliver of a moment, he let go of her mouth and she spit at him, but he clamped his hand over her face again before she could scream. The other man grabbed her from the side—their hands were all over her body, and her strength was no match for theirs.

This was happening. Right here, right now. Even if they

didn't leave her dead, they would kill her innocence, kill her virtue, and she would never be the same. *God! Where are You? Please, God.* She couldn't make a sound, but her spirit screamed. Begged. Pleaded. She would not give in to these animals. Let them kill her. She would not give in without a fight. She kicked, squirmed, punched, but nothing seemed to matter.

A loud bang came from behind her, like the door slammed open, then a crash. Something sharp hit her face, and then the men were no longer on her.

"Hold it right there!"

Alan!

He stood in the doorway, a Colt .45 pointed at one of her attackers. Right behind him, with a pistol pointed at the other, was Walker. She scrambled to pull the blanket around her and scuttled back against the wall, pulling her legs to her chest. She tried to make herself as small as possible. Somehow, her mind registered that one of her new chairs was in splinters on the floor. That her blouse—torn at the shoulder. Her skirt—unbuttoned, but still on.

More voices. Sam, she thought. Someone brought in the lantern from the porch and turned it up. She saw with her eyes, but she couldn't comprehend. None of it made sense.

And then there was Mary, her arms around Skye, rocking her back and forth, singing a Coushatta lullaby that Skye's first mother used to sing to her, and Skye tried to block out the shouting and the cursing and the fact that all these people were in her house, in her safe place. And then she was shivering, shaking violently, though she didn't feel cold.

Alan knelt in front of her and asked her something, but she couldn't make her mouth form words, couldn't even make her brain understand what he said, as if he spoke a foreign language.

After a time, Mary pulled on her arm and told her to stand up, and Skye obeyed. Mary fussed over her clothing a bit, then led her to the other cabin, where she took Skye into a back room and gently, matter-of-factly, spoke to her.

"Skye, I need you to tell me what happened. Tell me everything you remember."

Skye tried to form coherent thoughts, but she couldn't.

"Take your time. But I need you to tell me. Were you violated?"

Skye didn't want to relive what happened. She strained her mind, tried to make sense, tried to put things in order. "I-I don't know. I don't think so."

"Think hard, Skye. I need you to tell me. You've done nothing wrong, and even if they did violate you, you are still a good girl. No one can steal your virtue, because virtuous is who you are on the inside. But I need to know so they can be punished accordingly."

Skye forced herself to think back through the last hour.

The men, coming in the dark.

Grabbing.

Holding.

She fought.

Kicked.

Bit.

She could still taste that man's dirty, salty skin. Without warning, she knew she'd lose her dinner. Somehow, Mary was ready with a bucket, then a rag and a cool drink of water.

The trembling returned, her arms, her legs, violently shaking, and Mary sat with her, holding her, humming that lullaby until the trembling stopped. After a long time, Skye felt calm.

Her mind cleared.

And realization covered her like a bridal veil.

God heard her.

He answered.

"No. They didn't violate me. They were going to, but Alan

came in, and Walker, and...the next thing I knew, you were there, singing."

Tears filled in the grooves and lines on Mary's face, and she held Skye close and whispered, "Thank you, God. Thank you, God. Thank you, God."

CHAPTER 34

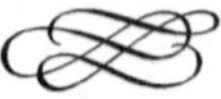

The sun had barely peeked over the horizon when Alan finally stood on Mary and Sam's porch. He knocked softly, just a gentle tap. If Skye was sleeping, he didn't want to wake her. But he had to know. He didn't want to know, felt nauseated just thinking about it, but he had to know the details so he could file a report with the sheriff's office. For the time, the two filthy swine were being held in the jail on the reservation, and Alan instructed the guards to make them as miserable as possible. The two miscreants cried like babies when Alan left. Apparently, they were convinced the Coushatta would scalp them, behead them, and hang their skulls out for the crows.

Alan said nothing to change their perception.

Mary cracked open the door, then held it wider and motioned for Alan to come inside. "She's asleep. Finally."

"Did she talk to you? Did they—?"

"No. They didn't."

Alan exhaled, and without conscious thought, he dropped into one of the ladder-backed chairs. "Thank God. What happened was bad enough. Thank God I got there before it was worse."

Behind him, a door scratched open. He turned, and there was Skye, her hair a mess, her eyes swollen, her cheek bruised and scratched. She was wrapped in a blanket. "Alan?"

He stood, took a step toward her and stopped. "I'm here."

Her eyes watered, and he wanted to take her in his arms, hold her tight, make everything all right. But after what she'd been through, he wasn't sure if he should touch her. Would that make her uncomfortable?

She dragged one arm across her eyes, wiping the tears. "Thank you for being there. I don't know why you were, but thank you."

All rational thought left him, and he had to be closer to her. He took one step, then another, and when she didn't flinch or draw away, he held out his arms in invitation. He'd let her decide.

Her eyes met his, and then she fell forward, her head on his chest, and she cried. And he cried, though he tried with every ounce of willpower to force those tears back inside. But tears have to go somewhere once they surface, and they ended up all over his cheeks, running into her hair as they held each other and he sobbed tears of relief and anger and gratitude and fear and every human emotion he could think of, all wadded up in his chest and spilling down his face.

And then they both calmed, as if their hearts beat as one, and he pulled back just enough to lift her face to his. "You're gonna be okay. It's gonna be okay. I need to go to Livingston, but I'll come back. I promise. Are you all right staying here with Mary and Tálwan for the time being?"

She nodded.

"Once I inform the sheriff of what happened and those miscreants are in jail, I'd like to bring you back to my parents' house. Just for a while. I can even take you back to Lampasas if that's what you want."

She didn't respond for a moment. Then she stiffened her shoulders, pushed them back, and lifted her chin. "Let me think about it. We'll talk when you return."

She turned, as in a daze, stepped back into the little room, and closed the door.

He watched her go, emotions warring within him. *God, I love that woman. I'm going to marry her one day.*

And I'll spend the rest of my days protecting her.

And somehow, in his spirit, he knew God was okay with that.

~

Skye slept harder than she ever remembered sleeping in her life. When she awoke, the sun was low in the sky, and Mary waited with a hot bowl of venison-and-squash stew. Skye ate slowly, then tipped the bowl and drained its contents. She helped clean the dishes, even as Mary fussed for her to sit down.

"I want to go back to my cabin."

"Are you sure?"

Skye nodded. She would not let those men steal her life from her. The longer she waited before going back, the harder it would be. "I'd like you to come with me, but yes."

"Why don't I go over first and straighten things up a bit? I can get some fresh clothes for you to change into."

"No. I need to see it. I need to remind myself of what happened, remind myself that I survived. I won't let them keep me from my home."

Mary covered Skye with a long, slow look, as if assessing her state of mind. "All right. First, let's comb your hair and get you cleaned up. It will make you feel better."

A half hour later, Skye stood in the front room of her cabin, Mary's supporting hand at her back. One of her new porch chairs lay in splinters across the floor. She touched the cut in her cheek. Had Alan used the chair to bludgeon her attackers? It was all a haze.

She walked to the center of the room, turned, and examined the contents. The ordeal had lasted how long? At the time, it felt like an eternity. In retrospect, it probably lasted less than ten minutes.

Her broom rested in its normal place, in the corner by the window. With squared shoulders and stiff chin, she retrieved it and swept up the mess. Mary didn't say a word, just started picking up the larger pieces and piling them in the fireplace.

It took less than five minutes to clean up an event that could have destroyed her. How could evidence of such an episode be eliminated so quickly? She knew the memories would take much longer to purge. But something inside told her the longer she kowtowed in fear, the harder it would be for her to recover.

Do not fear. I am with you.

God had been with her last night. More and more, she could see that He'd been with her even when she wasn't aware of His presence.

Mary stayed, but didn't talk. Just gave Skye space to process. Skye dragged one of the dining chairs out to the porch, and the two women sat and watched the afternoon sun play with the shadows of the pines.

After an hour or so, Alan rode into the opening in the trees. Mary stood. "I need to fix dinner. Are you okay?"

Skye nodded, and the woman rested her hand on Skye's shoulder for a moment before crossing the yard.

Alan looped Fiona's reins around the porch rail. "How are you?"

"Better than I thought I'd be at this point."

He ascended the steps, opened her front door, and looked

inside. He closed it and sat in the other chair. "Those two men are wanted for armed robbery and public disturbance in Silsbee, Beaumont, and Jasper. They also fit the descriptions for several other unsolved cases in the area. I don't think they'll be bothering anybody else anytime soon. If ever."

Skye soaked that in. Would they hang? If they were tried for attempted assault of a white woman, probably. For an Indian woman, doubtful. At least they were behind bars. "Will I have to testify?"

"Only if you want. Since Walker and I saw them in your house, we can make a case without your testimony."

She'd have to consider that. She wasn't sure she wanted to lay eyes on those monsters. She wanted to be brave. But she also had a need for self-preservation. She tipped her chair back, leaned her head against the wall. Mama would swat her for doing such a thing, but it was Skye's house, Skye's porch. Funny. Right then, aside from being a bit banged up, she felt fine. Strong. Even peaceful.

"Have you decided what you want to do? I went ahead and booked tickets on tomorrow's stage to take you back to Lampasas. The tracks out of Houston still haven't been repaired. No pressure. I just wanted you to have the option, and not have to wait another week for the journey."

"If I run home, I may not come back."

"No one would blame you."

"If I run home, I let them win."

"They only win if they destroy you. They won't win."

Skye rolled her head against the wood wall and looked at Alan. "I think I'll stay right where I am."

The look he gave her was part shock, part are-you-out-of-your-mind concern. "Skye. You don't have anything to prove."

"I'm not trying to prove anything. Or maybe I am. I don't know. All I'm sure of is that last night, things could have been much, much worse. But I prayed. I asked God to save me from those men, and then there you were. God protected me. And He will keep doing so. With God on my side, I'm in no more danger here than I would be in Lampasas. I think this is where I'm supposed to be."

Alan moved his gaze to some point across the yard. The muscles in his jaw twitched. Was he angry?

"Skye. Listen to me. You are the strongest, most amazing person I've ever met. I have no doubt about your ability to slay dragons or giants or mountain lions. But even with Mary and Sam and Tálwan right next door, you were vulnerable. What if I hadn't been here?"

"Why *were* you here, since you brought it up?"

Alan's face went from golden tan to tomato-red in a matter of seconds. "I've been camping in the woods. To make sure you were safe."

He mumbled those words, but she was pretty sure she'd heard him correctly. "You've been…what? You've been watching me? Every night?"

"Don't make it sound like I'm some kind of reprobate. I wasn't peeping in your windows, if that's what you mean. But a few weeks ago, I saw Clem in Livingston, and I got a bad feeling. I just wanted to be sure."

"And you didn't see fit to tell me about it?"

"Why would I alarm you when I wasn't even sure?"

"You were alarmed enough to camp out in the woods at night to make sure I was safe, but you…never mind." He had put his life in danger for her. She should thank him. Not scold him.

"I'm sorry if I didn't handle things exactly like you think I should have." Alan ran a hand over his head. "I didn't want to scare you. And I wanted you to be safe. If anything—" His voice broke, and he looked away. Swallowed. "If anything happened to you, I don't know what I'd do."

She tried to read what his heart meant. A few weeks before, she'd thought she could never trust him again. But after last night, after spending weeks camping outside when he could have slept in his own bed at his parents' house... Maybe he was just human. And humans make mistakes. Right about now, she felt like she could trust him more than any other person she knew. He'd *saved* her.

"Skye, I don't care about keeping my job. Let your uncle do what he wants. He can fire me, blacklist my name from ever working in the political arena again. I'll get a job shoeing horses or bailing hay if I have to. I just want you to be safe."

His words soaked into her spirit like rain into the parched earth. Did he mean it? She thought he did.

Her stomach growled. The wind whooshed and whistled through the pines, and the light breeze felt cold on her skin. The only other sound was Mary, at the fire pit, cooking something that smelled delicious.

Neither Skye nor Alan said anything for several minutes.

Finally, Alan turned in his chair. "I don't feel comfortable with you staying here alone. As Indian Agent, I'm in charge of finding a teacher and making sure that teacher is safe. You can either move back to Livingston with my parents or find a boarding house there, or...or you can get married and live here with your husband." He choked on that last part, as if the words tasted bad to him.

Her first thought was to rail at him for being ridiculous. To say that what happened the night before wasn't going to happen again. That he had no right to dictate where she lived. This was her house. That she bought with her own—well, with her Daddy's money.

But she bit back the words. She'd had a lifetime of practice, not saying what she wanted to. In that instance, it was wisdom. It gave her time for another idea to slip in.

Did she dare speak the thought aloud? Before she could talk herself out of it, she decided to be brave. She stood up, rested her fists on her hips, and gave him what she hoped was a teasing grin. "Then I suppose, Agent McNaughten, since it's your job to provide me with what I need to be a successful teacher, you'll just have to find me a husband."

She turned, descended the steps, and refused to let herself look back. Her heart pounded. Had she ever in her life been so brazen?

Mary was already placing venison and fried onions on plates when she approached, and Sam was helping Tálwan to their little outdoor eating area. Skye helped pass out the portions and tried not to visibly react when Alan took a seat on one of the hewn log benches.

She could feel him staring at her. But if she looked at him, she'd blush, and she wanted to keep the upper hand. Don't-look-don't-look-don't-look-don't…

She looked at those cool-water blue eyes that she could drown in if she didn't hang on to her senses. And he smiled.

And she smiled.

"I…um…I'll be sure and work on that supply order you just requested, Miss Stratton."

There it went. The blush that she could feel all the way from her ankles to her eyebrows. But she made herself hold his gaze. "Thank you. I hope it won't take too long."

CHAPTER 35

ONE MONTH LATER

Skye stood at the back of the church while Mama adjusted her veil. "You are the most beautiful bride I've ever seen."

"Thank you, Mama."

She felt beautiful, but not because of her veil, a delicate ivory lace with tiny pearls at the center of each embroidered rose. Not because of her dress, made of ivory satin with the same lace overlay, a scooped neck with tiny satin rosettes along the border, with gathered lace sleeves that hugged her arms to the elbows, then flared and fell to her wrists, with a cinched-in waist that emphasized her curves or the flared skirt that swooshed when she walked. Not because of the embroidered satin train that would trail half the length of the small church. None of that could make her feel any more beautiful than she felt, simply because she was loved.

Loved by a man who'd risked his life for her.

Loved by parents who'd chosen her through adoption.

And from the looks of the overcrowded church, more loved by her Lampasas, Texas, community than she'd ever realized.

The door to the sanctuary creaked open, and Aunt Allison stepped into the vestibule. "I know this is a private moment, and I'm sorry to intrude. But I have something for you." Her eyes were shiny, and she held out a small box.

Skye opened it. Inside was a silver necklace with a single pearl bead.

"It belonged to your grandmother. I thought you might like to have it, to wear today, if you want."

People never ceased to surprise her. "It's beautiful, Aunt Allison. Thank you." She unclasped it, and Mama and Aunt Allison helped attach it around her neck.

Aunt Allison smiled, touched Skye's cheek, and disappeared back into the sanctuary.

Daddy placed a hand on each of her shoulders. "As pretty as your mother, and prettier than all others." His eyes were moist, and his voice wobbled a little.

Skye rewarded him with a smile. She'd smiled so much over the last few days, her cheeks hurt. "I love you, Daddy."

"I love you too, baby girl."

Mama sniffled, dabbed at her eyes. "I'd better go find my seat." With one last look that held all the love a mother's heart could contain, she slipped through the sanctuary door.

The organ music changed from "Be Thou My Vision" to Mendelssohn's Bridal March, and Daddy held out his elbow. "It's not too late to change your mind, you know."

Skye giggled. "I know."

Yellow roses covered every available space. Where did they find roses at this time of year? But Skye hadn't questioned any of the wedding plans Mama and Daddy fussed over. All these trappings were more for their sakes, their way of pouring out their love. Skye would've been happy to find a justice of the peace. She just wanted, more than anything, to be Mrs. Alan McNaughten. And that wish was about to come true.

There he was, waiting at the front of the church, and Skye's breath caught. In all of creation, had any man ever been as handsome as Alan? She didn't think so. If Daddy hadn't walked with her, she might have cast dignity aside and run down the aisle.

She barely heard a word Alan's pa said as he led the ceremony, until she heard her name. "Do you, Alan, take Skye to be your wife...?" There were more words, but Skye's attention was on her husband-to-be. She watched his full, curved lips smile and say "I do," and she couldn't wait to kiss him.

It was her turn. "Do you, Skye, take Alan to be your husband...?"

"I do."

The congregation laughed, and she realized she hadn't let the man finish. Oops.

"By the power vested in me by God and the state of Texas, I now pronounce you husband and wife. You may kiss your bride."

Alan slowly, reverently lifted her veil and placed it around her shoulders. Placed his hand, ever so gently, behind her head. Tilted his head to the left, and leaned forward. She closed her eyes, and he offered the softest, gentlest kiss, like an angel's breath, and it was gone, along with her heart.

She opened her eyes, and she knew that *he* knew what she was thinking. She wanted more. Without warning, he leaned in again and kissed her, longer, deeper, and she wrapped her arms around his neck and drank in his sweetness.

James cleared his throat, and several in the audience coughed and chuckled, but Skye didn't care. She finished her kiss, then pulled back, flashing him a grin that promised more later. And she wasn't even embarrassed.

~

*A*lan knew he was marrying the most beautiful woman in the world. Even so, today, her beauty had ascended to a level formerly reserved for angels. It seemed the entire town of Lampasas—no, the entire county—had shown up for Skye's wedding. And even though he couldn't wait to get her all to himself, he wouldn't steal one moment of this day from her. He could see she was truly surprised at the outpouring of love and support.

It was a crisp November day, with the bluest sky he'd seen in a while. Lace-covered tables lined the borders of the church yard, and the center table held an elaborate three-tiered wedding cake with actual yellow roses arranged on top and trailing down the sides. Beside the main cake were several smaller cakes of the same design, enough to feed the massive crowd. Next to the cake was punch in a fancy silver bowl, and the rest of the tables held various dishes of whatever beans and meats and veggies the guests had brought to contribute to the potluck.

But it looked like Alan and Skye wouldn't get to eat. There were too many well-wishers, and each wanted a moment with Skye and her new husband. Most of them looked at Alan like he wasn't quite good enough for their darling, and he wasn't even offended. He was pretty sure they were right.

Halfway through the line, a small person lunged at Skye and buried his head in her dress.

"Charlie!" Skye knelt to the boy's eye level. "I'm so glad you came." She looked up at the boy's mother and a man.

"We wouldn't miss it," the woman said. "I'd like you to meet my husband, Roy."

Skye and Alan both shook hands with the couple and thanked them for coming. Then Skye looked at Charlie again. "I have a very important task for you."

"I'll do anything for you, Miss Skye."

"On that terrible night, I promised you a petit four—a little cake—and you never got to eat it. Promise me you'll eat at least two tonight."

Charlie's grin revealed a couple of missing front teeth. "Yes, ma'am."

When the line had dwindled almost to the end and most of the crowd stood around with plates of food and cups of punch, a group of two men and two women approached.

For the first time all day, Skye seemed uncomfortable, and Alan's protective instincts went on high alert.

"Miss Stra—pardon me. Mrs. McNaughten, could we have a moment with you and your husband around back?"

Skye's jaw tightened. She offered a gracious smile, but Alan wasn't fooled by his wife's words. "Yes. Certainly."

He placed a protective hand on her back, and they followed the foursome. Behind the church was a group of twenty or so men and women. One man stepped forward with an envelope. "Congratulations, Mr. and Mrs. McNaughten, on your marriage. We're here to apologize and to give you a gift."

Skye was stiff as a statue.

Alan interrupted the man. "What, exactly, are you apologizing for?"

"Skye knows." The man cleared his throat as if he'd continue his prepared speech.

"She might. I don't. And as her husband, I believe I have a right to know."

The man at least had the decency to look ashamed. "Times have been hard, you know. With the drought last summer, we could see our crops were suffering. Most of us didn't know how we'd make it through winter." He moved his eyes to Skye again. "When your Uncle Colt came to us offering cash if we'd keep our kids at home instead of sending them to school, we agreed.

We knew it was wrong. We could see what he was doing. But Colt Stratton is a powerful man, and we didn't want to cross him. And we needed the money."

Skye sucked in a breath, and Alan knew she was trying not to cry. How dare these people ruin her day!

The man held out the envelope. "Here is a written apology, signed by all of us. We never wanted you to get hurt. We love you, Mrs. McNaughten. Always have. We were just scared. Scared of Colt, and scared of not having enough funds to get us through. We're all ashamed of what we did. So here's an apology, along with all the money we took. We hope you'll accept it as a wedding gift."

Skye sobbed then, and Alan felt his fist tightening. "Come on, Sweetheart." He pulled her back toward the front of the church.

"No. It's all right." Her voice caught, and her face formed a vulnerable, watery smile. "I-I'm relieved to know the truth. I thought you all just didn't like me."

The small group erupted in a jumbled chorus of "No," and "That's not true," and "We love you."

And then, his beautiful bride was sobbing, and he couldn't stop the people from mobbing her...with love. With apologies. With well-wishes. And he knew, somehow, that this awkward moment was sent from God to further heal her spirit.

"Thank you." She wiped her tears and flashed that gorgeous, pure-hearted smile. "Please. Won't you all join the reception? There's plenty for everyone."

She stood there like she'd grown roots as the group thanked her and slowly disappeared around the building.

"Are you all right?"

"I'm better than all right. But I have one more thing I need to do." She tore open the envelope and pulled out the written page. Skimmed it, then handed it to Alan. "Hold onto this, please. I need to return this money to my uncle. I don't want anything to do with it."

Alan folded the paper and placed it in his breast pocket, then followed his bride back to the reception.

~

Skye held Alan's hand, practically dragged him around the church, ignoring a few good-natured comments about leaving the reception to take up that kiss again. She scanned the faces. There was Aunt Allison. Where was Uncle Colt?

There. Skulking in the shadows of the oak tree, south of the church building. Looking like he'd swallowed a mound of fire ants. Next to him was her cousin, Davis.

She wrapped the long veil around her arm, lifted her skirt, and traipsed through the grass. "Hello, Uncle Colt. Hello, cousin. I'm so glad you came today. It wouldn't have been the same without you."

Davis stepped away from his father. "You look real pretty today, Skye. I'm real happy for you."

"Thank you, Davis."

The seventeen-year-old tipped his hat and left, probably in search of more food.

Uncle Colt flashed his eyes at Alan before meeting her gaze.

"Congratulations."

"I know it's customary for guests to bring gifts to the wedding, but I have a gift for you."

His forehead wrinkled, but he said nothing.

She held out the envelope. "I believe this is yours. It's the money you paid people to keep their children at home instead of sending them to my class. It's the money you invested in my future, to ensure I'd feel like a failure, tuck tail, and run. It was given to me, but I don't want it." She offered him the envelope, but he wouldn't take it. So she dropped it at his feet.

She searched her uncle's face, looking for a shred of goodness there, but all she saw was a miserable old man. And instead of making her angry, it just made her sad.

"When Joseph's brothers shoved him in that pit, then sold him into slavery, they meant to get rid of him. They didn't care how they did it, they just wanted him gone. But God had a bigger plan for Joseph. What his brothers intended for harm, God intended for good. I've learned that's how God works, Uncle Colt. No amount of evil is bigger than His goodness. What you intended to harm me, God used to bring Alan into my life. And did you know I met my cousin? My great aunt? Because of what you did, I have not one, but two families who love me. You wanted me to feel like an outcast. Instead, I feel more loved and accepted than I ever have. So thank you."

She held his gaze and saw something like regret pass over his eyes, just for a sliver of a second. And instead of hate, all she felt was pity. And somehow, strangely enough, a little bit of love.

"You look like him, you know." His voice was gravelly, rough.

"Pardon me?"

"Your father. My brother. It's not that you're Indian. At least, that's not all of it. Looking at you reminds me of him. I loved my brother. We lost him when he married your mother."

They locked eyes, and Skye realized that his words were as close to an apology as she would get from this man.

"Be sure and try the cake, Uncle Colt. It's lemon custard. I'm sure it's delicious."

She took Alan's arm and left her uncle there, under the tree, lonely and miserable. But there was nothing she could do about that. Today was her wedding day, and she intended to enjoy every remaining second of it.

Alan drew her close, whispered in her ear. "I'm so happy you're finally my wife."

"Me too." A smile bubbled from deep inside like a brook that couldn't keep from sparkling. "One wedding down, one to go." Then she pulled her husband in and planted a sloppy, wet kiss on him. "Let's go have some cake."

<h1 style="text-align:center">EPILOGUE</h1>

Two Weeks Later

Skye stood facing Alan on the platform at the center of the reservation. This crowd was even bigger than the one at their first wedding. She felt beautiful in a bright red dress with delicate beads and colorful feathers lining the sleeves, collar, and hem. Alan wore a red shirt, and Chief Scott stood beside him, uttering words in Coushatta, then in English. Mary stood beside Skye, holding a tall vase with two handles.

At a specified time in the ceremony, Mary handed Skye the vase, which contained an herbal tea. Skye took a sip, then handed it to Alan, who also drank. Then, the two were to try to drink at the same time without spilling any of it. Slowly, carefully, they tipped the vase, and somehow they managed not to get it all over themselves. Skye tried not to laugh. She thought this was supposed to be a solemn moment.

Then Chief Scott said more words in Coushatta, and Mary picked up a beautifully-woven blanket of bright reds, yellows, and blues and wrapped it around both Skye and Alan.

"This is a symbol of your new life together. You are bound to each other, no longer two, but one." Mary whispered the words so only Skye and Alan could hear.

In the audience, Mama and Daddy, Cordell, Anita, and Uncle Lyndel sat on the same bench as Alan's parents. Skye looked around at the other faces, the dark-eyed faces of her once lost family, her grandmother's family, every one of them smiling, welcoming her home.

She felt Alan's eyes on her, and she wrapped her arms around his waist, covered by this bright, handmade, symbolic blanket, and she knew the covering she felt had nothing to do with the wool threads or the feathers on her dress, and everything to do with God.

She was wanted.

She was accepted.

She was loved.

Did you enjoy this book? We hope so!
Would you take a quick minute to leave a review where you purchased the book?
It doesn't have to be long. Just a sentence or two telling what you liked about the story!

Receive a FREE ebook and get updates when new Wild Heart books release: https://wildheartbooks.org/newsletter

ABOUT THE AUTHOR

This is the place where **Renae Brumbaugh Green** is supposed to provide impressive things for you to read. But since the most impressive thing about her is the fact that she almost won a car in one of those little fast-food scratch-off games one time, years ago, but she didn't actually scratch off the car until she found the card in her desk drawer, long after the deadline had passed, there's not much to say.

But if you really want to know about her writing stuff—she's the author of many books, made the ECPA Bestseller list twice, and has contributed to many more books. She's written hundreds of articles for national publications and has won awards for her humor.

She's married to a real hunk, and she's a mom to some amazing kids. She writes music, sings, and likes to perform on stage. She's a sometimes schoolteacher, a part-time chicken farmer, and an all-the-time wannabe superhero. Her favorite color is blue, unless you're talking about nail polish, in which case her favorite color is Bubblegum Pink.

To learn more about Renae, sign up for her newsletter or visit her website at www.RenaeBrumbaugh.com.

Lone Star Ranger (Texas Ranger Series, book 1)

Ranger to the Rescue (Texas Ranger Series, book 2)

Lassoed by the Lawman (Texas Ranger Series, book 3)

If you love historical romance, check out the other Wild Heart books!

Rocky Mountain Redemption by Lisa J. Flickinger

A Rocky Mountain logging camp may be just the place to find herself.

To escape the devastation caused by the breaking of her wedding engagement, Isabelle Franklin joins her aunt in the Rocky Mountains to feed a camp of lumberjacks cutting on the slopes of Cougar Ridge. If only she could out run the lingering nightmares.

Charles Bailey, camp foreman and Stony Creek's itinerant pastor, develops a reputation to match his new nickname — Preach. However, an inner battle ensues when the details of his rough history threaten to overcome the beliefs of his young faith.

Amid the hazards of camp life, the unlikely friendship growing between the two surprises Isabelle. She's drawn to Preach's brute strength and gentle nature as he leads the ragtag crew toiling for Pollitt's Lumber. But when the ghosts from her past return to haunt her, the choices she will make change the course of her life forever—and that of the man she's come to love.

~

Katherine's Arrangement by Blossom Turner

Marrying him is her only choice to save her family, but Josiah Richardson isn't at all the man she expected.

Katherine William's family was left destitute when their home was burned to the ground by Yankee soldiers, so the ready solution presented by the prominent Mr. Josiah Richardson seems almost too good to believe. He'll provide a home, work for her pa, and a new beginning for her family...if only Katherine will accept his proposal. A marriage of convenience is the last thing she wants, but there doesn't seem to be a better option for her family or herself. Setting aside her dreams of love, Katherine agrees to the arrangement.

The gentleman in Josiah Richardson can no more force his frightened bride into his bed, than he can force her into loving him, so he sets out to gently woo her. He works hard to befriend her, to earn her trust and win her love.

Katherine is pleasantly surprised to find herself drawn to the man she thought she would never love, until an unexpected friendship tears apart all they've worked for. Where once the promise of love had budded between Josiah and Katherine, now they wonder what to do with their so-called marriage. Is love strong enough to weave its healing power through two broken hearts?

~

Waltz in the Wilderness by Kathleen Denly

She's desperate to find her missing father. His conscience demands he risk all to help.

Eliza Brooks is haunted by her role in her mother's death, so she'll do anything to find her missing pa—even if it means sneaking aboard a southbound ship. When those meant to protect her abandon and betray her instead, a family friend's unexpected assistance is a blessing she can't refuse.

Daniel Clarke came to California to make his fortune, and a stable job as a San Francisco carpenter has earned him more than most have scraped from the local goldfields. But it's been four years since he left Massachusetts and his fiancé is impatient for his return. Bound for home at last, Daniel Clarke finds his heart and plans challenged by a tenacious young woman with haunted eyes. Though every word he utters seems to offend her, he is determined to see her safely returned to her father. Even if that means risking his fragile engagement.

When disaster befalls them in the remote wilderness of the Southern California mountains, true feelings are revealed, and both must face heart-rending decisions. But how to decide when every choice before them leads to someone getting hurt?